Deadly Demands

Penrose & Pyke Mysteries, Book 10

Rose Pascoe

Published by Flax Bay Books, 2026

Copyright

DEADLY DEMANDS

ISBN: 978-1067141301 (Paperback POD)
978-1067065096 (Epub)
Publisher: Flax Bay Books, New Zealand

Cover design: Rose Pascoe
Cover images from Adobe Stock Images

Contents

The First Victim

A soft bump, bump, bump roused Charlie Penrose Pyke from a deep sleep. He lifted his head from the pillow with the utmost reluctance.

Silence.

It was probably just the pups running riot again. Or a figment of the dream he'd been enjoying.

The faint light seeping past the curtains told him there was no hurry to leave his warm bed. However, a private detective who'd survived several attempts on his life couldn't afford to ignore an unexpected bump inside the house for the sake of a few more minutes of dozing. If there was an intruder on the stairs, he ought to hear a faint squeak, where he had deliberately loosened a few treads for exactly that reason.

Bump, bump, squeak … Bump, bump, bump, squeak.

Charlie sprang out of bed. His wife's side of the bed was empty. His first thought was that Grace must have needed the bathroom. At eight months pregnant, with a bladder the size of a prune, an uninterrupted night's sleep had become a distant memory for her. However, she had crossed her heart and promised to use the chamber pot at night, because attempting to descend the stairs in the dark was foolhardy for a woman whose centre of gravity was a foot further away from her spine than normal.

His second thought had him sprinting for the bedroom door. The bumping sounded exactly like a body being dragged down the stairs. He grabbed an old police truncheon as he passed the dresser.

In the dim light of the stairwell, Charlie saw his wife bumping down the stairs on her bottom, resting every few steps.

Grace turned at the sound of his rapid footsteps behind her. "Sorry to wake you, my love. I heard the front door slam and smelled something burning. It seemed safer to go down like this, because I cannot see my feet."

Charlie smelled it too. He sprinted past her down the stairs. A waft of smoke greeted him in the kitchen, coming from a frying pan that had been pushed to the back of the stove, away from the heat. He tipped the blackened remains of bacon into the scrap bin and poured water from the whistling kettle over the charred pan. A plume of steam joined the smoke, which he dispersed by opening a window and waving a dishcloth.

Blaze poked her nose around the doorway, whining an apology. Normally, Charlie could rely on his faithful border collie to warn him of anything amiss in the house, but she was busy with her boisterous litter of pups. A little over a month ago, Blaze had given birth with a pleasing lack of drama. Four tiny, plump sausages, blind and deaf, and entirely dependent on their mother. The newborn helplessness hadn't lasted long. A skittering of claws heralded the arrival of a tumble of black and white fur balls, falling over each other in their eagerness to leap upon this strange, large, two-legged creature who was treated as the pack leader by their mother.

Grace eased herself onto a chair at the kitchen table, looking at the burnt bacon as if she couldn't comprehend what her eyes were seeing. He couldn't blame her. Their housekeeper-cook, Mrs Brown, was widely admired as the best in the business. She had never burned so much as a slice of toast in his memory, let alone allowed the travesty of a single lump to linger in her porridge. Burnt bacon was unthinkable. Charlie feared their lives would fall apart if she ever left them. Certainly, his stomach would never recover from such a shock.

Picking up a ladle, he gave the porridge a tentative stir, encountering sticky resistance at the bottom of the pot that didn't bode well for the person who had to clean it. He ladled a serving from the top.

"I haven't asked how my three favourite people are this morning," Charlie said as he set the bowl down in front of his wife.

"The twins are resting after a vigorous night of using my bladder as a punchbag," Grace said. "Right now, I would willingly trade the pair of them for a full night's sleep, but I'll settle for a nice, strong cup of tea."

"Coming right up." Charlie reached for the teapot, but it held an over-stewed, lukewarm brew. He threw it out and started afresh.

Grace spooned up a glutinous lump and let it glop back into the bowl. She sighed and pushed her chair back. "I must see to Mrs Brown. Whatever illness or catastrophe has struck her, it must be dire for her to leave the stove untended."

"I'll do it, Grace. You'd better eat. I want to get you to your examination with plenty of time to spare."

Charlie had hired a gig to transport Grace to the medical school, because his wife struggled to haul herself onto trams or walk on Dunedin's steep streets. Today's practical examination was one of the last hurdles to Grace qualifying as the first female doctor in New Zealand. Normally, his wife could recite anatomy in her sleep, but her advanced pregnancy meant she faced more than the usual challenges to completing her qualification.

She shoved a spoonful of porridge into her mouth, grimaced, and reached for the sugar. "It'll be a miracle if I don't flunk the practical today. My brain's been functioning at the level of a bowl of custard ever since I fell pregnant. I shudder to think how I'll bend over the dissecting table."

Charlie murmured sympathetically. Her enormous belly was his fault, according to Grace, because large body size ran in his father's family. He was not stupid enough to remind her that her size was more likely because she was less than a month away from giving birth to twins, and twins ran in her family. Instead, he poured her a cup of freshly brewed tea and assured her that her brain was the envy of the medical school, before hurrying away to see what catastrophe had befallen their housekeeper.

Mrs Brown was nowhere to be found. Charlie couldn't imagine what had caused her to rush out of the house, leaving full pots and pans on the stove, and the front door unlocked. Whatever it was, it couldn't be good. He checked the tray near the front door for clues from the early mail delivery, but there were no urgent messages, or none that Mrs Brown had left behind. Nor had she left a note for them to explain her sudden departure.

Baffled, Charlie returned to the kitchen. "Vanished without a trace. Her shopping basket and favourite hat are still here."

Grace poured him a cup of tea. "It must be a wedding emergency."

"A wedding emergency? Sadie's wedding is weeks away." Weddings could be stressful, as Charlie knew all too well from the crises that delayed their own nuptials, but Mrs Brown and her daughter Sadie were far too organised and sensible for such disruptions.

"Maybe Sadie is ill, or having second thoughts about marriage," Grace said. "Auntie Anne is the only other person for whom Mrs Brown would abandon her post, but she would have woken us up if there was something wrong with Anne."

Charlie grunted his agreement as he shovelled down porridge. Mrs Brown was devoted to Anne Drummond, whom she had served for over two decades before Grace came to live with them in this house. Mrs Brown must have been young when she started with Anne, because she appeared to be not much over forty years old now, whereas Anne was well into her seventies. Grace's great-aunt suffered from arthritis and had an occasional bout of illness or fall, but otherwise she was as sharp as a scalpel. Even if something had happened to her, Anne's husband, Kenneth Drummond, was more than capable of dealing with an emergency.

Charlie glanced at the clock and pushed his concern aside. "I expect Mrs Brown will explain when she gets back. You've got more important things to focus on today."

By the time he gulped down breakfast, fed the dogs, and helped Grace to wash and dress, it would be time to leave. He hoped their housekeeper would be back soon, because he didn't want Blaze left alone for too long, this being her first litter. Especially as the pups had an annoying habit of breaking out of their pen and rampaging around the house.

Four hours later, Charlie reined the horse to a halt outside the medical school to pick up Grace after the examination. He didn't have long to wait. Within minutes, a clatter of boots and chatter headed his way. He gathered from the preponderance of grim and stunned expressions on the passing faces, all male, that it had been a challenging morning. Thus, he breathed a sigh of relief when Grace waddled out of the medical school with a smile lighting up her face. To be honest, he was relieved that she had made it out in one piece. Despite having a month to go until her due date, they both had a lingering fear that the stress of her final examinations might trigger the birth.

Charlie swept her up into an embrace before helping her onto the gig. "I take it the practical examination went well, Grace."

"The post-mortem was a doddle, and my live patient examinations couldn't have gone better. I suspect the patients felt sorry for me because they kept dropping subtle hints, like resting their hands on the sore part of their anatomy and winking when I was on the right track." Grace stretched awkwardly in the tight space of the gig and pulled at the fabric of her gown, which was stretched tight. "My feet and back are killing me. What news from home, Charlie? Did Mrs Brown say why she left in such a hurry?"

"Mrs Brown came back not long after I returned home from dropping you off. I tried to speak to her, but she brushed me off with a brisk apology, before flinging herself into making bread and scrubbing pans with a frenetic determination that discouraged further discussion. I retreated to the office, still none the wiser as to the cause of her disappearance."

The detective agency's office was next door to their home. At present, they weren't taking on any new clients, but there were still plenty of loose ends to tie up on various cases and the usual mail to answer. Refusing clients wasn't good for the agency's reputation, but his business partner, Alistair Stewart, had insisted on it for Grace's sake. Alistair was busy doing cloak-and-dagger work for the government in Wellington and had taken his wife, Lily, with him, promising they would be back in time for the birth.

"I'll have a word with Mrs Brown the moment we get home," Grace said.

Their housekeeper met them at the front door, with soapsuds up to her elbows and Blaze at her side. The collie's tail swept the floor in delight at their return, although she appeared a little more subdued than normal, perhaps because two of the pups behind her were covered in flour. Little devils – nothing was safe from their curiosity. Mrs Brown had seemed remarkably tolerant of these puppyish antics so far. Charlie wondered if they had been particularly naughty this morning, causing her to burn the breakfast and flee the chaos. If she resigned, he'd have to go down on his knees and beg her to stay.

"You have a new client," Mrs Brown said. "I know you told me you weren't taking new clients, but it's Mrs Mackenzie's daughter and she's crying. I've put her in the drawing room."

Charlie opened his mouth to say Mrs Mackenzie's daughter would have to take her problems elsewhere, crying or not, but Grace, Blaze and Mrs Brown all gave him The Look.

"Might we have some tea, Mrs Brown?" he asked, in an attempt to reassert a modicum of control.

Mrs Brown withdrew to the kitchen. Fortunately, Grace elected to join him, so Charlie didn't have to face a tearful woman alone. With any luck, Miss Mackenzie's problem would be a trivial matter or something the police could deal with.

In the drawing room, a pretty young lady paced up and down by the window, oblivious to their arrival. Charlie recalled Miss Mackenzie immediately. She and her mother often passed by, walking into town down High Street. Her gaiety and head of springy golden hair marked her out as memorable, even in a city with more than its share of redheads thanks to a strong Scottish heritage.

Their would-be client flinched at the sound of the door closing and hastily dabbed at her eyes with a crumpled handkerchief.

Grace hurried forward to take her arm and guide her to an armchair. "Welcome, Miss Mackenzie. I hope you don't mind if I put my feet up." Grace sank onto the sofa without waiting for a reply, propping her feet on a cushion.

Miss Mackenzie gaped at her. "Good heavens, Mrs Penrose Pyke, you look fit to burst at any moment." A furious blush spread across her pale, freckled skin at the impulsive outburst.

Grace waved away her apology. "I'm not due for another month. We're having twins."

Charlie drew up another armchair. "I'm sorry to tell you that we cannot take on any new cases, Miss Mackenzie. As you can see, we have our hands full at present. However, I can assure you that the local police force has –"

A sharp cry from their visitor cut him off. "No! I simply cannot go to the police. You have to help. I have nowhere else to turn."

"Perhaps you could tell us your problem," Charlie said. "I'll do what I can to provide advice."

Miss Mackenzie sank her head into her hands. "It's too dreadful. I'm to be married, you see."

Charlie waited for her to go on, but the tears had taken hold again, leaving her unable to continue. He hesitated to prompt her, dreading what she would say next. Their agency never dealt in marital affairs or other such matters of the heart, regardless of how distressed the client was. However, turning down desperate clients was never easy, especially with a marriage at risk.

"Have you discovered something that troubles you about your fiancé?" Grace asked gently. She caught Charlie's eye and tipped her head towards the door.

Charlie had heard the rattle of the tea tray too. He went to the door to collect the tray from Mrs Brown. She would not be offended at being excluded, knowing the matter being discussed would be confidential.

Miss Mackenzie answered without waiting for Mrs Brown to leave. "Oh no. Dougal is as perfect as ever. I love him with all my heart. It's only … I fear he may no longer wish to marry me." She extracted an envelope from her bodice. "Someone is threatening to expose a shameful secret, you see."

Mrs Brown fumbled the tea tray, rattling the cups and spilling milk on Charlie's hand. He steadied the tray before it fell to the floor and placed it on the table. Mrs Brown hurried out, closing the door behind her with a mumbled apology.

Charlie wiped his milky hand before taking the envelope from Miss Mackenzie's trembling fingers. The postmark – a useful innovation introduced seven years prior – showed that it had been posted in Dunedin city. The envelope and paper stock were cheap and of a type readily available at any stationer. The note was written in a simple, childish style by a firm but far from precise hand, as if the author had little practice at writing, or wanted to convey that impression. However, the words were far from childish.

The note read: *You're no daughter of Robert Mackenzie with your golden hair. Reckon that fire-headed boarder your mother doted on laid a cuckoo egg in the nest. Put £1 in the church charity box before the morning service on Sunday, or Dougal Matheson will hear of your shame.*

Acid roiled in Charlie's stomach. There were few crimes more despicable than blackmail, in his opinion. He passed the note to Grace. "Have you tried talking to your mother, Miss Mackenzie?"

"That's out of the question. The shame would kill her. If you cannot find the devil who did this, I'll have to pay up or call off the wedding."

"You'll do neither," Grace said. "I believe this foul person is simply making trouble. A jealous rival for Dougal Matheson's affections, perhaps. Red-haired children can turn up in any family, especially in those with Scottish ancestry."

Their client shook her head. "My father has black hair, and my mother's hair is dark brown. None of my brothers or sisters are gingers like me. I cannot count the number of times folks have teased me about being the golden sheep of the family."

"What about your grandparents?" Grace asked. "Inherited traits can skip a generation."

"I never knew them." Miss Mackenzie looked down to hide the fire in her cheeks. "I never thought about what it might mean before, but I think the note might be true. I asked my oldest sister about a boarder, and she remembered a man with hair like mine. She was only four at the time and has no memory of who the man was because he left before I was born. I searched my mother's memory box while she was out and found a locket with his picture opposite hers."

"We must talk to your mother, Miss Mackenzie," Grace said. "She is the only person who can clear this matter up. I can see why you don't wish to ask her, but she would be much more deeply upset if you called off the wedding or became entangled with a blackmailer. My husband will go to fetch her immediately, because there is no point in drawing out the agony."

Their client nodded, albeit reluctantly, and supplied an address, which was just around the corner. Charlie strode across the drawing room to the door in case she changed her mind. He opened the door to find Mrs Brown backing away, mortified at being caught eavesdropping. Not that he minded especially, as Mrs Brown was an unofficial member of their detective team, but snooping was not normal for her.

Mrs Brown followed him down the hall to the front door, stopping him before he left. "I know Mrs Mackenzie. It might be easier if I bring her here. It'll only take a few minutes if she's home."

Charlie returned to the drawing room to find his wife pouring tea and sympathy. She passed him a cup of black tea, having used the remaining milk in the jug for their guest.

"I was just saying to Miss Mackenzie that her fiancé will still love her no matter what," Grace said.

"It's not Dougal I'm afeared of," their client said. "His mother is already of the opinion that I am not good enough for her son. Mrs Matheson is a devout churchgoer. If she believes I am illegitimate, she will make her husband withdraw his consent to the marriage and order the minister not to marry us."

"Do you attend the same church as your fiancé, Miss Mackenzie?" Charlie asked.

She nodded. "Both of our families have attended the First Church all our lives. The mortification would be too much to bear for my mother if this dreadful slander is repeated in public."

Charlie understood her concern. An illegitimate child would be scandalous to the morally strict Scottish Presbyterian community, in which even unnecessary indulgences were frowned upon. Their principal place of worship, the First Church of Otago, was much admired for its magnificence, and yet many amongst the congregation had spoken against the "worldly extravagance" of its soaring Gothic design.

Miss Mackenzie twirled the cup in its saucer but didn't drink her tea. "One reason I haven't spoken of this to my mother is that the truth of the accusation is irrelevant. Once the rumour spreads, people will believe it, true or not. The only option is to find the blackmailer and beg for their silence."

Charlie couldn't fault her logic. The power lay with the blackmailer, especially where the accusation had a ring of truth to it. Condemned by beautiful golden hair – the injustice of it made his blood boil. Miss Mackenzie was right that they must stop the blackmailer as soon as possible. Time to set aside his anger and focus on the facts.

He picked up the letter again. Short as it was, it provided several avenues for investigation. "It's odd that the note said to put the money in the church charity box on Sunday. Blackmailers are usually greedy for money for themselves, rather than wanting money to be donated to charity."

Miss Mackenzie shrugged helplessly.

Charlie might be wrong because he had little experience with blackmail. Could the blackmailer be an overly moralistic member of the First Church congregation, seeking to punish perceived sin rather than seeking personal gain? But why would such a person wait for so many years to pass after Miss Mackenzie's birth, unless her betrothal to Mr Matheson had triggered the desire to see her punished? The disapproving mother-in-law sprang to mind.

Grace must have been thinking along the same lines. "Could it be that someone wishes to prevent your marriage? A jilted lover? A family member against the union?"

"I can honestly say I have not the least idea," Miss Mackenzie replied. "I've known my fiancé for ten years, since I was fifteen years old and he was seventeen. There has never been anyone but Dougal for me, and the same is true for him. Dougal's parents may have wished for a better match, but they are a decent and loving family. I'm sure this is not their work. Indeed, if Mrs Matheson had known this information, she would have stopped the courtship years ago. The handwriting is not familiar, and I know of nobody who would be so vile as to pen this threat."

"I might have put this down to an opportunist making wild accusations," Charlie said. "However, the note is very specific in mentioning the boarder who left your family home before you were born. That suggests someone with intimate knowledge of your family circumstances dating back over two and a half decades."

Miss Mackenzie spent the better part of a minute considering the matter. "I suppose friends and neighbours would have seen the boarder and remembered his fiery hair. Gossip lingers long in some minds, Mr Penrose Pyke. I expect there are many people who made snide comments about my hair colour when I was born, who are still around to pass their nasty whispers to others now that I am to marry well."

Charlie heard voices at the door and rose to add another armchair to the circle.

"Mrs Mackenzie," Mrs Brown announced, before closing the door behind her.

The newcomer went straight to her daughter. "Catriona, what is this about? Mrs Brown would only say you wished to hire a private detective for a private matter involving me. I am at a loss to imagine why."

Miss Mackenzie took her mother's hand and apologised for what she was about to say. With commendable bravery, she explained her situation and handed her mother the note.

Her mother blanched at reading the accusation, but her response was outrage rather than guilt. "Disgraceful lies! Catriona, my dear daughter, this mischief-maker is talking through a hole in his head. Your father was my one and only true love from the moment I spied him across the dance floor, just like you and Dougal."

"But, Mama, why does your locket have a picture of a golden-haired man rather than my father? And who is the mysterious boarder, if not the man in the locket?"

Mrs Mackenzie wrapped her arms around her daughter and laughed. "You silly ninny. Why in the Good Lord's name didn't you just ask me? The locket is my mother's, not mine, and the pictures are your grandparents. The boarder is no mystery either. Before you were born, my brother came to stay with us for a time. We had to keep his presence quiet because the coppers were looking for him. Rory was the black sheep of the family, being partial to a bit of sheep rustling. That's why we don't talk about him. Rory had a shock of golden hair that could light up a room, just like his father, while I'm the very image of my mother."

"Oh," Miss Mackenzie said. "I feel a fool. But a happy fool."

"It's not you who is foolish, my girl," her mother said. "If I catch the blackguard who tried to extort money from you, I will make him regret his cruelty."

Charlie stood up to see them out, immensely relieved at the quick resolution of the problem. "My advice is to tell your fiancé about this, Miss Mackenzie, in case the scoundrel follows up on the threat."

Miss Mackenzie squared her shoulders and sent him a radiant smile. "I will. With my mother's permission, I will wear the locket so I can show everyone my lovely golden-haired Grandpa. Thank you for your kindness, Mr Penrose Pyke. The letter had me so rattled, I've not been thinking straight."

Charlie returned the smile. There was nothing so heartwarming – and rare – as a client whose happiness could be restored so easily. But that didn't mean the blackmailer was off the hook. "If you see me on Sunday, Miss Mackenzie, please ignore me. I will do my best to catch the blackmailer at the morning church service."

"But surely there is no need now, Mr Penrose Pyke."

Much as Charlie wanted to agree with her, he could not let it pass. "On the contrary. Blackmailers rarely stop at one victim. They cast their bile wide to see how many they can catch with their wicked insinuations. There'll be no charge to you. I despise blackmailers. The scoundrel must be stopped before he or she targets someone else."

"Is there anything I can do to assist?" Miss Mackenzie asked. "I hate to think of others suffering as I have."

Charlie took a moment to consider her offer. "Would you be willing to pay the £1 demanded? I will need proof that the person I catch is the blackmailer. If you mark the banknote with your initials in small letters in one corner, the culprit will not be able to deny it was your money."

"I'd be delighted to do so. It would be a small price to pay to ensure justice is served." Miss Mackenzie rose. She hesitated, then darted forward and embraced Charlie. "Thank you for saving my marriage. Life without my Dougal would have been unbearable."

A Ripping Time

Grace trudged up the stairs while Charlie showed the Mackenzie ladies out. She wanted nothing more than a long nap after the intense pressure of her practical examination, but knowing there was a blackmailer on the loose left her too agitated to rest. No matter. With family coming for Christmas in two months' time, she had a list of tasks as long as her arm to complete, preferably before the birth of the babies upended their lives.

By the time she was at the top of the stairs, she was puffing like a geriatric mountain climber and reconsidering her plan to prepare the guest bedroom for visitors. Nor did she feel like revising for her examinations, although she ought to. After the meeting with Miss Mackenzie, she was reminded of a rumour about an essay question on inheritance. She'd have to find her notes on the subject later today, but she wasn't capable of any mental challenges at the moment.

What she needed was a nice, cheerful, brainless task. Tidying the nursery appealed, but she could hardly pretend it was a necessary task. She'd already arranged and rearranged the furniture and toys, stacked and colour-coded the piles of baby clothes, and removed any item that was small, sharp, precious, delicate, toxic, or chewable. In other words, almost everything one would normally find about the house.

Grace smiled at the memory of Charlie crawling around on his hands and knees, identifying hazards after the puppies were born. The list grew so long, he decided it would be easier to fence the pups into a pen than rearrange the house. In his view, the pen could do double duty, because by the time the pups were trained, the twins would be ready to crawl. Grace wasn't so sure a pen would be acceptable for human infants, although she could see his point.

She consulted her list of tasks and found one to suit her mood.

Charlie walked into the guest bedroom a few minutes later. He stared at her like a halfwit, shaking his head. His mouth opened and closed twice before he blurted out a question. "Grace, dearest heart, why are you standing on a chair, attempting to bring down a large box from the top of the cupboard?"

"I am sorting out the Christmas decorations," Grace said, stating the obvious. Honestly, how could he call himself a detective?

He moved beside her, taking the box. "Don't you think that a woman who can no longer bend over to put on her own boots has no business reaching for heavy boxes on high shelves?"

"Don't look at me like that, Charlie. I'm pregnant, not paralysed, and tinsel isn't heavy. I want the house to look festive when our parents arrive."

"Christmas is two months away, Grace. I will have plenty of time for decorating. Please promise me you will never get up on a chair again."

Grace adjusted her gown where it was straining over the bulge of her belly. "Once the babies are born, there will be no time to do anything beyond feeding, bathing, and changing them. I really must tidy the cupboards and dust the shelves before everyone arrives for Christmas. And those curtains could do with a wash."

Charlie gaped at her as if she were mad. "In the five years I have known you, Grace, you have never once expressed a desire to tidy cupboards, let alone dust and wash curtains." His hands fisted on his hips. "Your job is to stay safe for the sake of our children. Leave the climbing and lifting to me. We'll hire extra help to give the house a thorough clean if Mrs Brown and I can't manage it."

She huffed and took the second box of decorations from the shelf. When she shoved the box into his hands, the chair wobbled alarmingly. Charlie dumped the box on the floor and caught her as she lost her balance. A year ago, Grace had been so slim that her husband could lift her effortlessly with one arm. Now, he grunted and broke out in a sweat when he picked her up. Fortunately, he wasn't foolish enough to comment on her weight gain, but he did fumble as her ungainly mass toppled onto him.

When her feet touched the floor at an awkward angle, Grace heard an ominous ripping and felt a sudden freedom to breathe. Looking down, she saw a gaping tear in her gown that left an embarrassing amount of flesh visible. She couldn't suppress a howl of despair.

"Grace, are you hurt?" Charlie put a warm hand on her bump. "Is it the babies?"

"We're fine. But this gown was the last garment that still fit my bloated body."

Tears sprang to her eyes. Lately, she found herself crying at the silliest of things, like an adorable puppy antic or another gift of tiny bootees, but this truly was a crisis. She had grown out of the loose tea gown that had seen her through most of her pregnancy and the voluminous maternity smock made by Charlie's Aunt Lily. There was nothing left in her wardrobe except dust and clothes from her past life as a slim person.

Grace stifled a sob and made a half-hearted attempt at humour. "I'll have to attend tomorrow's examination wrapped in a bedsheet."

Charlie gave her a tentative smile, but it was clear he was holding back laughter. "The velvet curtains from the dining room might be more suitable than a sheet. We could pin them into a sort of Roman toga. I'm sure nobody would notice if you wore a cloak on top and carried a bunch of grapes."

"You'd better not be laughing at me, Pyke. I'm carrying two babies the size of circus elephants ..."

"... and it's all my fault. I know." Charlie hurried off, returning with a thick cloak to wrap her in. "I'm taking you to the dressmaker. If I have to go down on my knees and beg, you'll have a new gown before sunrise."

Grace forgave her husband for the circus elephants in light of his decisive action. "This is exactly why I fell in love with you, Charlie Pyke. However, I suggest a hefty bribe might work better than begging. The dressmaker has several assistants and seamstresses, but they are always frantically busy, and doubly so with the social season upon us."

The gig was still outside, which meant they arrived at the dressmaker's premises on lower Dowling Street within a few minutes. Grace was glad of the cloak and Charlie's arm around her as they descended the steep incline of High Street and hit the freezing blast of wind blowing up Princes Street. Typical spring weather for Dunedin – calm and sunny one day, squalls of freezing rain the next.

Charlie pulled her closer. "Don't despair, Grace. It will all be over soon. It'll be worth it when we have two gorgeous babies in our arms and you're a qualified doctor. What a celebration that will be."

She shivered, despite his reassuring presence beside her. He made it sound so simple, as if the exams were a trifle and the birth a moment's inconvenience. Grace was trying not to think about the birth, which was approaching with the terrifying speed of an out-of-control train. Or, in her case, two out-of-control trains trying to squeeze through a narrow tunnel at the same time. Anyone with a passing knowledge of anatomy would declare childbirth to be an anatomical impossibility.

Charlie was worried too, although he never mentioned it. How many times had they heard that old nugget: how hard could childbirth be when women did it every day? But Grace knew women died every day as well. In fact, one mother died for every two hundred births, while infant mortality was a frankly terrifying one death for every ten born alive. Grace told herself that her odds were better, because she was young, healthy, and surrounded by qualified helpers, unlike most mothers-to-be.

Her husband was sending anxious glances her way, so Grace beamed a saintly smile at him. The textbooks declared that an attitude of serenity was essential to ensure an easy birth. Unfortunately, the authors seemed to assume that pregnant mothers had nothing better to do than lie about on a pile of cushions looking serene and beautiful, nibbling grapes from a platter delivered by a servant like a vision from ancient Rome. Perhaps Charlie's idea of turning the curtains into a toga was not so silly after all. Grace had little hope that the dressmaker could accommodate her needs at short notice.

Charlie took her hand and squeezed the swollen fingers gently. "I'm sorry I broke my promise not to take on any new clients."

"You made the right choice. I hate to think of a malicious blackmailer on the loose. I'm only sorry I cannot help."

"There's nothing I can do anyway until the Sunday morning service." Charlie pulled the gig up outside the dressmaker's salon. "Miss Mackenzie seemed certain the letter writer was not a close acquaintance with a specific grudge against her and her fiancé, so my only lead is the drop-off point for the blackmail money at the church. Until then, I am at your command."

The dressmaker, Mrs Harper, leased the building next door to the Hallenstein Brothers clothing factory. The lower floor displayed garments of superior design and quality, at a price modest enough to be within the reach of the middle echelons of society. Mrs Harper's well-honed instinct for the perfect style and colour for each customer made her an institution amongst those in the know. Grace had heard women whisper that they would sooner give up their husband than their dressmaker.

Two women were waiting, chattering about an upcoming ball and eyeing up the gowns and accessories on display. A fidgeting gentleman sat on a chair in the corner. A husband, presumably, from the way he nervously fingered his wallet.

At the counter stood a middle-aged woman, elegantly dressed and coiffed, but wearing too much face powder for Grace's taste. Mrs Eliza Harper, the goddess of needle and thread.

"You will be the belle of the ball, Mrs Saunders," the dressmaker said, handing a parcel to a woman of statuesque proportions.

"You know I wasn't at all sure about that shade of blue, Mrs Harper, but I have to admit you have surpassed yourself." The lady beamed a delighted smile at the dressmaker before leaving.

Charlie took Grace straight to the counter. "Pardon me for interrupting, Mrs Harper, but we have an emergency." In his eagerness, he opened a flap of cloak, exposing Grace's flesh for all to see.

The waiting pair of ladies tittered, and the gentleman turned away. Grace heard a murmur of sympathy from one woman, but the other woman whispered in too loud a voice that it was an outrage that Grace allowed herself to be seen in public at all when she was at such an advanced stage of pregnancy, let alone in her current state of disarray.

Grace ignored them. She'd heard it all before. Lingering Victorian sensibilities of the more extreme kind dictated that women in their last trimester ought to be safely behind their own front doors in case their embarrassing condition caused gentlemen to become discomforted. Indeed, a special meeting had been convened at the medical school to determine whether she could continue to attend in her condition, after complaints that she would bring the institution into disrepute. Grace had argued that any medical student who could not cope with the sight of a pregnant woman ought not to be a doctor. She'd won, but the vote hadn't been unanimous.

Despite her own views, she had followed the advice to stay home as far as possible. Not because of any outdated notion of propriety, but because she would scream if she had to smile benignly at any more strangers who patted her belly and asked if she was overdue. At least strangers weren't as rude as her fellow medical students, who had taken to making quips such as *watch out, here comes a runaway hot-air balloon.*

Charlie ignored the tittering ladies. "My wife has an extremely important engagement tomorrow morning and nothing to wear. I will pay whatever it takes to make her comfortable and happy."

The crow's feet around Mrs Harper's eyes crinkled into deeper creases as she directed her remarks to Grace. "You're Mrs Drummond's niece, aren't you? I never forget a face or figure." Her gaze dropped, and the smile widened. "Although I must say your figure is rather altered from when I saw you last. It's Mrs Penrose Pyke, isn't it, if my memory serves?"

Grace nodded. "I apologise for coming without an appointment, Mrs Harper, but I am desperate."

"Of course. Anything for Mrs Drummond's niece. Come back in an hour, Mr Penrose Pyke."

When Mrs Harper turned to Charlie, Grace got a side-view of her powdered face. As she'd thought the first time she'd met the dressmaker, the powder was not artifice so much as a means of covering scars or pockmarks, perhaps from chickenpox or an accident.

Mrs Harper took her arm and helped her up the stairs to the second level, where the magic took place in a narrow, elongated room. Above them, Grace could hear a battery of seamstresses working away on sewing machines, alongside lace-makers and embroiderers. Perhaps they lived on-site, in the attic, like an industrious beehive.

The resemblance to a beehive became more obvious as Mrs Harper took Grace to the last free space at the end of the room. Young worker bees flitted here and there with design books, fabric samples, rolls of material, and finished gowns. In the half-dozen curtained-off booths Grace passed, a higher echelon of worker bees tended the customers – measuring, fitting, and demonstrating fabrics and styles.

A constant buzz of chatter filled the room, of which Grace heard snippets as she passed each booth. Compliments on a final choice, indecision over fabrics, whispered gossip. Most customers had brought along a friend or lady's maid to provide support and reassurance. A gown was an expensive asset, which would have to last the test of time. Mrs Harper and her staff always provided options to get the most from the purchase, such as a choice of matching shawls, overlays of lace, and accessories to make the gown suitable for diverse occasions.

"I must return to my other customers," Mrs Harper said, once she'd installed Grace in a curtained area with a comfortable chair and two mirrors. "One of my assistants will see to the measuring as soon as she can. Something simple, elegant, and … capacious. I have recently perfected a new design of gown. The system of pleats and drawstrings allows the gown to be worn at all stages of childbearing, as well as between children."

Clever, Grace thought. Many women's lives were a near-continuous round of childbearing until their bodies gave out. She shuddered. Her focus was on getting through her first birth, preferably wearing something other than a curtain toga. Thank goodness for Mrs Harper. Grace wanted to drop to her knees and thank this angel of mercy, only she feared she would not be able to get up again. Besides, she was too late. The queen bee had already taken flight, buzzing around her customers, handing out advice and compliments with cheerful efficiency. Mrs Harper had the knack of making each customer feel special and excited by the experience.

While Grace waited, she inspected the rip in the mirrors, concluding that the gown was beyond repair. She took a seat, grateful for the soft padding and generous proportions of the chair. A young girl brought her a cup of delectable tea, which was far superior to the ghastly dandelion-leaf tea Anne insisted she drink for her water retention. Grace would have preferred a few pints of fluid sloshing around her ankles over drinking dried grass clippings, but she'd deferred to Anne's wisdom most of the time.

She closed her eyes and enjoyed the moment of blissful peace.

With her eyes shut, the hum of chatter around the room distilled into snatches of conversation. Fortunately, Grace had excellent hearing. The two ladies in the adjacent booth were discussing the latest styles and colours with a worker bee. When the assistant left to gather samples in the requested shades of umber and chestnut, the talk turned to more personal matters.

"My husband's unmarried brother arrives next week," one lady said in a stage whisper. "I'm dreading it. I'll have to hide the port and brandy, or there'll be hell to pay. Goodness knows, it's taken me long enough to wean my husband off the bottle."

"You'll have to find an excuse not to attend church, Edna," the other lady said. "Can you imagine what the vicar would say when he sees the garish clothes your brother-in-law wears? It's unseemly. It wouldn't be so bad if he paid attention to eligible young ladies, rather than rakish young men. Disgraceful!"

A heavy sigh. "I cannot bear to think of him supping at my table. Let's not talk about him now. Did you see the simply massive bulge on the young lady who came in with the split in her gown? Honestly, one could see everything. What was she thinking, exposing herself in public?"

"I fear for the moral decay of our colony, Edna, I really do. And how will she push that enormous baby out? I wasn't half her size with my three, and thank the Good Lord for that."

"Talking of giant babies, have you seen the size of the Prendergast infant? Premature, her mother said. How can she expect anyone to believe that when the marriage was so hasty?"

"I blame the mother for bringing her daughter up without strict moral guidance. She still wears sunflower yellow, despite knocking on the door to fifty at least. I always say that a woman ought to be in muted colours beyond the age of thirty. It's simply intolerable. I'll bet she's one of those dreadful suffragists. Why on earth do women need the vote when they have husbands to guide them?"

Grace rolled her eyes and held her tongue. The enormity of the investigation Charlie had taken on suddenly became clear. A quarter of an hour in a dressmaker's salon had supplied her with enough gossip to make a blackmailer froth at the mouth. It would be the same at social gatherings all over the city – shops, afternoon tea parties, card evenings, dances, and parks. She'd heard a few shocking tales in doctor's surgeries too, and not just about undesirable medical conditions people would rather keep secret.

It would be the same for men in places like barbershops and clubs. Indeed, she had overheard three of her fellow medical students swapping yarns about shenanigans at their so-called gentlemen's club just this morning. Their cruelty toward one young student of her acquaintance was particularly egregious. It seemed they had lured the strait-laced, staunchly religious student to join them, telling him it was a musical soiree. They were still chortling over his hasty, red-faced exit as soon as he saw a stage full of half-naked dancing girls.

And then there was the servants' rumour mill, because few secrets could be kept from employees who were treated as if they were part of the furniture. Grace had dined at houses where private matters were discussed as if the room were empty of servants.

Grace now realised she had been wrong to assume the blackmailer must be a close associate of Miss Mackenzie, because she saw that gossip could travel far and wide in myriad ways. The blackmailer need not even know his victims, because the veracity of second-hand rumours mattered little. Their client was right to say that it wasn't about whether the claim was true, but whether the lie was believable enough to cause damage to the victim's reputation.

She parted the curtains to see what was going on. Mrs Harper was standing outside the curtains of the adjacent booth, frowning at the overheard gossip. The dressmaker looked as if she was on the verge of interrupting when an assistant arrived with fabric samples. She was a gaunt woman of similar age to Mrs Harper, who also had well-cut clothes and heavy powder on her face, which failed to hide her scars.

From inside the curtains, they heard a woman say she hoped they wouldn't be served by a disfigured assistant. The scarred assistant hunched her shoulders instinctively until Mrs Harper whispered a few words to her, bringing a smile to both their faces. The dressmaker looked over the fabric samples and selected three in shades of rich brown.

"Could you please find the design book and some fabric samples for a maternity gown, Miss Rudd?" Mrs Harper said loudly enough for her customers to overhear.

The scarred assistant hurried away, looking relieved that she would not have to serve the tactless ladies. With a flick of a finger, Mrs Harper signalled another woman to attend to Grace, after which she disappeared behind the curtains to assist the two gossips.

Grace ducked her head back into the curtained area as her designated assistant approached.

The woman cleared her throat before entering with a broad smile and twinkling eyes. "Good afternoon, Mrs Penrose Pyke. I'm Miss Kerr. My apologies for keeping you waiting. The social season is upon us, but people will leave it to the last minute to order their gowns." The dressmaker's assistant removed Grace's cloak and did a circuit around her. "Oh dear, oh dear. I see the problem. Let's get some measurements."

To Grace's horror, the assistant struggled to get the measuring tape around her belly. She mumbled an apology about having twins, but Miss Kerr took it in her stride. No doubt she had seen women of all shapes and sizes in her time, as Grace had in her medical career. Belatedly, Grace realised the difficulty lay with the woman's gnarled hands, although she didn't look to be much over thirty years of age.

Miss Kerr noticed the direction of her gaze. "I started as a weaver when I was fourteen. I was fortunate that Mrs Harper took me on when my fingers gave out."

Miss Rudd entered with a selection of fabric samples, before withdrawing again without showing her face. Again, the quick eyes of the dressmaker's assistant caught Grace's glance.

"Miss Rudd doesn't talk about it," Miss Kerr said, "but she had those burns when she arrived. Probably a kitchen maid. It's shocking what those girls have to put up with. Spit roasts, cauldrons of boiling soup, hot ovens. All the workers here have been rescued by Mrs Harper. Most of us would be begging on the street or worse without her. She even taught us our letters. Not that she'll accept any praise, because she says it is her duty to help others like her, when she has been so blessed with such success after a poor start to life. The woman is a saint."

Grace nodded. "My great-aunt is a great admirer of her work."

The measuring continued with a gentle stream of pleasant chatter from Miss Kerr. Before long, a low clearing of the throat outside signalled a new arrival.

"May I come in, Mrs Penrose Pyke?" Mrs Harper parted the curtain. "What do you think, Miss Kerr? Can we find a quick remedy?"

Miss Kerr ran her dressmaker's chalk gently around the gaping hole. "We could insert a panel on either side as a temporary measure, if we have any matching material. A new gown would take longer, of course, but if we work late, it could be done."

Her employer crinkled her brow, presumably trying to figure out how she could fit the work in when her team was so clearly run off their feet.

"Excuse me," said a soft voice from outside. Miss Rudd stepped inside the curtained booth, wielding an enormous armful of cloth in the most gorgeous shade of forest green. "I wondered whether the gown Mrs Thompson never picked up might suit, Mrs Harper. It is, as you'll recall, a generous size."

"Brilliant, Miss Rudd. The perfect solution." Mrs Harper must have seen the doubt in Grace's expression. "Mrs Thompson didn't require the gown because she gave birth early. It's a beautiful garment. She sent a note to ask me to sell the gown if I could, because this was most definitely her last child. Her eighth."

"As long as it's big enough to make me decent, I'd be delighted to buy it." Grace turned her grateful smile on Miss Rudd to thank her too, but she had already slipped away.

Miss Kerr unlaced the torn gown and pulled it over Grace's head. The green gown slithered over her body in a silky caress, slipping over her bump with ample to spare. A blessing on the generous proportions of Mrs Thompson and her premature baby, Grace thought, and an extra hurrah for her exquisite taste.

Mrs Harper gave a satisfied nod. "Note the fan pleating down the bodice, Mrs Penrose Pyke. The pleats can be gathered with this drawstring, expanding as required, and reverting to fit as an ordinary gown after birth. And here and here, you can see hidden splits to make feeding more accessible for your darling babies."

"Ingenious," Grace murmured, holding back the urge to embrace the clever dressmaker and her team of magician's assistants.

The dressmaker deftly adjusted the pleats and the discreet lacing that allowed for expansion of the side seams of the skirt. "These darts can be resewn after the birth too. There now, don't you look a picture." Mrs Harper pulled on another drawstring to gather the hem off the floor.

"You have worked a miracle," Grace said. "I'm so delighted I might have to name a baby after you."

Mrs Harper smiled. "I'm sure you have loved ones you'd rather name the child after, although I always did like the name Eliza. Now, might I suggest a better corset? I couldn't help but notice yours was pressing into your abdomen. We have some excellent designs that use supple, directional boning to provide better support. Miss Kerr?"

Miss Kerr trotted away, leaving Grace grinning like the Cheshire Cat. Perhaps not quite like the cat in the story, since she could not vanish at will, but she would certainly be a lot less noticeable for the wrong reasons in her new gown.

"Now, dear, take a seat while we wait and tell me how your lovely great-aunt is faring. I thought it delightful of her to pay for a wedding gown for her housekeeper's daughter. Such a marvellous, charitable lady. I've employed several workers through her women's refuge."

Grace didn't know that Anne had paid for Sadie Brown's wedding gown, but it didn't surprise her. Anne lived her life for the betterment of others, and Mrs Brown had been a faithful employee for many years. "Auntie Anne is one in a million. I would never have been able to pay my way through medical school without her support. She told me it's always a pleasure to support your business too, because you take on and train young women who would struggle to find other employment. And, of course, you are the best dressmaker in the city."

Mrs Harper's laugh was the sort that made others wish to join in. Despite the circumstances, Grace found herself enjoying the experience. Even more so when Miss Kerr returned with a corset that enhanced her comfort rather than detracting from it. Moreover, when Grace looked in the mirror, she didn't look like a green whale, thanks to the well-cut gown and shaped undergarment.

Mrs Harper clapped her hands in delight and departed with another radiant smile and a promise to send the bill.

Now that Grace could breathe again without rupturing a seam, she felt entirely capable of getting through the next month, despite the backache, swollen ankles, heartburn, breathlessness, and constant pressure on her bladder.

Charlie was waiting for her downstairs. His eyes lit up at the sight of her. "As beautiful as ever, Grace, but rather more presentable. Mind you, you would look perfect to me wrapped in a bedsheet." He leaned closer to whisper, "or wearing nothing at all."

"The feeling is mutual," Grace whispered back. "Thank you for rescuing me today, and for waiting so patiently."

Charlie took her out to the gig and helped her mount. "Actually, I went to the First Church to see the minister. I wanted to warn him about the blackmail and get his permission to watch over the charity box on Sunday."

"I suppose that makes sense, because the blackmailer will want to be on hand to ensure his victim pays up."

"And because I'm hoping that the blackmailer might also be a thief." Charlie flicked the reins gently to start the horse plodding its way uphill towards their home. "I cannot see someone resorting to blackmail only to have the proceeds go to charity, unless the person directly benefits from the charity. That's unlikely, since this Sunday's collection is destined for a Christian mission in the South Pacific. The alternative is that the blackmailer intends to steal the charity box during or after the service. I'm going to enjoy unmasking the culprit."

"The minister must have been appalled by such gross abuse of the church's charity," Grace said.

"Appalled, yes. But not surprised. The minister said he had been approached in the strictest confidence earlier today by a young man who was in a state of extreme distress. He had received a note threatening him with exposure if he did not put £1 in the charity box on Sunday. The young man denied any wrongdoing, but he could see that it hardly mattered if the rumour was circulated, as threatened. He is courting the daughter of a prominent family, who would not take kindly to any hint of scandal."

"The poor man," Grace said. "One pound would seem a small price to pay to stop a threat that could destroy his future happiness, just like Miss Mackenzie."

Charlie shook his head. "I fear that paying up once might only encourage the blackmailer to come back for more. The minister fears for the young man's safety, after the man said he would rather die than lose the love of his life. You can see why I despise blackmailers. They cause irreparable harm for little gain."

"I agree," Grace said. "He or she has to be stopped. Did the minister give you any indication of the accusation against the second victim? Or provide any other clues as to the blackmailer's identity?"

"It was a matter of a purported prior commitment to another young woman. The young man swore she was no more than the daughter of longstanding family friends, who had taken a fancy to him with no encouragement on his part. Unfortunately, the minister would not disclose the young man's name or situation. Discretion is understandable, of course, but finding the blackmailer would be easier if I could find the links between his victims. However, the minister did give his blessing to my attempt to catch the blackmailer on Sunday."

"I fear it may not be as simple as finding links between the victims." Grace told her husband about the gossip she had overheard while waiting to be measured. "Imagine how many morsels of embarrassing gossip might be gathered during a single day at the dressmaking salon. Or at any social event, from dances to card evenings. Or at gentlemen's clubs, or barbers, or indeed at any place where people gather. If one chooses to listen in, there is fodder for blackmail everywhere."

"All the more reason to catch the blackmailer on Sunday," Charlie muttered. "Who knows how many other victims there might be, too scared to speak out."

A black cloud hung over her husband's head for the rest of the ride home. He hated feeling helpless in the face of evil just as much as Grace did.

An Act of Charity

Six days later, on Sunday morning, Charlie joined Anne and Kenneth Drummond outside the First Church of Otago, half an hour before the start of the morning service. People had already begun to gather outside, chatting in clusters around the church grounds or admiring the view over the harbour. The church sat in soaring grandeur on the solid granite promontory of Bell Hill, towering over the harbour and the lower reaches of the city, proclaiming itself as the most important building in the city.

Kenneth, Anne's second husband, was Presbyterian, and Anne had joined him at his place of worship. Charlie was Anglican, but he had visited the pride of this staunchly Presbyterian community once before, in 1890, when extensive remediation work had been completed. It was a source of embarrassment that the building had to be fixed only a decade and a half after being completed. Dunedin's notoriously wild weather had taken much of the blame. The *Otago Witness* reported that leaks in the many-angled roof had left the interior severely damp and the magnificent wooden ceiling in an extremely unsafe state, because of dry rot in the bearing timbers.

Nevertheless, the First Church remained an awe-inspiring building, faced with pale Oamaru stone, with the eye drawn upwards from the massive wooden entrance doors to the lofty spire by way of turrets, pinnacles, and gables. The interior left Charlie speechless, because nothing in his humble upbringing in rural Central Otago could have prepared him for the vast space and the stunning beauty of the design.

However, their early arrival today had nothing to do with admiring the gorgeous rose window above the raised central octagonal pulpit, or the soaring organ pipes on either side, or the ornate gallery hovering over the rear pews, or even the magnificent wooden ceiling that rose to a steep pitch above arched support beams. Despite all these glories, Charlie was there to watch over one small, insignificant charity box.

At first, he thought the blackmailer must be insane to choose a church service attended by hundreds of people as the location for the blackmail payments. He soon changed his mind. The charity box was strategically located on a table in the narrow entrance foyer between the outer vestibule and the inner church. Arrivals would file past and make their donations, before entering the church proper. Once the service began, the foyer would be empty, and thus the charity box would be unprotected.

Indeed, the more he thought about it, the more brilliant the scheme appeared. The blackmail victim or victims would not stand out from the crowd as they filed past, slotting their "donation" discreetly into the box. Nobody would notice if the victim donated extra generously that week, especially if the money was concealed within a cupped hand. A point that had puzzled Charlie – the relatively modest sums demanded by the blackmailer – now made more sense. For all he knew, every person attending the service might have been sent a note. Everybody had their secrets, and what did it matter if some people ignored the note as a prank, as long as other people were worried enough by the blackmailer's insinuations to put money in the box. Even if nobody gave in to blackmail, there would still be donations to steal.

And that left him with another problem. He'd been sure the blackmailer would be watching to see if Miss Mackenzie did as she was told. But, if there were many victims, each of whom was told to put in a small sum, the blackmailer need only sit back at a safe distance and rely on some of his or her poisoned arrows to hit home. When the coast was clear, he or she could slip in and empty the box, perhaps leaving smaller denomination coins behind so that the loss was not noticed. The blackmailer could have been doing this for weeks or months. With such a modest amount asked of each victim, the chances were that it would be easier for victims to comply than to complain and risk being exposed.

Charlie inspected the charity box, but there was little to see. It was simply a box with a slot in the top, albeit made of beautifully polished mahogany. The rear of the box was discreetly screwed to the table underneath a velvet cloth to deter light-fingered visitors. Thus, the box could not be easily removed. Most likely, the blackmailer would pick or pry open the lock that secured the lid, unless he or she had a key.

Therein lay the next problem. Charlie's plan was to catch the blackmailer red-handed, but the blackmailer had made that almost impossible by his choice of location. On either side of the lobby, stairs curved upwards to the gallery seating, leaving no place to hide and watch. At the base of each staircase, a small room offered potential as an observation point, except that the angle of the doors did not allow for a complete view of the box on the table. The only viable option would be to squeeze his bulk behind one of the lobby doors, which opened inwards, opposite the table the box was on. Given Charlie's size, his chances of crouching unobserved were next to nil. If he did manage it, his muscles would seize from crouching in the awkward space.

Fortunately, a pair of young men arrived at that moment, carrying a tall display board hung with tapestries. The minister appeared behind them and directed the men to install the display at an angle to the base of the stairs. He nodded at Charlie, adding an upward flick of raised eyebrows to indicate he had foreseen the problem.

Charlie stifled a grin and returned the minister's nod. "What a blessing to have a display of such beauty and large dimensions."

"Thank you, my son," the minister replied, with a lilt of mischief in his deep voice. "It was inspired by 1 Corinthians 6:10. A blessing on you and all your endeavours, young man."

Charlie ducked into the church and took a Bible from the nearest pew. 1 Corinthians 6:10 read: *Nor thieves, nor covetous, nor drunkards, nor revilers, nor extortioners, shall inherit the kingdom of God.*

He put the Bible back with a chuckle and went to join Anne and Kenneth Drummond, whose role was to linger in the lobby as the congregation filed in. He asked them to make a list of every person who placed a donation in the charity box, especially those parishioners who appeared nervous or who were overly generous. Meanwhile, Charlie took his place behind the tapestry screen, adjusting it so he could see the charity box through a narrow gap between the hangings.

The congregation started to file in, at first in dribs and drabs, and then in a flood. At capacity, the church could seat over a thousand people, making the task ahead of them monumental. For all their carefully laid plans, Anne and Kenneth had no hope of recording all the names, because the majority slotted a donation into the box. From his hiding spot, Charlie silently cursed the charitable instincts of the congregation.

He was pleased to see that the golden-haired Miss Mackenzie was one of the first to arrive. She walked with a straight back on the arm of a young gentleman who couldn't keep his adoring gaze off her. Her mother walked behind them, arm in arm with another lady, who looked similar enough to the young man to be his mother. The younger generation had dressed for the joys of spring, whilst the older generation came wrapped in black stoles and capes, with stout gloves and hats also in black. Miss Mackenzie walked past the charity box and inserted her donation without looking back.

A few places further down the queue, a young man fretted with a banknote. From his furtive glances at the other parishioners and the sweat on his brow, he could be the young man who'd spoken to the minister about an accusation of impropriety.

Charlie had hoped Miss Mackenzie and the young man were the only victims. However, that hope was short-lived. Other members of the congregation looked around nervously before darting their hands to the slot in the top of the charity box. Several lingered, perhaps hoping to spot their blackmailer. With so many people in the lobby, queuing, exchanging greetings, and swapping news, they had little hope of achieving their goal. The situation was even worse for Charlie, whose view was obscured. He was also at a severe disadvantage, not knowing the parishioners.

The only moment of potential significance occurred when an older woman stumbled, grabbing the edge of the table, pulling the velvet cloth askew, and knocking over the vase of flowers beside the charity box. Charlie tensed, alert for trickery. Several women rushed to her aid, clustering around the scene and blocking his view. When they dispersed, the woman and the vase were upright, and the box was in the same position it had been in before the incident. Suspicious as he was, Charlie had seen the screwed-down and locked charity box and couldn't imagine how the stumble could have covered any thievery or other misdeed.

People kept pouring in. Most of them put a coin in the charity box. Charlie could only hope that they were not all blackmail victims, because interviewing every donor would be nigh on impossible.

At last, the flood of arrivals ebbed. Inside the church, the babble of voices subsided as the organist began to play. Anne flicked a glance at the tapestry screen, lifting her shoulders and palms in a gesture of hopelessness, before hurrying inside to take her seat beside her husband.

Charlie waited. And waited. He waited through glorious choral music and a hymn sung by the congregation. His feet itched for action, but nobody came for the charity box. He waited through an interminable sermon. Still, nobody entered the lobby. Charlie eased his muscles, which were seizing up from standing still. Inevitably, as the service droned on, his thoughts drifted to Grace.

She had stayed at home today, pleading tiredness. In theory, Charlie was glad she was being sensible in taking the time to rest and recover after a gruelling week of examinations. But it wasn't like Grace to leave the investigating to him, even though that was their agreement. He worried it was more than tiredness. Last night, he found her on all fours, groaning in pain and panting. False labour pains, she'd said, as if they were nothing to worry about. The stress of seeing her like that had sent muscle spasms through his own belly. Grace told him it was not uncommon for close couples to feel sympathetic pains. Divine justice for putting your wife through labour, she said, with a definite twinkle in her eye.

Charlie jolted himself back to his vigil as the last hymn thundered to an end. A door squeaked open, and several people hurried out, but none dallied. Inside, he could hear church notices being read. Then, the door opened again to disgorge the bulk of the departing congregation. The service was over. The charity box remained untouched.

Anne and Kenneth Drummond were the last through the door, along with the minister and a fine-boned but barrel-waisted gentleman. The latter was middle-aged and of sombre demeanour, wearing an equally sombre suit of the type worn by a respectable man from the middle orders of society. A man with an indoor occupation, perhaps clerical, judging from his slim, ink-stained fingers. He walked several steps behind the minister, as if deferring to his reverence.

The quartet looked at Charlie expectantly, but all he could do was shake his head. Unless he had missed a sneak thief of exceptional skill during a moment of distraction, not a soul had entered the lobby, let alone touched the charity box.

The rotund gentleman, his expression masked by a thicket of greying whiskers, looked to the minister for instructions. His deference and hesitancy told Charlie that the minister had apprised him of the situation.

"May I introduce Mr Landsburgh," the minister said, "who kindly volunteers his services to keep the church accounts."

Landsburgh drew a key from his pocket. He stood to one side as he opened the charity box, so his actions were clearly visible – a further sign he knew the stakes. With a quick twist of the key, the box lid hinged open. The height of the box meant Charlie had to lean over to see inside to the pile of coins and one or two banknotes. A sizable haul, reassuring him that he hadn't missed anyone emptying it.

Charlie nodded to the minister and saw his own relief reflected in the release of tension across the minister's face.

"Proceed, Mr Landsburgh," the minister said.

The man scooped the donations into a drawstring bag and locked the charity box.

"Thank the Lord for small mercies," the minister said. "A blackmailer in my congregation would have been a heavy cross to bear. I expect one amongst us has resorted to unacceptable methods to raise funds for our much-needed mission in the Pacific, if it was not merely an irresponsible trickster out to ruffle feathers."

"Let us hope we have no recurrence of such despicable behaviour," Mr Landsburgh said. "I suspect none would dare, after your rousing sermon today reminding the congregation of the Lord's abhorrence for those who seek to profit from the misery of others."

Charlie was reluctant to write the blackmail off as an unfortunate enthusiasm to raise more money for charity. Besides, even if the motive wasn't personal gain, extorting money by threatening to reveal a secret was still a crime. However, it was hard to argue against the minister's opinion, no matter what Charlie's gut was saying, because the plain fact was that the money hadn't been stolen. It was a weight off his shoulders. His client's problem had been resolved, and he had every reason to walk away and focus on what was truly important to him – getting his wife safely through the next few weeks.

He shook the minister's hand. "My apologies for causing distress. You'll contact me, I hope, if any other parishioners report blackmail attempts?"

"I will, although I trust it will not be necessary. My congregation is filled with honest, hard-working people, devout in their beliefs. Of course, there will always be the occasional bad apple, as Adam and Eve were the first to discover."

The minister and the volunteer bookkeeper retreated into the interior of the church, while Charlie joined Anne and Kenneth Drummond outside. He was about to suggest they go home, when a sudden thought had him running back into the church. The minister had returned to the pulpit, where he was gathering his notes.

Charlie slowed to a striding walk, because running inside such a magnificent church seemed ungodly, and he didn't wish to be smitten by a lightning bolt from above before he met his firstborns. "My apologies, but I need to see the charity collection again."

"Follow me," the minister said, tucking his notes under his arm and leading the way through a door behind the pulpit.

Beyond the door, a corridor led to the vestry and parish hall at the rear of the main body of the First Church. The minister showed Charlie into a study lined with books, where Mr Landsburgh was busy counting pennies, having sorted the donations into piles of the same denomination. The highest piles were the low-denomination copper coins, with a fair haul of silver, such as sixpences and shillings, as well. There were only two £1 banknotes.

"May I?" Charlie asked, inspecting the two banknotes for the initials Miss Mackenzie had agreed to put on her donation.

The minister put down his sermon notes on another desk and came over. "Is there a problem, Mr Penrose Pyke?"

"I asked my client to put a mark on her banknote so we could prove the case more easily against the blackmailer if he was caught in the act. Neither of these two notes is marked." Charlie's eyes flicked to the bookkeeper and back to the minister.

The bookkeeper's pallid face turned beet red under his whiskers. "I sincerely hope you are not accusing me of taking the marked banknote, sir."

The minister was quick to intervene. "I'm sure Mr Penrose Pyke meant no such thing, Mr Landsburgh. There cannot be the slightest suspicion of your involvement, considering your exemplary history of volunteering at the church." The minister turned to Charlie. "Mr Landsburgh is a respected senior clerk at the Bank of Otago. He has my complete confidence."

"You may search my person if you harbour doubts, young man." Landsburgh rose and stepped forward, his chin elevated and lips pursed. His head was at Charlie's shoulder level, but his affronted dignity made him seem taller.

Charlie had no wish to make an enemy of a respected churchgoer. "I wouldn't dream of it, sir. I merely wished to be certain of my facts when I discussed the matter with my client. No doubt she forgot to mark the note. An easy oversight under the strain of the situation."

With a bow, he took a step back, despite knowing that Landsburgh could have stashed some of the money elsewhere while he had wasted time dithering in the lobby. The man seemed an unlikely suspect, but Charlie had long ago learned that the most respectable of men could hide dark secrets.

"Mr Landsburgh, perhaps you would be so good as to satisfy my curiosity," Charlie said. "Is the sum donated substantially more than previous weeks' collections?"

The gentleman consulted his tally. "It's difficult to say, since the charity box is usually opened only once a week, after the Sunday evening service. However, I would say the sum collected is less than expected rather than more. It's getting harder and harder to part people from their money in these tough times."

"For once, I am relieved to hear it," the minister said. "A low total sum surely means that the blackmail is not widespread. We know of only two victims, after all. Is that not so, Mr Penrose Pyke?"

"Indeed. Well, I can do no more. Let us hope this is the end of it." A forlorn hope, in Charlie's view. Blackmail was usually driven by greed and vindictiveness, traits that did not vanish after a single bite of the apple.

He thanked them and hastened out, hoping he was wrong. It might be no more than a storm in a teacup, although Miss Mackenzie and the young man certainly wouldn't see it that way, when both had been threatened with the loss of their future marital happiness.

Frustrating as it was to face a dead end, there was little more that Charlie could do. He wished he'd stayed home with Grace, who was enjoying a nice, long sleep in a warm bed.

A Day of Secrets

Grace woke up feeling refreshed after a lie-in on Sunday morning. She'd barely noticed Charlie leaving, although she felt the touch of his lips on her forehead and heard him whisper a few words to the twins about being good and looking after their mother while he was out. Although she teased him about his conversations with his unborn children, she was just as bad when nobody was listening.

She picked up her textbook, intending to use the quiet time before everyone returned from church to revise for her general medical examination. Her last examination ever, all going well. Hallelujah. After an hour's reading, hunger forced her downstairs. Besides, she ought to check on Blaze and her pups, who were suspiciously quiet this morning.

Blaze looked up at her from the pen in the kitchen. Her lolling tongue and bright collie eyes seemed to laugh at Grace. Look at me, her expression said, I gave birth to four pups on the kitchen floor with ease, so surely you can manage a mere two?

Only three pups were in the pen. Inevitably, it was the smallest, liveliest one who had escaped again. They'd named her Spark, because she was a bright, curious little imp, just like her mother. After a quick search of the kitchen, Grace found the escapee beside the stove, chewing on a slipper. She put the pup back with her littermates, ensuring the gate to the pen was securely fastened.

"No more escaping, you little ratbag."

Spark regarded her with interest through the bars of the pen. The pup looked so sweet and innocent that it was impossible to be cross. Grace cleaned up a puddle and a scatter of chewed items, including a carrot, a dishcloth, and the slipper, foolishly left within reach.

A wet nose bumped against her bare foot. Spark looked up at her with big, winsome eyes, the other slipper dangling from her jaw. Grace put her back in the pen. They had a staring contest. Grace turned her back. Sure enough, when she whipped her head around, there was Spark, slithering out through an impossibly narrow gap in the bars by the wall.

Grace wedged a tray into the gap. "If you're that clever, little pup, why didn't you put the roast in the oven?"

Spark prodded the tray, wrinkled her nose at Grace, then curled up into a ball and pretended to snooze. Grace went to find Mrs Brown, who was normally home from her early service at the Anglican church by now. Finding the house deserted, Grace rolled up her sleeves, donned an apron, and set to work preparing the meat and vegetables. Cooking was not high on her list of skills, but her great-aunt and her husband were coming for Sunday lunch, and Grace reasoned that her cooking was better than raw meat.

As she peeled potatoes, Grace wondered again at Mrs Brown's uncharacteristic absence. None of the possibilities were palatable: illness, worry over Sadie's wedding, annoyance at the chaos caused by the puppies, frustration with something Charlie or Grace had done. The meal was in the oven without Grace identifying either the problem or the solution. She put the kettle on, hoping to find inspiration in the swirl of tea leaves.

She would simply have to sit Mrs Brown down and ask what the problem was. But first, Grace would insist on hiring extra help. A maid-of-all-work came in daily to see to the routine cleaning, while Charlie saw to the heavy work, such as beating rugs, chopping firewood, making up the fires, and maintenance. A gardener came by once a week, and the heavy laundry and linens were sent out. Nevertheless, there was still a huge amount of work left for Mrs Brown, including shopping, cooking, baking bread, preserving, washing smalls, and managing the household.

Until now, Mrs Brown had refused offers of more help, but when the twins arrived, there would be far more work to do, and Grace would be less able to assist. At the very least, they would need to hire a nursery maid. Grace intended to work a few hours at Doctor Harvey's surgery as soon as she was able, and Charlie needed to get back to his work as a private detective.

She tried and failed to imagine how women coped with several children and no help. If Anne Drummond hadn't been so welcoming to Grace, and the private detective business hadn't proved to be more successful than they had dared hope, that would have been their future too.

The front door opened and closed softly as the kettle began to whistle. Grace poked her head around the kitchen door. "Morning, Mrs Brown. Tea's almost ready."

Mrs Brown shot Grace a startled glance and mumbled something unintelligible as she hurried past to her room.

Grace gaped after her retreating back. Mrs Brown was wearing black clothes, complete with a black hat and veil. She rarely wore black, preferring sombre grey against starched white for the house, and soft browns for visiting. Grace's heart sank into her boots. Was she in mourning? Their housekeeper had never mentioned any relatives. As far as Grace knew, she was alone in the world, aside from her daughter, Sadie. Mrs Brown's husband had died at a tragically young age over two decades ago, leaving her a widow with a young child. Thus, if she was in mourning, the deceased must be one of Mrs Brown's many friends in the servant and church communities. It certainly explained their housekeeper's distraction over the last week. But why would she keep such news to herself?

A second thought followed hard on the heels of the first, to Grace's shame. If the deceased friend lived outside of Dunedin, perhaps Mrs Brown would need time off to travel to the funeral. Of course, her bereavement came before all other considerations, but the thought of coping without Mrs Brown in the last few weeks of her pregnancy sent an icicle of dread down Grace's spine.

She waddled down the hall to Mrs Brown's room. Her suspicion was correct. The funeral must be out of town, because their housekeeper was packing her carpetbag. Not knowing what to do, Grace returned to the kitchen.

Mrs Brown reappeared in her usual grey and white a few minutes later, without the carpetbag, just as Grace was putting the final touches to the tea tray and tidying up her mess.

"A cup of tea would be lovely, thank you, Mrs Penrose Pyke." Mrs Brown sniffed, her body stiffening like Blaze's did when she detected the scent of a criminal. "Oh, my dizzy lord! The roast! I'm so terribly sorry, it quite slipped my mind this morning."

"Don't fret, Mrs Brown, it's in the oven. I expect Charlie will be late home anyway, because he is attempting to catch a blackmailer at the First Church."

Mrs Brown looked a little weak at the knees, so Grace pulled out a chair for her and poured tea made to her exacting standards: one teaspoon of leaves per person and one for the pot, steeped for four minutes precisely, turn the pot three times each way, milk in first, then tea, and woe betide the infidel who suggests a little sugar would sweeten her up.

Their housekeeper closed her eyes as she took a first sip. "Ah. Perfect. Just what I needed." Her eyelids fluttered open. Deep brown eyes met Grace's gaze. "Thank you for seeing to the Sunday meal."

"It's the least I can do after all you do for us, day in and day out." Grace decided there was nothing for it but to dive in. "Mrs

Brown, if you have suffered a bereavement, or indeed any other misfortune, you only need ask and we will do whatever we can to support you. Time off, assistance, anything."

To Grace's horror, a tear glistened in the corner of Mrs Brown's eye. With anyone else, a hug might have been appropriate, but their housekeeper liked to maintain proper boundaries.

Grace covered her shock with babble. "Charlie and I have been wanting to talk to you about getting extra help. A respectable young woman with childcare experience, we thought. She could help me prepare for the arrival of the babies and take some of the workload off your hands. We ought to have been more diligent in our search for Sadie's replacement, for which I apologise."

Mrs Brown's daughter, Sadie, had been their maid-of-all-work until she left to pursue a higher post as a lady's maid. They had a devil of a time replacing her, because Mrs Brown had trained Sadie well. The first maid they hired lasted a week before she left, after complaining about comings and goings at all hours, and having to serve Orientals. They were pleased to see the back of her, because she had been rude to Charlie's beloved Aunt Lily, who took after her Chinese father. The second maid lasted three weeks until an incident with a knife-wielding criminal late one night. Being a maid to a private detective was not for everyone, Charlie had sighed. The maid herself put the matter more succinctly as she threw clothes into her suitcase: "I'm not staying here to be murdered in my sleep."

"A new maid?" Mrs Brown drew a deep breath. "How thoughtful of you, Mrs Penrose Pyke. However, I am sure I can manage. Most of those flibbertigibbet girls who pass themselves off as trained maids do no more than get under my feet. As for my unforgivable lapse, I can only plead that I received a piece of unpleasant news. A trifling personal matter, but I spent a little longer at church than usual this morning to reflect upon it. I can only apologise and assure you I shall not shirk from my duties again."

Before Grace could think of how to draw out the discussion, Mrs Brown rose. "Why don't I take your tea into the drawing room, Mrs Penrose Pyke? You can have a nice rest while I make the mint sauce." Without waiting for a reply, she left with the tea tray.

Banished from the kitchen, Grace could do no more for now. She gathered up the pups and retreated to the drawing room. But her bladder couldn't take any more liquid, and it was a fine day, so she changed her mind and took the pups to their outside pen to allow them to experience the wider world. Then she settled down in a sheltered spot to enjoy the spring sunshine, with half an eye on the pups and the rest of her attention on her notes on the science of inherited traits.

Grace found the subject fascinating because she knew from her own family that children with the same parents could be very different. A sensible older brother, a teasing second brother, a pious third brother, and the tearaway twins. God help her and Charlie if their twins resembled her twin brothers – she'd have to abandon them on the steps of a church to save her sanity. Her babies gave her a boot in the ribs. She rubbed her belly and promised she was only joking.

Blaze's litter showed the same diversity of character. The largest pup, Caesar, was mostly black, and preferred to sit and watch his domain with a regal gaze. The next largest was a dreamer, most often to be found contemplating some new delight, such as a daffodil or a manure pile, as if it held the answers to the mysteries of the universe. He'd been named Byron and sported a white chest as regular as a starched white shirt under a black tailcoat. The larger of the two females, Sage, loved to stalk beetles and skinks, passing like a shadow through the herb garden with a quivering nose and stealthy steps. Spark was the smallest, with a lightning bolt of white down her face and a lopsided puppy gait. Despite her size, she was the most curious and energetic of the pups and always at the centre of the mayhem.

Grace had made it almost to the end of her revision when a broad band of shade passed over her, jerking her out of her concentration.

Charlie smiled down at them. "Ah, my delightful and rapidly expanding family. Ready for lunch, Grace? The Drummonds are here." He held out a hand to help her up, before gathering the pups. "Good to see you looking so well, my love. I have an irrational fear that your labour pains will start the minute I leave the house."

"Don't even think about that happening, Charlie. These babies need to stay where they are until I'm good and ready." Not that she'd ever be truly ready.

When they entered the drawing room, Grace was surprised to see that a lean young man had joined their group. It took a second to recognise him as Johnny Todd, whom she had first met hawking kindling on the street almost five years ago. Disreputable as he had looked back then, he had twice the brains of most lads and had proved himself time and again as a helper on various cases. But never had he looked like this – hair slicked down, starched white collar, boots polished to a shine – for all the world as angelic as a choirboy.

Johnny flourished his cap in a jaunty arc. "How do, Miss Bones?"

"I am well, thank you, Johnny Sticks," Grace replied, acknowledging the old nicknames they'd used at their first meeting. She kissed Anne and Kenneth Drummond on their cheeks and took a seat, eager to hear how the blackmail investigation had gone.

Mrs Brown appeared with a tray of glasses and a jug of lemon barley water. "Lunch in twenty minutes."

Their housekeeper hurried out of the drawing room with little more than a polite nod to their guests, despite her long years of service to Anne. She closed the door behind her, which surprised Grace.

"Mrs Brown seems … out of sorts," Grace said to Anne. "Has she said anything to you?"

"I expect she is fretting over Sadie's upcoming nuptials." But Anne's gaze went back to the closed door, and her frown gave away her concern.

"Shall we get business over before we eat?" Charlie suggested. "I engaged Johnny to circulate amongst the congregation as they waited outside the First Church this morning. I'm hoping he's going to tell me that he heard no whispers of blackmail, so we can put this sorry affair down to a jealous rival of Miss Mackenzie."

Grace hadn't known about Johnny joining the investigation, but it was a good plan. As the one day of rest, Sunday was a time to catch up with friends and neighbours before church. Thus, the Sunday morning service was the perfect time to exchange news and gossip.

"No such luck, Copper Charlie," Johnny said. "Half the bleedin' congregation was whispering about wicked accusations. I reckon if outrage could fuel Jules Verne's giant cannon, he really could have got to the moon."

Johnny was proud of his reading skills and adored the inventiveness of Verne's writings. However, he was prone to exaggeration at times.

Charlie raised an eyebrow. "*Half* the congregation?"

"I heard five groups discussing malicious notes and half a dozen others clammed up as soon as I got within cooee." Johnny pulled a notebook out of his pocket. "Let's see now. A fat old lady with a face like a bulldog, fair hissing with anger at being wrongly accused of short-changing her customers."

"Mrs Gilchrist, the proprietress of Gilchrist's Haberdashery," Anne said, holding back a smile. "She scanned the waiting parishioners with a bulldog glare before she put money in the charity box. It's fair to say that she believes charity begins at home, so donating was out of character."

Johnny moved on to the next person on his list. "A pretty young woman with golden hair, who was being consoled by a love-struck young man. They were joined by another young woman, who was close to tears. Ordinary-looking, twenties, brown hair."

"The golden-haired lady is our client, Miss Mackenzie," Charlie said. "We can ask her about her friend. Go on, Johnny."

"Old Tulloch, the grumpy coalman, and his even grumpier wife. Reckon he looked frightened. From what I hear, you can take your pick of things to blackmail him for. If it can make him money, he'll do it, although he doesn't stray too far onto the side of outright crime. His wife was urging him to put a token sum in the box when I wandered past them, so they would be seen to be paying. How much, and for what indiscretion, I don't know. Tulloch seemed more interested in finding the blackmailer and beating him to a pulp."

"I know the man you mean," Kenneth Drummond said. "Not a pleasant fellow. Tulloch put money in the charity box, and he certainly didn't seem happy to part with the coins. Frankly, I don't know why he bothers to attend church when he has no intention of following the teachings."

"You're right there, Mr D.," Johnny said. "Old Tulloch will plead in vain outside the pearly gates before being cast into the fiery pits of Hell, from what I hear. His missus and all. Let's see now. After that, I overheard a trio of young fellows, dressed too prettily and far too pally with each other, if you take my drift."

Anne and Kenneth exchanged glances. "We saw them make donations, but they are relatively new to the congregation and we haven't been introduced. One of them was so nervous that he fumbled a coin. It was a shilling, and I'm sure he put several of them in the box, as did his friends."

Johnny consulted his notes. "The next potential victims were that pompous ass, Mr Morton, and his friend. They were talking in low voices, but I could tell they were angry, and I overheard the word blackmail. It seemed to me they must both be victims, because they seemed equally angry, rather than one consoling the other."

"Can you describe Morton's friend, Johnny?" Anne said.

"Short, plump, bushy beard, dressed like an undertaker."

"Sounds like Mr Landsburgh," Charlie said.

"Both men are volunteers at the church," Kenneth said. "Morton and Landsburgh share the not inconsiderable task of keeping the church accounts. They are both employed at banks as bookkeepers and have impeccable reputations. I cannot believe that either could be a victim of blackmail."

Grace didn't share Kenneth's optimistic view of human nature, because even respectable gentlemen had their secrets. However, there might be another explanation. "It's possible they were discussing the blackmail, rather than being victims of it. How did you know Mr Morton's name, Johnny?"

"Morton plays the high and mighty, but I happen to know he wears a wide sleeve to play poker at his club." Johnny caught the puzzled looks on their faces. "He cheats at cards, I mean. Not a professional cardsharp. He's only been spotted once, as far as I know, and he passed it off as a momentary lapse of judgement after a run of rum hands."

"How do you know about his cheating?" Grace asked. She knew Johnny had tentacles everywhere in Dunedin through his various legitimate enterprises, including a team of messenger boys, and he had many contacts amongst doormen and security guards at the various clubs. They needed to hear the details, because any lead was worth following up at this early stage of the investigation.

"Heard it from a fellow who works for the club Morton belongs to." Johnny grinned. "Old Mortie was mortified at being caught. My friend was having a good laugh about it, because Morton has a reputation for being strait-laced and God-fearing. However, he felt the cheating was out of character, so he let Morton off with a warning."

"Just a warning? Your friend didn't make an official report of the incident?"

"Morton offered him a generous tip to turn a blind eye, and my friend has a brood of children to feed. He saw no harm in it, just that once. Morton hasn't been back to the club again, nor any of the other clubs, so it appears he has learnt his lesson."

"Holy smoke," Anne said. "I wouldn't have pegged Morton as a cheat. He's been a church stalwart for decades. So upright he'd give a flagpole a run for its money. The same goes for Landsburgh, as far as I know, although I am not personally acquainted with him."

"Landsburgh's been a pillar of the community since he transferred here from Auckland a few years ago," Kenneth said. "Both he and Morton put money in the charity box, but I think it was only a couple of coins. Even if they were shillings, it's not an unusual sum for men of their standing, and not enough to suggest a blackmail demand. Why are you so interested in those two, Charlie?"

"Landsburgh was the man who opened the charity box after the service and counted the donations. Nobody else had access to the open box. I would have searched him, only the minister vouched for him as an upstanding citizen. The cocky devil even offered to turn his pockets out if I doubted his integrity. Perhaps his anger before the service was feigned. He could be the blackmailer, not a victim."

"I confess I am shocked," Kenneth said, "although I suppose it had to be someone from within the First Church congregation. Landsburgh is usually a pleasant, sociable fellow, always doing the rounds before church, greeting people and asking after them. I can imagine him as the type of person others might seek out for advice on their problems. But a wicked crime like blackmail seems like an inconceivable leap for a man of his character. Why would he need the money, when he has a good position at the bank?"

Grace was inclined to agree, especially as Landsburgh could have helped himself to any amount of money from the charity box with ease while he was doing the weekly count. There was no need for him to resort to a crime as sordid as blackmail.

"I'm not accusing him," Charlie replied. "I'm simply following the evidence as it presents itself. I'll have to speak to the minister again. He and I can have a quiet word with Landsburgh to decide whether the bookkeeper is an innocent party, a victim, or something worse. If the latter, our investigation might ensure he never does it again, even if we cannot prove a case against him. Carry on with your list, Johnny. The minister will also need to be made aware of the extent of the crime."

Johnny ran through several other groups on his list who had cut short their conversation when he passed by, which might or might not mean anything. Anne and Kenneth recognised most of them by their descriptions and confirmed they had made donations.

"The trouble is," Anne said, "most people put money in the charity box. Several people appeared furtive, in that they seemed to be very alert to the people around them. I cannot help but think we are missing something."

"I agree," Charlie said. "With so many victims, it seems inconceivable that the total collection was rather less than usual, according to Landsburgh. If he didn't pocket the higher denomination donations, how else could a portion of the money have been taken? The only suspicious incident was the woman stumbling into the table the charity box was sitting on. I cannot imagine how it could be relevant when she had neither the time nor the opportunity to take money from the box, because other ladies rushed forward immediately to help her up. Do you know who she was?"

Anne cast a worried glance toward the door before she leaned forward to whisper a name. "Mrs Car–". She jumped as the door opened.

Mrs Brown entered and handed Charlie a message. "Shall I hold back lunch, Mr Penrose Pyke?"

Charlie opened the note. "No need, thank you, Mrs Brown. Whenever you are ready is fine." He waited for Mrs Brown to leave before he continued. "Miss Mackenzie writes to thank us for our help. You'll be pleased to hear that she told her fiancé, and he declared nothing would come between them and their wedding vows, even if the gossip had been true. She also confirms that she put a marked note in the charity box and mentions that her friend received a blackmail demand as well. The friend was told to put a shilling in the box, or face being exposed for wearing silk undergarments under her austere outer clothes."

Grace stifled a chuckle. How absurd that anyone would care about a secret taste for silk. However, it was not a laughing matter for the young lady concerned, especially if her parents held strict religious and moral views. "One has to credit the blackmailer with a wealth of knowledge. Not to mention a fine understanding of the varied sums appropriate to the alleged indiscretion. A shilling for the minor wickedness of silk underwear, a pound for the disgrace of being illegitimate. Given the church connection, I wouldn't be surprised if the blackmailer was on a moral crusade to make people atone for their sins."

"I cannot reconcile a man like Landsburgh with a knowledge of a girl's preference for silk underwear," Kenneth said. "Or intimate knowledge of a coalman's secrets, for that matter. Sounds more like gossip-mongering or servant tittle-tattle to me."

Grace was inclined to agree, but, right now, she was concerned about the odd behaviour of Anne and Mrs Brown. "Auntie Anne, you were about to tell us the name of the woman who stumbled against the charity box. I'd like to know why you looked so ill at ease when Mrs Brown entered the room."

Anne's eyes flicked to the door again before she replied in a low voice. "Her name is Mrs Carmichael. Not a nice lady, but I cannot see how she could have tampered with the charity box. Her friends were beside her in an instant, steadying her and picking up the fallen flower vase."

"Not nice?" Grace prompted.

"Mrs Brown worked for her before she married Mr Brown. It's a long story, but Mrs Carmichael was far from an exemplary employer. It's a long time ago – a quarter of a century ago, in fact. Water well and truly under the bridge and out to sea, as far as I am concerned. Mrs Brown refuses to utter her name, and I have no wish to upset her by talking about that woman in her hearing. I'd love to know what Mrs Carmichael was threatened with to make her as nervous as she seemed at church today. Whatever it was, she probably deserved it."

The bell rang in the dining room, signalling that lunch was ready.

Charlie rose and helped Grace up. "I'll visit Mrs Carmichael after lunch. The other victims too, although I suspect they will be reluctant to talk to me. I'm not sure what to do about Landsburgh. He doesn't strike me as a likely blackmail suspect, so I want to be very sure of my facts before I speak to the minister about him. Come, let's eat."

Anne put out her walking cane to hold him back. She struggled to her feet and came right up in front of them, worry adding years to the many lines on her seventy-six-year-old face. "The odd thing is, I could swear I saw Mrs Brown at the First Church this morning. Only, that's impossible, because she is Anglican and because the woman I thought was her was wearing black."

Charlie lowered his voice to Anne's barely audible whisper. "Mrs Brown never wears black. It's as if she is determined not to be seen as a widow. I didn't see her face in the crowd."

"She was wearing a veil," Anne said. "She slipped in with a crowd of women, behind my dressmaker and her many assistants. Two of Mrs Harper's workers wear veils to church to cover their unsightly facial scars, so one more veiled woman didn't stand out. I must have been mistaken. The woman slipped out early, so there was no chance to speak to her."

Grace's innards clenched in a way that had nothing to do with premature contractions. "Mrs Brown came home late this morning wearing a black dress and veil. I assumed she must have suffered a bereavement and didn't wish to talk about it. Mrs Brown was so distracted that she forgot to put the roast on."

Anne and Charlie's sharp intakes of breath said it all. Mrs Brown hadn't forgotten to put on the Sunday roast in living memory. She'd sooner forget to breathe.

A Suspicious Stumble

After lunch, their guests didn't linger. Johnny departed as soon as the jam roly-poly plate was scraped clean, claiming business of his own to attend to, and Anne and Kenneth left soon after.

Grace leaned on the gate while Charlie helped them into their buggy. She couldn't help but notice the way Charlie rubbed the small of his back as he farewelled their guests. Always a sign of a tingling down his spine, which meant he had a nasty feeling about this investigation. Anne seemed to share the instinct, because she leaned across from the buggy and squeezed his shoulder.

If two of the cleverest people she knew felt uneasy, Grace was not about to let Charlie walk into the lion's den alone. Anne had given them an address on lower Maitland Street for the Carmichael residence, and there was no time like the present.

"Do you mind if we borrow your buggy for the rest of the afternoon, Auntie Anne?" Grace asked.

Charlie shot her a suspicious glance. "What for, Grace? It's a lovely afternoon, and I could do with a walk."

"I'm coming with you to interview Mrs Carmichael, of course. Don't look at me like that, my sweet. I've had a restful morning, and my brain will explode if I try to cram any more knowledge into it for tomorrow's examination. A distraction is exactly what I need."

"Why don't you come with us now, Charlie?" Anne said, as if the matter was settled. "You can bring the buggy back as soon as you have delivered us home. Don't scowl, young man. You'll need a lever to get the Carmichaels to answer highly personal questions about their indiscretions. Who could refuse to talk to a woman who looks as if she'll give birth on their sitting room floor if she is thwarted?" Anne chortled but soon turned serious again. "Please don't discuss your visit with Mrs Brown. The merest mention of Mrs Carmichael's name will cause her great distress."

Charlie knew better than to argue. He waved them off and walked after them, sparing the horse the burden of dragging his bulk up a steep hill.

Grace returned to the house. Mrs Brown's bedroom door was emphatically shut, so Grace did the final tidying and securing of wily canines, before waiting at the gate for her husband's return. She used the time to plot a strategy to extract information from reluctant lips, and to puzzle over Mrs Brown's extreme aversion to Mrs Carmichael. Their housekeeper was liked by all and sundry, and she generally returned the favour.

Ten minutes later, Charlie helped Grace into the buggy, a task that involved much manoeuvring on his part and undignified grunting on her part. The trip to the bottom of Maitland Street didn't take long, but the time passed in heavy silence. If Anne was correct in seeing their housekeeper at the First Church, there could only be two reasons. The first was that Mrs Brown had suddenly renounced her Anglican faith after four decades. The second was that she was another of the blackmail victims.

Neither option seemed remotely plausible. Mrs Brown was the epitome of respectability. Unless she was being accused of producing the occasional roast potato that wasn't perfectly crisped, Grace was at a loss to explain it. On the other hand, Mrs Brown was an intensely private person, who kept to the rigorous boundaries between mistress and servant, although she must have known that Grace and Anne, and now Charlie, considered her part of the family.

The best explanation Grace could come up with was that Mrs Brown might have been forced to borrow from an unscrupulous moneylender to pay for her daughter's wedding. Grace would never forgive herself if that were the case. She resolved to discuss an increase in wages with Charlie tonight. And they would have to settle the pressing matter of hiring extra help for Mrs Brown.

Charlie pulled the horse to a halt outside a large house near the bottom end of the road. Although the house must have been grand when it was built, it showed signs of slipping into disrepair. Grace wondered if the Carmichael family was having money troubles. Naturally, being a suspicious lady detective, this led her to wonder if they had resorted to blackmail. Of course, the far greater likelihood was that their fortune had suffered during the recession, like so many others had.

"How are you going to convince them to talk to you?" Grace asked, as her husband helped her down from the buggy. "Despite Anne's claim about my pregnant presence, I can't see the type of grand folk who live in a house like this agreeing to air their dirty linen in front of a private detective."

Charlie helped her up the path and rang the bell by the door. "I anticipated the problem yesterday and armed myself with a secret weapon."

A man came around the side of the house, carrying a shovel and wearing muddy boots and rough working clothes. A tall, handsome fellow with broad shoulders, who wore his sixty-odd years with the bearing of a man twenty years his junior. Odd that a gardener would work on a Sunday afternoon, Grace thought, and even odder that he seemed so confident, as if he owned the place.

"Can I help you?" the man said.

"We'd like to talk to Mr and Mrs Carmichael," Charlie replied.

"You're talking to him."

Charlie reached out to shake his hand. "Charlie Penrose Pyke. I've been engaged to investigate a matter on behalf of the First

Church. I have a letter signed by the minister, if you would like to see it."

Mr Carmichael cast a suspicious eye over Charlie. "If this is about me not coming to church on a Sunday, I've not changed my mind since the last time the good reverend sent a delegation. Easter and Christmas are enough for me, especially as my wife is devout enough for both of us. I've got my business to tend to. Tools don't sharpen themselves, and Sunday morning is the only free time I get to do it."

"It's nothing like that, Mr Carmichael. In fact, it's your wife we need to speak to about a church matter."

The mention of tools clicked with the surname in Grace's brain. This man must be the owner of Carmichael's Ironmongery, purveyor of tools, stoves, grates, bedsteads, tinware and cutlery, and all manner of other items made of iron. The shop was a few minutes away on Princes Street.

"It's a matter of some delicacy," Grace said. "If we might go inside?"

Mr Carmichael strode past them and pushed the front door open, bellowing for his wife in what Grace's mother referred to as an outside voice. With five sons and a daughter, Grace's mother had more reason than most to insist on inside voices within the confines of the house.

"There's no need to shout, dear." A sour-faced woman appeared from a room further down the hallway. She faltered at the sight of them, straightening her spine and raising an inquiring eyebrow. "Oh, visitors. Do come in. Please excuse my husband's muddy attire. He does love to potter in the garden."

She glared at her husband's feet, and he promptly kicked off his muddy boots. Carmichael's wife was dressed in a dark gown with a hint of lace at the neck, as befitted a respectable lady of sixty, and looked as if butter wouldn't melt in her mouth. Her shawl was the only discordant note, a deep maroon shade trimmed with a ribbon the colour of a pumpkin. Not a combination Grace would have chosen, but each to their own taste.

Mrs Carmichael hesitated in the hallway, eyeing up Grace's enormous belly and Charlie's respectable attire. Her raised eyebrow told Grace she was struggling to place their status and therefore whether she ought to invite them in for tea or interrogate them in the hallway.

"Good afternoon, Mrs Carmichael," Charlie said, flashing her a charming smile. "Mr and Mrs Penrose Pyke, at your service. I was just telling your husband that we have been engaged by your minister to investigate a situation of grave concern to the church. Our sincere apologies for calling unannounced on a Sunday afternoon, but the matter is urgent. I have a letter of authority if you wish to peruse it."

Mrs Carmichael sprang to attention as soon as he mentioned the minister. "Naturally, I will do whatever is required to assist the church, although I cannot imagine what can be of such urgent concern. Please come through to the parlour."

The parlour appeared to be reserved for rare guests, judging from the musty tinge in the air. The furniture would have been grand twenty years ago, but it showed signs of wear. Unfortunately, the deep scarlet fabric of the armchairs clashed dreadfully with a most unfortunate choice of lime-green for the cushions, and the dusty pink of the antimacassars.

Mrs Carmichael waved them to the best armchairs by the window. "Tea?"

"I'll see to it," her husband said, "since it's you they want to speak to. Maid's day off," he added to Charlie.

Grace didn't particularly feel like more tea, but they did want to speak to Mrs Carmichael alone. She flicked a look at Charlie, who rose to examine a sailing ship in a bottle sitting on the mantelpiece.

Mrs Carmichael seemed pleased by his interest. "It's a model of the ship that brought us to this colony, all the way from Scotland. Nothing like the easy journey the later arrivals enjoyed on steamships. I thought I should go quite mad in that tiny cabin with our three daughters. We have a son too, but he was born here."

Grace recognised the gambit for what it was – a subtle positioning to determine the status of her guests. There remained a bone-deep pride among the families of the early colonists, who had earned easy wealth by gobbling up the lion's share of land and resources before the waves of later immigrants arrived. The first settlers, as they called themselves, ignoring the fact that the native Māori population had been here long before the British arrived. The mention of travelling in a cabin emphasised they were not amongst the majority of lowly wage workers travelling steerage class, who shared a crowded bunkroom under the deck.

Fortunately, this was a game in which Grace held all the aces. "My grandparents came to New Zealand in 1840 on a ship very like that one. They were among the very first English settlers." A little humility helped too. "My grandfather was the ship's surgeon, and my grandmother belonged to a shipping family. Practical people."

Mrs Carmichael nodded eagerly, as she settled comfortably into her armchair, the rapport firmly established. "My husband made the model. A practical man, as you say, with the ambition to make his fortune. He saw the need for equipment for the gold rush, you see. Spades and pickaxes and whatnot."

"A wise move on his part. My husband's father and grandfather were the same. No point toiling in freezing rivers panning for elusive gold when the real money was made selling wares to the miners."

Charlie raised an eyebrow ever so slightly, but Grace ignored it. Mrs Carmichael might not be so ready to talk if she knew the truth – that Charlie's grandfather was a Chinese miner turned market gardener and his father was a rural policeman.

He put the bottle down with great care. "It might be best to leave you ladies to your conversation. I confess I am eager to hear about Mr Carmichael's experience of crafting this fine model ship."

Grace settled further into her armchair, one hand resting on the mound of her belly. "We are fortunate women, are we not, to have successful husbands who are not too proud to make tea when their wives have important matters to discuss."

Their hostess was practically purring by now. "You mentioned a church matter, Mrs Penrose Pyke."

"A matter of great delicacy, I'm sorry to say. The minister has been made aware of some unpleasant incidents. Blackmail letters sent to several members of the congregation." Grace paused to observe Mrs Carmichael's reaction. The colour had drained from her face. If her fingers dug any further into her palms, there would be blood on the pink antimacassar. The only question that remained was whether she was a victim or the blackmailer. Given her reaction, Grace placed her bet on her being a victim.

"How dreadful," Mrs Carmichael said, when she had recovered enough to feign nonchalance.

Grace left a momentary pause for Mrs Carmichael to reconsider her answer. When the silence dragged, Grace leaned forward, opting for a sympathetic tone. "Other respectable people have been targeted by this disgraceful criminal. We need to talk to all the victims, in order to uncover the identity of this scoundrel. Whatever you say will be held in the strictest confidence, Mrs Carmichael. You may discuss the matter with your minister if you would prefer."

Mrs Carmichael looked towards the window, although it was unclear whether she did so to avoid Grace's scrutiny or out of concern for being overheard. "It was such a trivial matter … but, of course, one has one's reputation to protect. As a devout Christian, I mean."

"A trivial matter?" Grace leaned further forward, encouraging the disclosure, but she had left her run too late. The thump of heavy feet in the hallway signalled the return of the men.

Mr Carmichael burst into the parlour. "Apparently, there is a blackmailer running riot through the church congregation. Outrageous. Of course, I told Mr Penrose Pyke that we had no reason at all to be targeted by this rogue." He must have seen the tears glistening in his wife's eyes, because he went down on one knee and took her hand. "Vera? What is it?"

"I received a blackmail note, Richard. I didn't want to bother you with such a trifling matter."

A bloom of angry red flushed across her husband's cheeks. "You had no right to keep that from me. Blackmail is never trivial. If you'd told me about it, I'd have hunted the scoundrel down myself and shown him the blunt end of my knuckles."

"No need for that, sir," Charlie said. "It's my job to apprehend the blackmailer. May I ask what the letter said, Mrs Carmichael?"

Mrs Carmichael's fingers flicked over her sleeve, as if brushing aside a minor annoyance. "An entirely ridiculous claim that I ill-treated servants on occasion. I pride myself on being firm but fair."

"What servants?" her husband grumbled. "We've only one maid-of-all-work, and she hasn't the brains to clean a grate properly, let alone to write a blackmail letter. Ugliest woman this side of Glasgow."

"It cannot be our present maid, dear," his wife said. "She's illiterate."

"Servants can be a fickle, ungrateful lot," Carmichael went on, as if his wife hadn't spoken. "Honestly, girls get the silliest notions into their heads. I blame those cheap, sordid novels one sees everywhere these days."

"That last maid we had is the more likely culprit, in my opinion," Mrs Carmichael said. "She ripped my best shawl with her clumsiness, and I had to dismiss her. I never trusted her. Irish Catholic, and too quick with her tongue to her betters."

Her husband grunted his agreement. "Second ugliest woman this side of Glasgow. Is it so difficult to employ a maid who is both competent and pretty?"

Grace tried not to show her disgust at their prejudices in the interests of advancing the investigation. Mr Carmichael was no different from most men, who thought nothing of judging a woman solely by her appearance and her usefulness as a wife or servant. Grace could see why Mrs Brown had not wished to remain in service to the Carmichaels all those years ago.

"Do you still have the letter, Mrs Carmichael?" Charlie asked.

"Heavens no. I burnt it."

"Good thing, too," her husband said. "Trying to cadge money off respectable people. It's a disgrace. A good flogging is what's needed. Do you know where the Irish girl went when she left here, my dear?"

"She had a sister in Wellington, as I recall," Mrs Carmichael said. "However, if other members of the congregation have also received letters, I suppose it cannot have been her, or indeed any of our former servants. Why would this criminal send a letter full of lies to me? And how did you come to know of my situation, Mr Penrose Pyke?"

Nervous as she'd been about being revealed as a blackmail victim in front of her husband, Mrs Carmichael seemed doubly ill at ease now. Far more nervous than one would expect for an accusation of ill-treating a maid. A fair proportion of the city's households would brush that off as a trivial matter or justify it as a necessary reprimand for correcting a maid's inattention to her duties.

"I was observing the charity box at the church on Sunday morning," Charlie said. "I take it from your reaction, Mrs Carmichael, that the letter you received requested you put money in the box, just as the other victims were asked to do. May I ask the sum demanded?"

Mrs Carmichael's eyelids twitched like a rabbit trapped in a corner with a fox approaching. She swallowed the lump in her throat and failed to meet her husband's steely gaze. "It was a trifle. A couple of shillings. I thought it better to pay than to have the worry resting on my shoulders. I would have donated to the worthy cause anyway."

She was lying. Grace was sure of it. However, she was not sure if Mrs Carmichael was lying about the amount of the blackmail demand or something else.

"How dreadful for you," Grace said, leaning forward to draw the victim into an intimate one-to-one. "It must have been deeply upsetting, Mrs Carmichael. Is that why you stumbled when you were putting the coins in the charity box?"

Again, Mrs Carmichael hesitated before responding. "There was such a crush of people in the lobby at this morning's service. I don't know why they didn't move through into the church in an orderly manner like normal. Someone jostled me from behind, and I tripped on the hem of my gown. It was mortifying. I knocked over a vase of flowers in front of half the congregation. The beautiful velvet cloth on the table was completely soaked."

"Just as well you had the charity box to steady you," Charlie said.

"It was my friend who steadied me. It all happened so fast. Without her quick reactions, I would have fallen to the floor. All I could think about was how Mrs Yates broke her hip when she took a tumble last year."

"Well, let's hope we've seen the last of this rogue," her husband said. "Cheer up, my dear. I can see Donald coming up the path. Light of his mother's eye, our son."

Mrs Carmichael wiped her eyes, but it was her delighted smile that transformed her. "Light of both our eyes."

"Too right. A man needs a son to follow in his footsteps. Isn't that so, Mr Penrose Pyke?" He winked at Charlie and nodded at Grace's belly. "Most important thing in the world, a pretty woman to bear sons."

Charlie mumbled something noncommittal. Grace caught his eye to show her understanding. Her husband had made it clear from the day he found out about her pregnancy that he'd be delighted with whatever children they were blessed with, whether girls or boys.

Mrs Carmichael looked daggers at her husband, but Mr Carmichael failed to register her rebuke.

"Donald has picked himself a fine filly," Mr Carmichael said. "They're to be married next year. We'll soon have a grandson to be proud of."

"She is a lovely lady," Mrs Carmichael said. "Not like some of the young women today, who flutter their fans at all the young men in the most shameless manner. And her uncle is a member of the Dunedin Club. Our Donald has made a fine match."

Her husband rolled her eyes. Grace had no trouble guessing why. The Dunedin Club was a bastion of old wealth, accessible by invitation only. Originally a club for high-country runholders when they were in town, with the decline in mutton and wool prices, membership had been extended to include city gentlemen.

However, the solid oak door remained firmly closed to the likes of a moderately successful ironmonger with a socially ambitious wife.

The front door slammed. Donald breezed into the parlour, embracing his mother, to her obvious delight. After kissing her cheek, he said, "Why are you in the parlour, Ma? You know the décor gives me heart palpitations."

"We have visitors." His mother gestured behind him.

"Good afternoon, Mr Carmichael," Charlie said. "We were on our way out. May I offer you congratulations on your upcoming nuptials?"

Donald's face lit up. "The happiest day of my life was when my beloved agreed to be mine. We're getting married on my birthday, so I never forget my wedding anniversary."

"Men," his mother said. "As if he could forget, it being St Valentine's Day too."

The Carmichael men exchanged amused glances, as if to say that kind of frivolity was for soft-hearted romantics, not real men. Young Donald was a chip off the old block, with his father's blue-grey eyes and good looks, and his mother's air of gentility. However, his sartorial style marked him out from either of his parents, elegantly dressed as he was in a well-tailored suit. A deep red cravat added a touch of colour, matching the fine red stripe of his elegant midnight blue waistcoat.

"We'll leave you to your family," Charlie said. "Thank you for your time."

"You make sure you catch this blasted scoundrel," Mr Carmichael said as they left, but his focus was already turning back to his son as the door closed behind them.

A Shocking Twist

Charlie heaved Grace into the buggy with practised ease and flicked the reins to set the horse for home.

"I'm certain Mr Carmichael had no inkling of the blackmail before I told him," Charlie said, as soon as they were out of earshot of the garden.

"Whereas his wife was far more concerned than she admitted," Grace said. "I think Mrs Carmichael was understating the seriousness of the accusation against her or the amount demanded by the blackmailer. I could be wrong. Given her social aspirations, it might simply be horror at the thought of scandal, no matter how trivial, especially with her son about to marry the niece of a Dunedin club member."

Charlie was grateful, as ever, that Grace had no such pretensions. "I feel sorry for her husband, who has no desire to be measured by such standards. He is proud of the business he has built and the fine house he has provided for his family."

"Rightly so, although I do wish Mr Carmichael's attitude to women might be more appropriate to the times. I'll bet he was outraged at the notion of women getting the vote. Probably one of those brutes who protested outside the suffrage meetings." Grace nudged his ribs. "How fortunate for me that I fluttered my fan at a more enlightened gentleman."

"I'm no more a gentleman than Richard Carmichael," Charlie said, returning the nudge. "And it was more like a fluttering of the sheet covering a corpse than a fan, as I recall."

Grace laughed. "How could you resist such an alluring signal? It's good to be back out in the fresh air. I'm glad the son's arrival gave us an excuse to leave."

Charlie would have loved to let the matter rest there, but their path led home towards the issue of Mrs Brown's unusual behaviour. It had to be tackled, sooner rather than later. "I can see why Mrs Brown did not care to work for the family, especially if the wife considers ill-treatment of servants a trivial matter."

"And yet Mrs Carmichael considers herself an exemplary Christian. I keep going back to my earlier thought, that the blackmailer might be on a crusade against perceived immorality. Christian forgiveness and love for all mankind seemed somewhat lacking in her character, and the aging furniture and peeling paint might indicate a financial motive."

Charlie saw his wife's point. It was not at all hard to imagine Mrs Carmichael as a potential blackmailer rather than a victim. "You talked to her. What does your instinct say, Grace?"

"That she was lying about something. However, I'd have to say her reaction was consistent with being a victim. She certainly seemed genuinely distressed at being blackmailed. What she said about falling after being jostled by the crowd rang true as well. Even if she staged it, I cannot see how she could have removed money from a locked charity box in such a brief moment of confusion, especially as she was instantly surrounded by helpers."

"I agree." Charlie said. "I cannot see the husband as a blackmailer either. His shock when I told him about it was genuine, and he has only the slightest connection to the First Church. Frustrating, but we cannot expect miracles in a single day. It's the removal of Miss Mackenzie's marked banknote that is driving me to distraction. I'll go back to the scene of the crime tomorrow, while you are completing your last examination ever."

"Assuming I pass. As soon as we get home, we must talk to Mrs Brown."

But Mrs Brown was busy cooking when they arrived home a few minutes later, and she made it clear she didn't want them under her feet in the kitchen. The sharpness of her tone indicated that whatever was troubling her had not been resolved, but the meal choice – Charlie's favourite shepherd's pie with a caramel sponge for pudding – suggested she was not cross with them. He vowed to get to the bottom of it later that evening.

Grace seemed relieved at the delay. She fell asleep on the sofa – feet up to ease her swollen ankles and torso up to prevent heartburn. The resulting V-shape around her bulge looked hopelessly uncomfortable.

Charlie went out into the garden to reflect on what he had learned about the blackmail so far. He ended up with a long list of questions and no answers. Meanwhile, Blaze lay contentedly by his side, while the pups cavorted around them. Charlie's spirits rose at the uncomplicated pleasure of their doggy delight in his presence. Sometimes, he wondered if he would tire of the frustrations and unpleasantness of being a private detective. Risking encounters with vicious criminals was all very well as a single man, or even in partnership with Grace, but soon they would have a family to protect.

By the time he returned indoors with an armful of squirming collies, the table was set for dinner. The wafting aroma from the kitchen left him weak at the knees from hunger. The serious discussion with Mrs Brown would have to wait until he'd been fortified with her delicious cooking.

After dinner, he called Mrs Brown into the drawing room and thanked her for another splendid meal. She sat on the edge of the seat, a dishcloth clutched like a lifebelt. Charlie didn't have to be a detective to know something was worrying her, but he feared saying the wrong thing would make it worse. The dishcloth was suffering a fierce twisting in Mrs Brown's hands. Grace fidgeted too. Perhaps he ought to start by insisting on increasing her wages, which ought to smooth troubled waters.

"Mrs Brown," he began, "I fear we have been remiss in –"

The dishcloth dropped from their housekeeper's hands as she rose from her seat, cutting his sentence short. "I'll make this easy for you, Mr Penrose Pyke. I am painfully aware that my work has been unsatisfactory. I also know you went to see the Carmichaels this afternoon." She dug into her apron pocket and produced an envelope. "My resignation."

"What? No, you cannot resign. Wait. Please, let me explain, Mrs Brown –"

"There is nothing to gain by discussing the matter, Mr Penrose Pyke. I know what they told you, and I will not bring shame on this household." Mrs Brown ran from the room, leaving a stunned silence behind.

The door to her bedroom closed with a bang. Charlie's mouth opened, but no words filled the gaping hole.

Grace was the first to recover. "Holy smoke. What a disaster. Anne will throttle us if we lose Mrs Brown. I'll go and beg her to stay."

Charlie waited on tenterhooks. He paced the drawing room as Grace knocked gently on the housekeeper's bedroom door, getting no response. The silence drew out. Grace knocked again, harder.

He could stand it no longer. Charlie joined her outside the door and pleaded for Mrs Brown to come out. "I was only going to say we'd been remiss in not increasing your wages."

Grace pushed the door, which swung open to an empty room. "Charlie, her carpetbag is gone too. I saw her packing it earlier today. I thought the black dress meant she'd suffered a bereavement and assumed she must need to leave town for a few days for a funeral." She clutched his hands. "Go after her! It's nearly dark, so she cannot have gone far. Sadie's place of work or Auntie Anne's house."

Charlie didn't need any persuasion. Losing Mrs Brown was a disaster of the first order. She cannot have been gone for more than a couple of minutes at most. With luck, if he was quick, he'd see if she was walking down High Street towards her daughter or up towards Anne Drummond. He barged through the front door at speed, leaping over the steps and vaulting the gate onto the street.

Advanced as the twilight was, he could still see far enough to know she hadn't gone downhill. He raced up the hill and around the corner to the Drummonds' house, pounding on their door like a demon possessed. Kenneth Drummond's valet answered the door.

"Is Mrs Brown here?" Charlie asked before the door was half open.

"Is that you, Charlie?" Anne appeared at the door to the sitting room. "Why would Mrs Brown be here at this hour? What's wrong?"

"Mrs Brown has left us! I tried to talk to her about what was upsetting her, but I made a mess of it. She said she knew we'd been to see the Carmichaels and handed me her resignation. I have to find her and beg her to stay."

Shock jagged across Anne's face. "It's my fault. She must have overheard me mentioning her former employers. Mrs Brown never talks about them, but I know there was some unpleasantness that caused her to leave their employ."

Right now, Charlie didn't care about past unpleasantness, although he was sorry for whatever Mrs Brown had suffered. "I don't think she's gone to Sadie. Where else would she go?"

Kenneth Drummond joined them, his boots on and ready for action. "Lavender House?"

Charlie ought to have thought of that first. As a women's refuge, it would be the obvious place to spend a night. But was it too obvious? If she didn't want to be found, Mrs Brown could have gone to one of her many friends, who would have taken her in without asking questions.

Anne frowned. "She is a very private person. Whenever anything troubling happens, the first place she goes is to Mr Brown's grave. She likes to talk her troubles through with him."

Mr Brown was buried in the Southern Cemetery, about a mile away, past the far end of Maitland Street. Charlie had his doubts. "It's getting dark. No sane person goes there at night."

A fleeting smirk twitched Anne's lips. "*Mrs Brown* isn't afraid of a few wee ghosties, Charlie."

He wasn't either, or at least not enough to stop him from going after Mrs Brown. But rumours of strange happenings in the city's oldest graveyard were enough to spook the most sensible of people.

Kenneth slipped past his wife. "You take the cemetery. I'll take Lavender House."

"Go down Eglinton Road, Charlie," Anne advised, "if you want to catch her before she gets to the graveyard. Mrs Brown never walks past the Carmichaels' house, and it's almost as quick the other way. Mr Brown is in the Catholic Section. We'll meet you back at your house." She reached out to catch his arm before he left. "Bring her home safely, I beg you."

Charlie dashed off, desperate to catch Mrs Brown before anything happened to her. He cut down Stafford Street and took a shortcut through the Town Belt to Eglinton Road. She was nowhere in sight, so he doubled his speed on the downhill section.

As soon as he reached the first graves, he left the road, not wanting to run past her in his haste.

He ought to have asked for better directions, because the Southern Cemetery covered a vast area. It was the first of the new style of multi-denominational public cemeteries, since traditional small graveyards within church grounds were no longer practical. Thus, there were different sections for each denomination. Anne said Mr Brown was in the Catholic section. He had a vague idea that was closer to the far end of Eglinton Road, but he wasn't certain. He forged on through the cemetery.

By day, it was a pleasant place, dotted with a multitude of trees and meandering paths, with views of the harbour and peninsula. By night, it was a maze of paths and creepy shadows. He stumbled in what he hoped was the right direction, going down into hollows and up again, constantly forced to change direction as the rows of graves went first one way and then another. Tall crosses and tombs, graceful by daylight, loomed menacingly. The deepening night meant he could barely see a few yards ahead. More than once, he tripped over lumps of stone and marble.

The clawed limbs of overhanging trees seemed to reach out for him as he hurried past. He breathed a little faster, telling himself he was only out of breath after running. Somewhere in the dark, he heard a spine-tingling keening. Foolishly, he'd run out of the house without a weapon. Charlie picked up a broken branch. Much good it would do him against ghosts. Not that he believed in ghosts.

Somewhere ahead of him in the dark were the graves of seventeen Māori warriors. Local legend had it that at least one of them had risen from the grave to torment anyone who dared violate their final resting place. In the daylight, he was sympathetic to their plight. They were proud men, wrenched from their families in the 1860s and forced into hard labour in freezing Dunedin, after being captured during the Taranaki land wars, far to the north. By night, the prospect of an avenging Māori warrior, ghostly or otherwise, turned his blood cold.

The keening grew louder as he moved south. Something touched his forehead. He jumped back and lashed out with the branch, shaking his head at his foolishness when he realised it was only a tangle of leaves dangling from a tree.

At last, he found a path into the next section of the cemetery, where the keening resolved into weeping. A woman weeping. That he could deal with, or so he hoped. Another few steps and he saw the woman on her knees beside the plainest of graves. A solid human form, not a ghost.

"Mrs Brown, it's Charlie."

Her head whipped around, her hand to her mouth, too slow to stifle a scream. She jumped to her feet and grabbed her carpetbag.

He came close enough to read the lichen-dappled inscription on a simple plaque. Nothing more than a surname, Brown, and a date from over two decades ago. No "dearly beloved husband and father", no "rest in peace", not even a first name or a birth date. Just one more unexplained mystery in a day full of them.

"Please don't make me chase you, Mrs Brown. I've come to apologise for the misunderstanding. Grace and I wanted to meet with you to tell you how much you mean to us. We want to increase your wages to reflect how hard you work. And to insist we get help, because when Grace has the babies…" Charlie stopped gabbling out his apology and stepped towards her. "Please, don't leave us. We're sorry about the chaos the puppies have caused and anything else we have done to upset you. The late nights, the disruption our detective work causes to your routine, the mayhem. You've been a saint to put up with us."

Mrs Brown sank onto the edge of her husband's grave, her head in her hands.

Charlie sat down beside her, putting his arm around her shaking shoulders. Silence seemed best until she was ready to speak.

A flash of light caught his eye. It bobbed back and forth between the graves, getting closer by the second. He stood, putting his bulk between the apparition and Mrs Brown.

"Oi! You there! Whatcha doin' in my cem'tery in the dead of night?"

Hardly the dead of night, Charlie thought, but he knew there had been problems with wild behaviour in the cemetery. Drinking, vandalism, debauchery. He could see the man holding the lantern now. A shotgun protruded from the crook of his other arm.

Charlie spread his palms to show he was unarmed. "Good evening, sir. Are you the sexton?"

"Aye." The sexton came up to them, holding the lantern up to their faces unsteadily. The brandy fumes on his breath could have lit a fire, which explained the weaving course he had taken up the hill towards them. He looked from one to the other, a smirk curling his lip. "You can take your filthy game somewhere else. Gawd lad, that slattern is old enough to be yer mam."

It took a second for his meaning to sink in. A young man and a middle-aged woman found alone in a graveyard in the dark. Charlie gave the sexton the full force of his sternest constabulary glare. "I am Detective Penrose Pyke. Mrs Brown, who is a family member, wanted to visit her husband's grave after a distressing day. We're leaving now."

Mrs Brown clearly didn't like the look of the sexton, because she hooked her arm through Charlie's and pulled him up the hill without further ado. They reached Eglinton Road in less than a minute. Charlie felt a fool for having stumbled through the entire length of the cemetery when he could so easily have come down the road and saved himself the ordeal.

They walked arm-in-arm for several minutes until Mrs Brown broke the silence. "Thank you for coming to my aid, Mr Penrose Pyke. And for pretending to be family to protect my honour."

"You *are* family to us, Mrs Brown. Let's go home and talk in comfort. I'm sure it's what your husband would want." Charlie hoped that might comfort her, but he was embarrassed to admit how little he knew of her past. Few people were as fortunate as he was in his love for his spouse, and many women suffered worse than a lack of affection. But surely, Mrs Brown must have loved her husband if she still visited his grave.

Her voice came from beside him, but it seemed miles away, an echo of her usual self. "He's not my husband. That grave is just a place I go to pretend that I am a respectable widow. Not for me. For my daughter, Sadie, who never knew her father."

Charlie sucked back a gasp. "Whatever troubles you've had in the past, your home is with us now, for as long as you wish. Losing you would be unbearable."

Mrs Brown continued to stare into the distance, leaving Charlie with the ominous feeling that her troubles were very much in the present, and she doubted his resolve.

A Tragic Tale

Every tick of the mantelpiece clock drove Grace to distraction. Their housekeeper's sudden resignation had floored her. She had hoped Charlie would be back with Mrs Brown long before now and that it would all be a colossal misunderstanding.

With a rush of relief, Grace heard the key turning in the front door lock. However, it was the tap, tap of her great-aunt's cane she heard in the hallway, not the brisk patter of Mrs Brown's tread or the solid thump of Charlie's boots.

"Any news, Auntie Anne?" Grace said, as soon as her great-aunt entered the drawing room.

"Charlie came to see if Mrs Brown was with us. I sent him to the cemetery. Kenneth is checking at Lavender House. I was worried about your being alone, Grace."

Grace waved her concerns aside. "It's Mrs Brown that I'm worried about. Do you know what's behind this, Auntie Anne, because I'm flummoxed. Her resignation seems to have something to do with our visit to the Carmichaels, although they never mentioned her when we talked to them."

Anne sat opposite her, her face drawn with worry. "I'm not sure how much I should say. Mrs Brown is entitled to her privacy. If she wants you to know, she will tell you herself."

"Perhaps it would save her embarrassment if you told me. Whatever the problem was, it's better I hear about it from you than someone else."

"I suppose there's some truth in that." Anne drummed her fingers on the armrest, then came to a decision. "Twenty-five years ago, after Mrs Carmichael dismissed her without notice, I found Mrs Brown crying on a street corner. She was alone in the world and pregnant. I took her in, and she has rewarded me a hundredfold with her loyalty."

Grace knew it had to be something bad to cause so much distress, but this was far worse than she had imagined. "Mrs Brown, pregnant and alone? How can that be? I thought her husband died when Sadie was a baby?"

"That's what I told everyone to make it easier on her," Anne said. "The truth is, she was never married to Sadie's father. The woman you know as Mrs Brown has lived her life in fear that one day her shameful secret would be discovered."

Her great-aunt was obviously reluctant to go on, which left Grace fearing the worst. Anne had said Mrs Brown left the Carmichaels' household after some unpleasantness. Prior to Mrs Brown's shock resignation, Grace had assumed Mrs Carmichael had been impossible to work for. But now, Grace recalled Mr Carmichael's distasteful remarks on his preference for pretty maids. If Mrs Brown had left their household alone and with child …

"Auntie Anne, I have to ask. Did Mr Carmichael take advantage of her? Is that why Mrs Brown was left alone and pregnant? Is that why she hates the Carmichaels so much?"

"Goodness, no. Nothing like that. My understanding is that after she was dismissed, Mrs Brown sought sanctuary with the young man she was courting at the time. Of course, she wasn't Mrs Brown back then. She still isn't, legally speaking, since she never married. Evie Fleming, her name was, but the lad was called Hugh Brown. They were in love, and he promised to marry her and live happily ever after."

"But?"

"Hugh Brown took advantage of her, and then left her for another woman," Anne said. "The other maid in the Carmichael house, who had been stepping out with Hugh before Evie arrived. I didn't want Evie to be tainted with the shame of being a fallen woman with an illegitimate baby. She had suffered enough. I found a grave in the Southern Cemetery of a man with no relatives, who shared the surname Brown. It seemed a safe option, because so few people knew about Evie and Hugh. We told anyone who asked that Mrs Brown's husband had died tragically after Sadie was born."

Grace's heart went out to young Evie, deserted and with a baby on the way. No wonder Mrs Brown was fiercely loyal to Anne, who had rescued her from a disastrous situation and given her respectability and a caring home.

Kenneth Drummond arrived at that moment, with the news that Mrs Brown was not at Lavender House. Anne and Kenneth must have sensed Grace needed time to come to terms with the revelation about Mrs Brown's past. Kenneth set to work lighting the fire to bring much-needed warmth and comfort to a grim evening, while Anne disappeared into the kitchen, returning several minutes later with a jug of hot chocolate and cake. Comfort food.

The key scraped in the lock again. Charlie's voice and two sets of footsteps.

Grace and Anne embraced Mrs Brown like a long-lost relative, before sitting her on the sofa between them. Kenneth bustled around with plates and cups, before making a tactical retreat from the drawing room. Charlie hesitated, unsure of his welcome into this enclave of female solidarity.

"I'd like you to stay, Charlie," Mrs Brown said.

It was the first time she had called him by his first name. To Grace, it felt like a momentous shift in their relationship. She wondered what had happened at the Southern Cemetery.

"Did Mrs Carmichael tell you about my past?" Mrs Brown asked.

"They didn't say a word about you, I swear," Grace said, "and we didn't ask. However, I badgered Anne until she told me you were unhappy at the Carmichaels' house. I don't doubt it, having met Mrs Carmichael."

"I also told Grace that Sadie's father left you," Anne said softly. "It was time for them to know, and I thought it might be easier for you if I did the telling. They are investigating several incidents of blackmail. The blackmailer demanded that the money be put in the charity box at the First Church. But I suspect you know that already."

Anne let the sentence hang.

"You recognised me at the church this morning," Mrs Brown said. "I wondered if you had. I expect you'd like to see the blackmail note I received the morning I fled the house, foolishly leaving the porridge pot on the stove."

She dug into the contents of her carpetbag. When Mrs Brown showed no signs of handing the note over, Charlie went over and took it from her hand. He read it and handed it to Grace.

It was much as Grace had expected after Anne's account of Mrs Brown's past, except for the large sum of money demanded: *I know what you are, Evie. Put £5 in the First Church charity box before the morning service on Sunday, or everyone will hear of your shame.*

Mrs Brown sat wringing her hands. "My name is Miss Evie Fleming, not Mrs Brown. I had hoped that Evie's sullied reputation was long forgotten, but it seems not. You can see why I must resign. Your reputation will suffer too if word of my shame spreads. Goodness knows how I can face my Sadie after lying to her all these years about her father, even if I did it to protect her. I will never forgive myself if Sadie's fiancé hears of it and rejects her."

"Mrs Brown," Grace said, "there is no question of you leaving. It is no shame on you if your young man deserted you. It is his shame alone."

"But a child out of wedlock …"

Grace held up a hand. "I can't count the number of children I know who were born less than nine months after marriage, or outside of marriage entirely. Your life has been exemplary, and Sadie should be immensely proud of you, not least for your good sense in sheltering her from mean-spirited slurs."

"The accusation in the blackmail letter is very broad," Charlie said. "If it wasn't for the use of your first name, I would doubt that the blackmailer had any specific knowledge of events. We have seen other blackmail letters that were almost identical. Maybe the blackmailer is simply relying on speculation and gossip rather than fact, hoping that a few of the general hints will hit home."

"There now, nothing to worry about," Anne said.

"I'd like to believe you are right," Mrs Brown said, "but nobody has called me Evie since I left the Carmichaels' house twenty-five years ago. Genevieve is my given name, but I never use it, even amongst my friends."

To her shame, Grace realised that in five years of daily contact she had never asked Mrs Brown her first name, because Mrs Brown had always been so rigid about her place in society. As a housekeeper, it was normal to be called Mrs, regardless of marital status.

"Who knew you as Evie back then?" Charlie asked.

"Mr and Mrs Carmichael, their cook, the other maid, delivery men, and the very few other servant girls I knew from the local neighbourhood. I had no family in Dunedin. My parents died, and my uncle sent me away into service in the city, because they could not afford to keep me. I wasn't with the Carmichaels for very long, and I had little time off to make friends. Once I left their household, I never used the name Evie again."

"Hugh Brown knew you as Evie too," Grace added.

"Hugh delivered to the house. He was the fishmonger's son. He'd been stepping out with the other maid, Bess, but transferred his affections to me. Silly little fool that I was, I thought it was love at first sight. Madly in love we were, right from the start. Made for each other, like you and Charlie. Or so I thought."

Grace glanced at Charlie. She had been through the agony of doubt about his love for her when he left her after resigning from the police force. The devastation she'd felt would have been even worse if he'd left her for another woman, never to return. It was little wonder that the pain was still stark in Mrs Brown's eyes all these years later. The last thing she needed was to be reminded of it so cruelly by a blackmailer.

"The other maid must have been angry when Hugh left her for you," Grace said as gently as she could. "Could she have been angry enough to blackmail you all these years later?"

"Bess was furious, all right," Mrs Brown said. "I suspect her of telling lies to Hugh's parents to set them against me. When I left the Carmichaels' household, I had nobody to turn to except Hugh. He promised to marry me."

Grace couldn't stand the sight of her misery. She leaned closer to Mrs Brown, embracing her awkwardly around the baby bump. "Hugh was a fool to leave you."

"Bess was prettier and livelier than I was. She was also a disgraceful flirt, and all the delivery boys fancied her. Even so, I believed Hugh loved me, until Bess and Hugh ran away together. He didn't even break the news to me himself or leave me a note. I kept expecting him to turn up, full of remorse, but he never did. I was hopelessly naive back then."

"What about Hugh's family?" Grace asked. "Would they not help you in your hour of need, Mrs Brown?"

"Hugh's parents refused to see me. They'd always been against the match, what with Hugh being a young man with prospects and Catholic as well. I'd promised to take his faith, and I meant it. I tried to make them tell me where Hugh had gone so I could talk to him, but they called me a wicked slut and shut the door in my face. Hugh must have told them we had been intimate."

A fishmonger's son and a maid seemed a fair match to Grace. They must have been very young, which was probably another reason for Hugh's parents to disapprove of the match. However, their disapproval did not excuse their shocking rejection of Evie when she was desperate.

Pain crumpled Anne's already age-wrinkled face. "I should have told you at the time, Mrs Brown, but I didn't want to add any more heartache to your life. You see, I visited Hugh's parents myself after Sadie was born, because I couldn't understand why they had refused to see you, and I thought they would change their minds if they knew they had a grandchild."

Mrs Brown looked hopeful for an instant, but Anne's expression silenced the question on her lips.

"I'm sorry to say my visit only made matters worse," Anne said. "Hugh left his parents a note to say he was running away with Bess to Australia, because he had been told you were carrying another man's child. You can see why I didn't tell you. I know he loved you, and I suspect Charlie was correct. Bess told him a lie about the father of your baby to get him for herself."

Mrs Brown shook her head. "I heard the rumour that they had eloped, but it cannot be because Hugh thought I had been unfaithful to him. Hugh left me soon after I came to him after being dismissed. Nobody could have known I was carrying a child then, since I didn't know myself for another three months. You were the first person to know, Mrs Drummond, when you found me crying on the street corner. I was sleeping rough and had little to eat, but my belly just kept getting bigger."

"All the more reason to think Bess was making up a lie about you," Grace said. "What better way to turn Hugh against you than to make up a story about Evie having another lover."

A truly horrible lie. Hugh Brown really was a fool for believing Evie could be with child to another man. He cannot have been the decent man Mrs Brown believed him to be. Grace tightened her grip on Mrs Brown, who had collapsed against her shoulder, weeping.

Through her sobs, Mrs Brown said, "How could he have doubted me? I never lay with any other man and only once with Hugh. I loved him."

Grace didn't doubt the truth of her statement. She couldn't believe Evie was the type of girl to flaunt herself, unless her character had changed completely since then. It sounded far more likely that the other maid had lied to Hugh to get him back. If Grace ever got her hands on her … but that would not happen if Bess and Hugh had run away to Australia. The very fact that they had fled so far from home suggested guilty consciences for their deceit.

Charlie cleared his throat to break the uncomfortable silence. "My profound sympathies, Mrs Brown. Rest assured, I will do everything in my power to find the blackmailer and stop him from revealing your past. The fact that so few people knew you as Evie is extremely helpful to the investigation. The blackmailer must be one of them, or an associate of one of them. I can interview the Carmichaels again tomorrow and attempt to track down the other people who knew you back then. No one need know that you are Evie."

Grace suspected her husband was focusing on the nuts and bolts of the investigation to draw attention away from Mrs Brown's distress. To have lost her betrothed and the father of her child must have left deep scars on her heart.

But Mrs Brown wasn't finished with Anne's admission. "Were Hugh's parents certain the note came from their son?"

Anne was on the verge of tears too. "I'm sorry to say there was no doubt in their minds. Hugh's note was scrawled on a scrap of brown paper from the fish shop they owned. He had left it on the table in their home – a home to which only he and his parents had a key. His parents were devastated by his sudden departure."

Charlie heaved himself out of the armchair as if his body weighed a ton. "I'm deeply sorry that we have had to open old wounds, Mrs Brown, but there is one more question I have to ask. Did you pay the amount demanded by the blackmailer? If so, in what denominations of banknotes or coins?"

Mrs Brown's head dropped a little lower until her chin was on her chest. "I hoped that if I paid, the problem might go away and no one else would hear of my past. A vain hope, I'm sure. I rolled up five one-pound notes tightly and pushed them into the box under my palm so nobody would see."

Charlie offered his hand to help Mrs Brown up. "I suggest we leave it there for tonight, because you need to rest. Grace does too, because she has her final examination tomorrow morning. We will leave it up to you to decide what name you would like to use in the future, although it might take a while for us to get used to anything other than Mrs Brown."

A sad smile flitted across their housekeeper's lips as she rose. "Mrs Brown will be fine. Hugh Brown was the only man I ever loved. He was the kindest, sweetest man I'd ever met. Everyone liked him. He was clever too. Too clever to be a fishmonger forever. No matter what he did, he will always be Sadie's father and the love of my life. I wish now that I had told Sadie the truth, because once the blackmailer spills my secrets, my daughter will hate me."

He clasped their housekeeper's hand in both of his. "No, she won't. If Sadie hates anyone, it will be the blackmailer. But I promise I won't let the blackmailer ruin your life, not while I've got breath in my lungs."

"I'm relying on you, Charlie," she replied in a surprisingly firm voice. "For all our sakes, but most especially for my daughter Sadie, so her wedding isn't tainted with scandal. And I would like to stay on with you, if you'll have me."

Grace kissed her cheek. "Of course you must stay. This is your home and we wouldn't cope for a single day without you. What's more, we're going to get extra help and increase your wages to reflect your vital role in the household. We've taken you for granted for too long, my dear Mrs Brown."

Sleight of Hand

On Monday morning, Charlie took Grace to her final examination. The journey passed in silence. Grace had slept poorly, partly from worry about Mrs Brown being blackmailed and partly because of a painful bout of cramp. Or rather, she said it was cramp, but Charlie suspected it might have been more of the false labour contractions. Now, she was staring straight ahead, murmuring what might have been an incantation. He leaned closer and realised she was listing the bones of the body – an old habit Grace had long used to focus her thoughts.

Needless to say, he hadn't slept much either. The prospect of having a child had brought him boundless joy over the last few months, but, as the due date drew nearer, fear threatened to overwhelm other emotions. He tried to focus on the blackmail case as a useful distraction, but that path led to even darker thoughts.

Outside the examination room, Charlie gathered his wife in his arms and kissed her, ignoring the catcalls from the other students. "I'd wish you good luck, but I know you're the smartest and best-prepared student in the room. In three hours, you will have completed all the requirements to qualify as a doctor, and I will be the proudest husband this side of the moon."

Grace clung to him. "Thank you, Charlie. Frankly, I'll be happy if I can squeeze my baby-belly under a desk for three hours without my waters breaking. I plan to write quickly and not fret too much about overthinking the answers, in case I have to leave early. If I can just shut out everything else and concentrate, I know I can do it. I *have* to do it."

"Should I wait?"

"Definitely not." Grace patted her bump. "I was joking about my waters breaking."

"I'll be back to collect you in plenty of time, just in case." Her light-hearted reply didn't fool him, but Charlie also knew that nothing short of a baby dropping onto the floor under her desk would stop his wife from completing her medical degree.

He returned to the hired gig, determined to show the same single-minded focus on the blackmail case. His simmering hatred of the blackmailer had increased to boiling point since finding out that Mrs Brown was a victim. However, looked at rationally, Mrs Brown's involvement was also a major step forward in the investigation, because so few people knew her as Evie. Someone must have recognised their housekeeper as the long-vanished maid. All he had to do was find that person.

He recalled the blackmail note: *I know what you are, Evie. Put £5 in the First Church charity box before the morning service on Sunday, or everyone will hear of your shame.*

The wording was suggestive. I know *what* you are, not I know *who* you are. Linked with the comment about shame and the large sum demanded, it suggested that Evie had been targeted as a fallen woman who would pay handsomely to keep that fact a secret. Nobody knew Sadie Brown was born out of wedlock, because Evie had told no one but Anne that she was with child, and Anne had been rigorous in setting up the story of Mrs Brown's supposed marriage to Mr Brown before Sadie was born. Even Grace hadn't known the truth, despite her close relationship with Anne and Mrs Brown.

Thus, the fallen woman accusation must link back to the note left by Hugh Brown, which said he believed Evie was carrying another man's child. Who had told Hugh? And why had he believed a lie about the woman he loved? It must have come from someone he trusted – someone in a position to know for certain that Evie had been with another man. Mrs Carmichael was a possibility, because Hugh would view her as a respectable woman who would have had nothing to gain by dismissing Evie so suddenly unless she believed the accusation to be true. Mr Carmichael or another household member seemed less likely, but still possible. The other person in a position to know was the other maid. Bess had a reason to lie, because she wanted Hugh for herself. And she had succeeded, because Hugh and Bess had run away together.

Of course, the person who told Hugh about Evie's supposed betrayal was not necessarily the blackmailer. Mrs Carmichael might have gossiped about the maid's shocking behaviour to any number of other people over the years until it reached the flapping ears of the blackmailer.

Stewing on it wasn't getting him very far. After tossing and turning last night, Charlie had made a sensible, practical plan for this morning. What he needed was evidence based on solid, step-by-step detective work. First, he would direct his attention to the puzzle of how the blackmailer had taken the blackmail money. He now knew for a fact that Mrs Brown had inserted five one-pound notes in the box, and Miss Mackenzie had put in a marked one-pound note, none of which were in the charity box when the donations were counted. After he solved the puzzle, he would interview victims, suspects, and eyewitnesses until someone gave him the lead he so desperately needed.

Thus, his first stop was the First Church. He hoped that re-examining the box would provide a distraction from the tiny, annoying voice in his head, which reminded him, in the stern voice of an objective policeman, that Mrs Brown should not be ignored as a suspect. She had reason to hate at least one victim, Mrs Carmichael, and probably knew many others through her contacts below stairs. And she was seen, veiled, in the First Church, where she had no cause to be.

He halted the horse at a hitching post under the trees to one side of the church, giving the horse a nose bag with a few oats in expectation of a long day ahead.

Fortunately, the minister was in his study. Charlie informed him that the number of blackmail victims had increased substantially since they last spoke. He mentioned the oddity of the missing marked banknote and asked if he could examine the charity box. The minister came with him, confessing both concern and intrigue.

The box still sat in plain view on the table in the church lobby, convenient to the congregation filing past into the church. Charlie tested the lock and screws, but they had not been tampered with. The screws meant the box could not have been switched for another, even in the melee of Mrs Carmichael's stumble. He had been watching the box throughout, except after the donations were removed for counting. Unless the culprit was Mr Landsburgh, the money counter, it seemed impossible that any money had been taken. And yet it had happened.

"Nothing vanishes without a trace," he muttered.

"Only God can achieve such miracles," the minister replied, "although I'm told magicians manage it, too."

Charlie held back an ungodly curse. After the church service, it had seemed as if the blackmail was limited to one or two victims, and, with Landsburgh making a fuss, Charlie hadn't pressed the matter. But now he knew that money had definitely vanished, it was a different story. Could it really be so simple? The oldest magician's trick of all – the box with a false bottom?

The minister produced the key from his pocket. They both looked in the open charity box, but it appeared to be an ordinary, empty box, taller than it was wide. Charlie reached his hand in and measured the internal height. Only when he put his hand against the outside of the box did the deception become apparent, because there was a significant disparity between the outside height and the inside depth of the box.

He prodded the false bottom to see if it would swing open, but it was firmly set in place. And yet, the blackmailer would have to access the money in the bottom without too much fiddling. The only spot where the bottom didn't touch the sides was in one corner.

"If only I had a thin piece of wire," he muttered.

"Ask, and it will be given to you; seek, and you will find." The minister disappeared into the church, returning with a hatpin.

"Did this appear by divine miracle?" Charlie asked.

The minister returned his smile. "God provides in many ways. In this case, He ensured that our lost property box was full of dropped hatpins."

It worked a charm. With the hatpin inserted into the gap, the false bottom flipped up easily on well-oiled hinges, which were concealed underneath. The box's maker had done a fine job of the carpentry, although the design was simple enough. The bottom compartment was empty, which meant someone had removed the money sometime between the end of the Sunday service and this morning.

A closer examination showed the false bottom could be held open with a clever hook that could be turned from the outside with a brush of a hand against what appeared to be an external decoration. Any money inserted into the box would drop all the way through to the bottom. The blackmailer had only to twist the hook to release the false bottom, trapping the money in the concealed compartment. Any further money would drop into the upper part of the box, disguising the trickery.

If the blackmailer triggered the mechanism when half the congregation had passed by, half the money would be his or hers for the taking, leaving the rest for the church. The man counting the money would scoop out what he saw, never realising there was more hidden underneath. The blackmailer had to be present to trigger the mechanism, but that got them no further ahead since they already suspected the person was a member of the congregation. Perhaps even a person pretending to be a victim, to deflect suspicion.

His first thought was the woman who had stumbled against the box – Mrs Carmichael. Grace had been sure she was lying about something, and Charlie was not disposed to think well of her after her cruel treatment of Mrs Brown long ago.

The minister let out a whistling breath. "Well, gracious me. One has to admire the ingenuity, if not the motive. This person could have been stealing from the charity box for months. Do you think a few small coins were not enough for this sinner, so he turned to blackmail to increase the size of donations?"

"It's possible," Charlie said. "Greed has a way of escalating. The person couldn't expect to get away with it forever. Demands for small amounts were unlikely to be reported, but eventually somebody would balk at the principle and want the blackmailer stopped. I'm puzzled by how the blackmailer could ensure his victims were in the first half of the congregation to pass the box. The mechanism must have been tripped during the procession into the church, because we know that a considerable sum of money was put in after the false bottom was closed to fool us into thinking nothing was amiss."

"I'm afraid that is no mystery. People are creatures of habit, Mr Penrose Pyke, as I am sure you are aware. Most people arrive early for the social exchange of news and pleasantries before the service. Of that group, the gentlemen and ladies enter the church first, followed by the families in trade, with the wage workers and poor folk last. Everyone sits in their usual pew, too. Class distinctions are not something I encourage, but old habits and conventions persist."

Charlie had to admit a grudging admiration for the cleverness of the scheme. The blackmailer need only target the wealthy and sociable people, who were the very people most likely to have enough money and social standing to be the targets of blackmail and who would also enter the church first.

"And don't forget that the charity box is normally opened after the evening service," the minister added. "If you hadn't come to us, Mr Penrose Pyke, and we had kept to that routine, the amount of money above the false bottom would have been greater and the removal of the larger sums below less obvious. Ingenious, especially as the blackmailer could choose his time to return for the money. He faced almost no risk of being caught, even if we discovered the secret of the box."

Charlie didn't need reminding how firmly the odds were stacked against him. There was no point in lamenting his short-sighted focus on catching the culprit in the act. "Unfortunately, this discovery only complicates the investigation. We are further from identifying the blackmailer than ever."

The minister locked the box. "I have faith in you, Mr Penrose Pyke. The blackmailer does not know you have discovered his secret. Next time, you will get him. It is a great burden to know we have among us a person who would stoop so low as to blackmail his fellow worshippers and steal from charity. Who would do such a thing?"

Charlie treated the question as rhetorical, since no man of God needed a lecture on the nature of sin. "Can you tell me who had access to the church in the twenty-two hours between the Sunday morning service and now?"

"There was the usual evening service, which was well attended, but I expect you mean access when the church was empty." The minister gave a hopeless shrug. "The church remains open until late in the evening. I stay here all day on Sunday in case any of my congregation wishes to see me, but I was mostly in my study out the back. We have many visitors. The devout come in between services to seek a moment of quiet reflection and prayer. Others come to marvel at the glory of the church. Our splendid volunteer ladies come in to refresh the flowers and tidy the hymn books. The Sunday school teacher stays on to tidy and prepare for next week. It's often busy, but there are always quiet times too."

"Could you make a list of the people you recall, please?" Charlie didn't hold out much hope, but every avenue was worth exploring. "I assume the church is locked overnight?"

"The main doors are. I try to remember to lock the back door when I leave, but I confess my head is often full of other, less earthly, matters." The minister gave a hollow little laugh by way of apology.

Marvellous, Charlie thought. The church might have been open on Sunday night for all of Dunedin to traipse through. The back door led to the parish hall and study, where the keys were on open display. If the inner door to the church itself was ever locked, he'd eat his hat.

He gritted his teeth. "Has anyone visited this morning? I seem to recall seeing two women cleaning when I came in."

"That's correct. Our volunteers on the cleaning roster are usually the first in on Monday mornings. Mrs Harper, the dressmaker who has premises over the road, is marvellous about supplying volunteers from amongst her workers. They are all such fine, Christian ladies."

The minister led the way into the church, where one woman was moving along the pews, dusting the glossy woodwork and tidying the hymn books, while another woman mopped the floor around the altar.

"Miss Kerr, may I ask for a minute of your time?" The minister introduced Charlie and explained the purpose of his visit.

Miss Kerr gave him an open, unaffected smile. "Mr Penrose Pyke? I served your wife last week. She looked lovely in that maternity gown, although I can't imagine she'll be needing it much longer."

"No, indeed. The twins are due at the end of the month."

"How lovely for you. Now, how may I help you, sir?"

"I'd like to know if you saw anyone in the church this morning. Specifically, anyone near the charity box."

"I didn't see anyone else," Miss Kerr replied, "but I did give the box a good polish. Grubby fingerprints all over it after Sunday. I do wish people would wash their hands before church."

Charlie could hardly blame this woman for her diligence. There would have been far too many fingerprints to be of use to the investigation anyway. "Were you the first to arrive this morning?"

"Miss Rudd was here before me," she said, pointing to the lady with the mop. "I overslept after a late night putting the final touches to a wedding gown." Miss Kerr put a gnarled hand on his arm. "Miss Rudd has burn scars on her face. She doesn't like folks looking at her."

"Thank you for the warning, Miss Kerr." Charlie knew that Mrs Harper had a fine reputation for taking on women workers who might otherwise find work difficult to obtain. Many people had an unreasonable aversion to people with deformities from injury or illness, which meant they had to work twice as hard to prove their worth.

Charlie and the minister approached the second cleaner together. Again, the minister introduced him, but this time the minister was the one to ask if the church had been locked and whether she had seen anyone near the charity box.

Miss Rudd kept one side of her face turned away, but she answered his questions readily. "I found the door unlocked when I arrived this morning. There was a man by the back pew when I came in. A rough-looking man in filthy clothes. He left as soon as I entered the church."

"Homeless men sometimes spend the night," the minister told Charlie, "especially when it's cold or wet. It would be uncharitable to turn them away."

"Are you able to describe the man, Miss Rudd?" Charlie asked.

"Heavy build, rough worker's clothes, cloth cap, hands so black he looked like he hadn't washed them for a month. I didn't like the look of him one bit, so I didn't go close enough to see his face. I'm afraid that's all I can recall."

"Was he carrying anything?"

"Now you mention it, I don't believe he was carrying any bedding or even a blanket, and I didn't find any bedding in the church. How odd. Perhaps he came to pray rather than sleep after all. I think he had a small bag, but I can't be sure."

"Thank you, Miss Rudd," Charlie said. "Your observations have been most helpful. Did you see anyone else alone near the charity box?"

"Nobody suspicious. I assume it was Mrs Harper who unlocked the door, because she had been in to check the vase that had been knocked over next to the charity box. A tiny chip, hardly noticeable, she said. And, of course, Miss Kerr cleaned the lobby."

"Thank you for your time," the minister said. "The lady who knocked over the vase promised to replace it when she spoke to me after the evening service, but I told her there was no need."

Charlie waited until Miss Rudd returned to her mop. "I believe Mrs Carmichael was the lady who knocked it over. Was she here for the Sunday evening service as well as the morning service?"

"She is one of my most devout parishioners," the minister said. "Mrs Carmichael seemed unusually distracted yesterday. She appeared quite agitated and stayed after the service to pray on her own. I confess, I wondered if she was another of the blackmail victims."

"I'm afraid so. One of many, I fear."

"It's a dark day when churchgoers are not safe from criminals. Is there anything else you need from me to advance your investigation, Mr Penrose Pyke?"

"Not that I can think of. Once again, thank you for your time."

Charlie tried to console himself with discovering the secret of the charity box, but it was a hollow success when the perpetrator was as far from his grasp as ever. Still, Mrs Carmichael's presence at the church after the service struck him as suspicious. She had something to hide, he was sure of it. And the rough man warranted further inquiry too.

He hurried back to the gig and went to pick up Grace. All going well, she should be flying high over the last hurdle to her medical degree, metaphorically speaking.

Past Trauma

Grace's pen flew across the page as fast as the ink would flow. She'd always imagined the final examination for her medical degree would be an intelligent and considered rendering of the sum of knowledge she had gained during her years of study. Instead, the words disgorged onto the page from the unconscious depths of her brain against a backdrop of physical discomfort. Her legs ached from sitting still, her belly cramped from being squashed under the desk, her breathing wheezed from compressed lungs, and her hand was ready to fall from her wrist from writing so quickly.

Annoyingly, her last-minute frenzy of revision of inherited traits was not needed. The medical students she'd overheard must have been playing a trick on her, as they had done so often since she had first shocked them with her female presence in what they saw as their exclusive domain. No matter, the examination was challenging but fair.

When she turned to the final question, she smiled. Obstetrics. Now there was a subject she knew far better than her male colleagues. *What proportion of first babies are born early?* Easy. Only five percent, she wrote with a flourish, and thank God for that.

Ten minutes later, she had finished, with her waters unbroken and her sanity more or less intact. She handed in her paper and exited the room. Rows of heads looked up, startled at her early departure. Grace breezed past with a superior smile, hoping it conveyed her astonishment that they were taking so long over such simple questions. The fake smile disappeared as soon as she reached the door. Doctor Beechworth, one of several lecturers supervising the examination, frowned as he watched her leave. She nodded to him to indicate that she was fine.

Outside the room, she slumped onto a nearby bench seat, doubled over with the cramping in her belly.

Doctor Beechworth followed her out. "Grace? Are you having contractions?" As an obstetrics and gynaecology specialist, and a family friend, he was a welcome sight.

"I don't think so. Just a little cramp from sitting uncomfortably. It's easing off now that I can stretch out."

He watched her closely, no doubt noting her panting breaths but seeing only mild discomfort. "Did you finish the paper?"

"I did, although with rather less attention to detail than normal."

"Probably just as well in your condition. Don't tell anyone I said this, but the professors have been taking bets on whether you would make it to the end. I'm due a tidy sum for putting my faith in you."

Grace grinned. "A couple of little babies weren't going to stop me finishing my qualification, even if I had to cork them in." Easy to joke about it now, of course.

"I want you to rest up from now until the birth." Beechworth had his hands on his hips, making it an order, although he said the words kindly. "Avoid stress. Giving birth to twins is no Sunday picnic. Call on me at the first sign of any medical issues. Excessive dizziness, breathlessness, nausea, headaches – you know the symptoms. I'll come to you as quickly as I can. Once your contractions begin in earnest, come directly to the hospital. I have a private suite with all the latest innovations, including pain relief. If chloroform was good enough for Queen Victoria, it's good enough for you too."

Avoid stress? Not much chance of that, Grace thought. "I'll do my best. Thank you for looking out for me, Doctor Beechworth.

As you know, my preference is to give birth at home, but I will not take any unnecessary risks. It is a great comfort to know you are close by. Something tells me these babies aren't in the mood to be squashed much longer."

Beechworth eyed her dubiously. "I was pleased to hear your husband agreed not to take on any dangerous cases at such a critical stage."

"I expect Charlie will be outside soon, waiting to take me home to a haven of tranquillity." Grace crossed her fingers behind her back, wishing it were true.

"Hm. I'd better get back inside. Make sure your husband knows how critical these last few weeks are. Rest, rest and more rest. Goodness knows you deserve it after finishing your degree." Beechworth gave her one last appraisal, then returned to his post.

Grace lingered another ten minutes until the cramp passed, and the scrape of chairs inside the examination room told her that her moment of peace was over.

A flood of students surged past her, many with expressions of granite, others already dissecting their answers and slapping their foreheads over stupid mistakes made in the heat of the moment. Grace waited for the flood to subside, not wishing to be knocked over.

Charlie met her on the steps. Relief washed over his face at the sight of her.

Grace punched her fist into the air. "Last examination ever!" She shot him a beaming smile, not wanting to worry him. If she told him about the cramp and breathlessness, he'd lock her in their bedroom and order her to rest. Not that a lock would stop her, because she could pick a lock blindfolded.

He took her arm and helped her down the steps. "Home, Grace? Or should I take you to Doctor Harvey to ensure that all is well?

Don't think you've fooled me with your smiles. I can see you are in pain and exhausted."

She couldn't get anything past her husband. Served her right for marrying a detective. "Home. Doctor Beechworth assured me all was well."

"So, can I call you Doctor Penrose Pyke?"

"I do love the sound of that," Grace said, "but I cannot officially claim the title until I receive confirmation of the results. I'm sure you'll be as relieved as I am to see the back of my studies. You've been a saint for putting up with me."

Charlie's grin was as wide as his face. "We ought to celebrate, when we can find a quiet moment."

"A quiet moment? Charlie, dearest, it'll be twenty years at least before we have a quiet moment. Did I not mention we are having twins?"

"Twenty years," he said dreamily. "I wonder what life will be like in 1914. Perhaps the tales of Jules Verne will prove prophetic, and we'll have cannons shooting rockets to the moon."

"I'm glad you have so much faith in human nature, my love. If man invents long-distance rockets, you can be sure he'll be shooting them at other nations and not at the moon."

"Cynic. Can't I hope for peace and prosperity so our daughters can discover cures for all known diseases?"

Grace liked the sound of that, although her main hope was of a more short-term variety – to deliver a pair of healthy babies with the minimum pain. "Don't you want to be like Mr Carmichael and have a son following in your footsteps?"

He shrugged. "If that's what our son or daughter wants, I wouldn't object. Can you imagine one of our girls in Detective Inspector Wallace's chair ordering her sergeants around?"

"A woman in the police force? Gracious, Charlie, what have you been imbibing this morning to generate such wild fantasies?"

"Nothing but the natural stimulant of a minor success. I've solved the mystery of the vanishing blackmail money." Charlie told her the trick of the charity box and how they would have to rethink the investigation because anyone could have accessed the box. Mrs Brown's blackmail note had become more vital than ever, because it was their best chance of narrowing the field of suspects.

When they arrived home, Grace was happy to allow Charlie to help her to the sofa and fuss over her. As he was propping her up with the plumpest cushions, Mrs Brown bustled in with a tray of tea and delicacies to celebrate the end of her medical studies. Grace had planned a list of jobs to do but decided to enjoy an hour of utter indulgence instead – maybe even several hours.

However, something in the way Mrs Brown shuffled her feet and looked nervously at Charlie made Grace suspect she wanted a moment alone with her. Charlie must have noticed it too, because he announced he had to return the hired gig and wouldn't stay for tea.

Mrs Brown handed her a cup and a plate of her favourite treats. "He's a fine man, your husband."

"Yes, he is," Grace said. "The very best. But he is still a man. And sometimes a woman needs to talk through her problems with another woman."

"Quite so. Charlie is lucky to have such a clever wife. Fortunately, he knows it."

"As if I'd let him forget." Grace nibbled on a slice of rhubarb crumble cake, waiting patiently for Mrs Brown to gather her courage. It couldn't be easy, if it was something she couldn't discuss in front of Charlie.

"I want the blackmailer caught, whatever it takes," Mrs Brown said. "I have been silent for long enough, mainly to shelter Sadie, but also for my sake. Even Anne Drummond doesn't know the whole truth, for all that she has been my saviour in every way."

Grace put the cake down and brushed crumbs off her lips. "Whatever you say will remain confidential, unless you would like me to pass on any information relevant to the investigation."

"It's about Hugh's decision to leave me because someone convinced him I was carrying another man's child. I've mulled it over and decided you cannot possibly solve this case without knowing the facts."

"Why don't you tell me the full story from the beginning?" Grace nodded encouragingly, even though she had a bad feeling about where this was heading.

Mrs Brown settled back in the armchair and gazed out the window. When she spoke, it felt as if she was telling the tale of another girl called Evie, rather than her younger self. A fairytale, which started once upon a time. Like all fairytales, Grace suspected there would be wicked wolves and evil witches, so she looked away and pretended it had happened in a land far, far away.

"I was eighteen and impossibly unworldly when I came to Dunedin to work for Mr and Mrs Carmichael. They employed me and Bess as maids-of-all-work, but it soon became clear that I was better working downstairs and in the kitchen, because the woman they had hired to cook was lazy and useless. I didn't like Cook, but I enjoyed cooking. Bess was better at the upstairs work, acting as a lady's maid to Mrs Carmichael and seeing to the usual tasks. Bess had a lively personality and coped better with Mr Carmichael's teasing ways too."

Again, Grace's stomach churned with the feeling she knew where this was going, but it seemed she was wrong.

"Don't get me wrong," Mrs Brown said. "I liked Mr Carmichael. He was always very friendly with us maids, stopping for a chat and a laugh, as if he was one of us rather than one of them. But I was a shy lass back then and not used to his hearty manner and friendly pats on the shoulder as he passed us on the stairs. He was a working man, not a master, but his wife made up for it with her airs and graces."

"Mrs Carmichael received a blackmail note accusing her of ill-treating servants," Grace said. "That is what she said, anyway. I'm sure she wasn't telling the full truth. She did not mention past events involving you and Bess, only a maid she dismissed recently for ripping a shawl. But I have to know – was Mrs Carmichael abusive towards you, Mrs Brown?"

"Not physically. She never gave us a beating, which is more than I can say for my uncle before he sent me away. Mrs Carmichael was strict, though, and never one to spare a word of praise. She didn't speak to me unless it was to reprimand me for not polishing the silver properly or serving a meal that didn't meet her standards. The other maid, Bess, didn't have such a hard time of it, because she could dress the mistress's hair better than anyone else. Bess was friendly towards me, but she and Mrs Carmichael made it clear that I was the lowest in the pecking order. I took no offence because it was true. Bess had been there longer and acted as a lady's maid."

Grace waited patiently for Mrs Brown to continue in her own time, sensing that she was struggling to put long-suppressed memories into words.

Mrs Brown shuddered. "It was the coalman who caused the problems. He was on good terms with Mr Carmichael, which made him act above his station. A ladies' man that's what he called himself – but any lady would run a mile from him. He liked to push up against us girls and whisper racy comments in our ears. Disgusting. When I complained to Cook, she told me to ignore him, because he was only teasing and meant nothing by it. She fancied him, although I cannot imagine why."

"His behaviour was completely unacceptable," Grace said. "The cook ought to be ashamed of herself for allowing it to go unchecked."

Mrs Brown hung her head. "I know that now, but I was young and naive back then. The coalman convinced me that it was my fault for being too sensitive and unable to take a joke."

If Grace had a penny for all the male medical students who said those very words after playing a prank on her, she could feed a poor family for a month. "Typical bully, blaming the victim for his own inexcusable behaviour. Did you speak to Mrs Carmichael about it?"

"Mrs Carmichael refused to hear any complaints from the maids. Cook was supposed to be in charge of us, which meant our welfare was in her hands. I asked her to take the matter up with Mrs Carmichael, because I was scared of the coalman."

"What happened, Mrs Brown?" Grace asked, hoping to hear the coalman got what was coming to him, but fearing the worst.

"Nothing. Cook said she had spoken to the mistress. According to Cook, Mrs Carmichael didn't believe me and blamed me for leading him on. Avoid the coalman if you don't like him, she said. As if I could when he was hanging around the kitchen at all hours. There was nobody else to turn to, because Mr Carmichael and Tulloch were firm friends. I often heard them laughing in the garden when the coal and firewood were being delivered. Raucous male laughter. Bess said she found postcards of naked ladies in Mr Carmichael's study, and I am sure I saw money exchanged between them on several occasions. Tulloch was the type to do anything for a price."

Tulloch the coalman? The name rang a bell. It took Grace a moment to recall that he was suspected of being a blackmail victim. Johnny had said Tulloch would do anything for a price too. Coincidence, or was the blackmailer deliberately targeting people associated with the Carmichael household?

Another visit to Mrs Carmichael would be necessary, although Grace doubted she could manage it without letting loose her fury at the woman who had ignored a young maid's desperate plea for help.

Mrs Brown paused. Grace dreaded to think what she was unwilling to say, fearing that Tulloch had taken advantage of her. Worse still was the possibility that Hugh's note was correct, and Sadie's father was not Hugh Brown. All she could do was offer support and reassurance.

"With our work at Lavender House refuge," Grace said softly, "we both know what many women suffer at the hands of violent men. Understanding that the woman is not to blame is the first step in healing. Whatever you have suffered, Mrs Brown, know that you are loved."

"That means a great deal to me, Grace."

Mrs Brown kept her eyes averted as she found the courage to continue her story. "I'd gone up to Mr Carmichael's study to stoke the fire before the Carmichaels returned from an evening out. Tulloch was there, sipping port and looking at those awful postcards as if he were lord of the manor. He grabbed me before I could run away and pinned me against the wall. He said I would regret it if I told anyone what I had seen. When he pushed against me, I kneed him in the privates and ran down to the kitchen. I told Cook what he had done, but she just slapped me hard for making up wicked stories."

Grace passed a handkerchief to Mrs Brown as she finally allowed tears to flow. She wanted to cradle their housekeeper in her arms, but instinct told her that Mrs Brown needed to unburden herself of the past before she sought comfort.

When the tears dried to hiccoughing sobs, Mrs Brown took a long breath and continued in the same emotionless voice as before. "Tulloch came down to the kitchen too, and Cook could see from his anger that I hadn't been lying about what happened in the study. He wanted to hit me, I'm sure of it, but he held back. Tulloch pushed me against the wall with a hand at my throat and told me he had the power to destroy me if I didn't keep my trap shut. Cook took his side, saying she'd have me fired if I said a word."

"What did you do?"

"I ran to my room and put a chair against my doorknob. As you can imagine, I didn't sleep a wink. By dawn, my bag was packed. I wanted to run away then and there, but I owed it to my mistress to explain. Besides, it seemed unfair that I would get the blame for what Tulloch did. Without the wages I was owed, I didn't have sixpence to my name. And, if I didn't get a reference, I wouldn't get another position as a maid."

"Did you talk to Mrs Carmichael?" Grace asked.

"I didn't get a chance. Cook got to her first and spun her a load of lies. Mrs Carmichael stormed into my room in her dressing gown and laid into me. I've never seen her so furious. She called me all sorts of names for getting drunk and bringing a man back to my room while she was out."

Grace had to clench her fists to restrain her anger. "Did no one stand up for you?"

"It was my word against Cook's. Bess had the night off, which meant she wasn't there to witness what happened between me and Tulloch. But Bess did go to fetch Mr Carmichael, who tried to calm his wife down. Mrs Carmichael wouldn't let her husband interfere with what she saw as her domain. She threw me out. To be honest, I was glad to go. Mr Carmichael saw me to the door and gave me a couple of shillings, which was all he had in his pocket. Those coins meant the world to me. With no family or friends to go to and no hope of finding a new position without a reference, the only person I could seek help from was the young man I had been stepping out with, Hugh Brown.”

Despite the traumatic events she had just revealed, Mrs Brown's lips curled into a slight smile as she spoke his name.

Grace could see that she still loved him after all these years, despite everything that had happened. “What did Hugh do?”

“I told Hugh the truth, that Tulloch did no more than put his hands on me and threaten me, and that Cook lied about me having a man in my room. Hugh was furious at how I had been treated, but his first instinct was to shelter and support me, bless him. Hugh promised to marry me straight away. He said he'd been wanting to ask me but was worried I'd think it was too soon. Silly man, he thought he had to make something of himself before he married, as if I would only marry him for money or position. The family fish shop was already doing far better than it had been when his parents managed the business side of it. His father was good with fish, but hopeless with money. Hugh was clever as well as kind.”

Tulloch and the cook now vied for the top spot on Grace's list of most loathsome potential blackmail suspects. Tulloch's immorality, greed, and links with both the Carmichael family and the First Church fitted the nastiness of blackmail perfectly. But the cook had now been revealed as a lying schemer too. Mrs Carmichael had cast Evie out heartlessly, but it seemed her actions were based on the lies the cook told her about Evie. In fact, Mrs Brown had more cause to blackmail Mrs Carmichael than the other way around.

Charlie could deal with Tulloch. Men like him were bullies. Charlie's size and authority would bring him down a peg or two. Grace also wanted to confront the cook about her cruelty to the servant girls under her care, if they could find her after all this time. Mrs Carmichael no longer had a cook, so their former employee could be long gone or even dead by now.

But right now, Grace's main concern was Mrs Brown's welfare. "Thank you for having the courage to tell me, Mrs Brown. Knowing what happened all those years ago might be the clue we need to find the blackmailer. Once he or she is apprehended, you can focus on the joy of Sadie's wedding without the worry of the blackmailer spreading malicious rumours."

Mrs Brown shook her head. "You don't understand, Grace. When I think back to what Miss Mackenzie said, I realise she was absolutely correct. It is not the truth that matters, but whether the gossips will believe the lie. If Mrs Carmichael never doubted Cook's story that I lured a man to my room, why should anyone else doubt it? If the police go after Cook and Tulloch, they will keep lying until the cows come home. My security all these years has depended solely on my anonymity, and now that is gone too. What if the blackmailer does as he has threatened to do? What if Sadie's fiancé is told she is illegitimate? Her future happiness could be destroyed in an instant."

Much as she hated to admit it, Grace feared Mrs Brown had a point. If Charlie put the thumbscrews on Tulloch, he would be sure to tell all and sundry that Mrs Brown was a slattern and a liar. In fact, Tulloch could say she was trying to seek revenge on him and Mrs Carmichael and thus try to pin the blackmail on her too. It sounded all too plausible, especially because there were few people who knew as much about all levels of Dunedin society as Mrs Brown. Many investigations had relied on her knowledge of the goings-on above and below stairs. Grace wanted to believe that Mrs Brown's reputation would shield her, but it was more often the woman who took the blame when accusations of impropriety were hurled.

Grace suddenly realised she had been silent for too long and Mrs Brown might take that as agreement. "Nobody would believe Tulloch and the cook over you."

"Mrs Carmichael did. Hugh and his parents believed I was carrying another man's child. If anyone found her birth record, they would see that Sadie was conceived around the time I was thrown out of Mrs Carmichael's house for having a man in my room. Overhearing Miss Mackenzie saying she was the odd one out in her family with golden hair … it made me think about Sadie. She has bright blue eyes, like Tulloch, while Hugh and I have brown eyes. Nobody will believe Tulloch never got near my bed, or any other man for that matter. If this becomes common knowledge, my reputation will be ruined forever, as will Sadie's."

Grace was thankful she had been reading up on inheritance for her medical examination. "Sadie's blue eyes prove nothing. Brown-eyed parents can have a blue-eyed child, as long as there are blue eyes in both family lines."

"I cannot remember my father, but my mother had brown eyes like me. I cannot recall Hugh's parents. It was a long time ago, and I only met them briefly twice. It doesn't matter anyway. As Miss Mackenzie rightly understood, it is appearances that count. At least she has a mother to defend her and a locket showing a golden-haired grandparent."

Mrs Brown looked Grace in the eye. "I hope you don't despise me. Hugh's parents wouldn't shelter me after I was dismissed without a reference, so we had no choice but to go to a cheap hotel, where we could only afford one room. I loved Hugh, and he said he loved me. Bess told me you can't fall pregnant the first time."

"Bess was wrong," Grace said. "That dreadful old wives' tale has caught many an innocent young lass. As for despising you, how could I? When you are young and in love, temptation is a constant, even for those who are not in the awful situation you faced. I know exactly how you felt. As you know, I had every intention of waiting until I graduated before marrying, but that became impossible when Charlie returned to Dunedin. Waiting any longer to get married seemed intolerable."

Mrs Brown embraced her until she was breathless. "It's been a joy to witness the pair of you so happy, Grace. Charlie reminds me a little of my Hugh. In character, I mean, because Hugh was about as different from your husband in looks as it was possible to be. No taller than me and whip-thin, with a mop of sandy hair and a grin to make your heart wobble. Hugh's lack of faith in me was the worst moment of my life. Charlie would never have deserted you on the say-so of a girl like Bess or Cook's lies."

Grace wasn't so sure. "As you know, Charlie left me once, simply because he felt he could not support me in the manner he thought I deserved. He would not have stayed in Dunedin if he had been convinced that I loved another man. Indeed, it took a long time to persuade him that I preferred a penniless policeman over a wealthy suitor, despite my obvious preference for him."

"Charlie came back to Dunedin in the end."

"Only because Alistair conceived the idea of a private detective agency. My dear Mrs Brown, regardless of Hugh's motive for leaving, you still have your lovely daughter, Sadie. She is a blessing – a gift born of love – and you need never be ashamed of that." Grace paused, uncertain how to proceed. "Do you wish Charlie to close the investigation to prevent any of this from becoming known?"

Mrs Brown reeled back, shocked. "Good heavens, no. Keeping secrets does no good, and letting evildoers run rampant is unconscionable. That is why I am telling you the full story, Grace, so you and Charlie can find the blackmailer and bring him or her to justice, whatever the consequences."

"In that case, I promise you we will move heaven and earth to track the culprit down." Grace stood and helped Mrs Brown up. "Now, I absolutely insist you take the rest of the day off and do something nice for yourself. A stroll in the botanic garden or a visit to a tea shop with a friend, perhaps. Maybe buy yourself a new hat for Sadie's wedding. It can be our Christmas present to you. We're so looking forward to her wedding."

Mrs Brown looked at Grace as if she had taken leave of her senses. "Goodness me, no. It's past one o'clock, and I haven't served your lunch yet. I've a hearty soup bubbling on the stove and fresh bread rolls. After your examination this morning, you must be starving. And then there's the grocer to see and the evening meal to cook, as well as the house to scrub and polish to a shine before the babies are born."

Mrs Brown swiped a handkerchief across her tear-stained face and hurried away. Once-upon-a-time Evie was gone and Mrs Brown was back, on the surface at least.

To Grace, Mrs Brown had always seemed ageless and imperturbable. Now, she knew Mrs Brown's forty-four years of life had been anything but easy. The scars on their housekeeper's heart would likely never heal. Grace felt an overwhelming desire to have her husband at her side.

Right on cue, the frantic yipping of excited puppies told her that Charlie was home.

The Coalman

Charlie sat down to lunch with his wife, who was as subdued as he had ever seen her. He soon found out why when Grace revealed Mrs Brown's traumatic past. From the halting manner of her narrative, he suspected she had left out the most harrowing parts for the sake of their housekeeper's dignity. By the time Grace finished, his blood was pumping red hot over Mrs Brown's treatment at the hands of Tulloch, and the blind eye turned by the cook. Not just a blind eye, but outright lies to protect Tulloch at Evie's expense.

He shoved his half-empty soup bowl away. "I'm off to pay a visit to Tulloch at his coal yard. I already had him on my list as a possible blackmail victim, but now I wouldn't be surprised if he is the villain. He fits the character of a blackmailer, and he is one of the very few people who knew Mrs Brown when she was Evie. A coalman is also a good match for the man the dressmaker's assistant described seeing in the church during the period the charity box was emptied."

Grace clamped a hand over his wrist. "I can see you're furious with Tulloch for what he did to Mrs Brown, but don't take any risks. He'll be strong after a lifetime of shovelling coal, and he won't fight by gentlemen's rules. Please, Charlie, be careful. Our children need their father."

Much as he appreciated his wife's concern, Charlie had dealt with tougher adversaries than an aging coalman. However, he would need a police presence for what he had in mind. His best friend, Detective Sergeant Declan Kelly, was just the man for the job.

"I'll be careful, Grace. I promise. I'm hoping Declan will be available for a delightful amble to the coal yard with me."

Grace clutched his wrist for a moment longer, then removed her hand to take up her spoon. To Charlie's expert eye, his wife's apparent restraint was all on the surface. He'd lay short odds that on the inside she was as furious as he was. Furious enough to do something rash.

He rose and went around the table to kiss her. "The same goes for you, Grace. No rushing off to accost Mrs Carmichael or the cook while I am out. I'll deal with them in due course."

"I promise you, tackling those foul people is the very last thing I want to do this afternoon. The very thought of them makes me feel nauseated, and I don't mind admitting I'm exhausted. Go, Charlie. Catch this swine and squeeze him until he squeals."

Charlie headed down to the central police station, contemplating what he would do when he got his hands on Tulloch. He'd need DS Declan Kelly on hand to make an arrest, if he could find just cause to throw the coalman behind bars. More importantly, he'd need Declan there to calm the situation, because Charlie had seldom felt angrier than he had at hearing of the man's abhorrent behaviour towards Mrs Brown. He reminded himself several times that they had no evidence to indicate Tulloch was the blackmailer. Unfortunately, there was no law against being a nasty, vicious scumbag, more's the pity.

As luck would have it, Declan was at his desk in the detective room, his broad back hunched over a pile of outstanding arrest warrants.

Declan jumped when Charlie clamped a hand on his shoulder. "Blimey, Pyke, don't creep up on me like that. What'll my family do if I drop dead of heart failure?"

"Mourn you for six months, after which Moira will marry a rich, handsome man who works regular hours, and they'll all live happily ever after?"

Declan punched his shoulder, but his lips twisted into a grin. "Call yourself a friend? To what do I owe the honour of your esteemed presence, Detective Pyke? Is it about the blackmail case?"

After Miss Mackenzie's visit, Charlie had alerted Detective Inspector Wallace and his team to the presence of a blackmailer in town, but he hadn't updated the police on the latest developments in the case. Wallace had already caught sight of him and was eyeing him up hopefully over a pile of files. He and Declan shared a loathing of paperwork and a bear-like physique. They loathed blackmailers too, and the prospect of throwing one in prison was far superior to signing off a monthly arrest report.

With a jerk of his head, Wallace summoned them to his office and gestured for them to sit. "Morning, Pyke. How are the collie pups coming along?"

"Thriving. They're still young, but one shows great potential." Charlie had promised his former boss the pick of the litter to be trained for tracking criminals. He thought Sage might suit, because she had her mother's curiosity and a sharp nose for scents. The idea of giving up any of the pups pained him, although he knew it was inevitable.

Wallace gave a satisfied nod, before raising a bushy eyebrow. He was not a man to waste words. "News, Pyke?"

"I'm here about the blackmail case. Since we spoke, we've discovered several other victims and made some progress in identifying suspects."

"Several more victims? Not good news, Pyke." Wallace pushed aside a pile of official documents and picked up his pen. "If it's not simply a case of jealous rivalry involving your client, then I must insist it becomes a police matter."

"Understood, sir." Charlie outlined his investigation, while Declan and Wallace took notes. "To be honest, it would be a relief to hand over the interviews of the potential victims to the police. There's a lot of legwork still to be done, such as finding out who delivered the notes, who set up the charity box, and what, if anything, links the victims. However, I want to continue my investigation on behalf of one victim."

"Your client, I presume," Wallace said. "That's fine by me as long as you share any leads."

"My initial client's situation is resolved. I'm now working on behalf of Mrs Brown."

Both policemen looked up sharply. They respected Mrs Brown almost as much as Charlie did, and not just for her delicious gingerbread.

Charlie wished he could leave Mrs Brown out of the discussion, but her situation was also by far the best lead, because so few people knew her as Evie. He outlined the relevant facts, including her relationship with Mrs Carmichael and Tulloch, but leaving out the details Mrs Brown would wish to remain private. Nevertheless, Wallace and Declan looked as if thunderclouds had amassed over their heads by the time he finished with his proposed plan of action to snare Tulloch.

"Agreed," Wallace said. "I want this brute taken down. But strictly by the book. We'd all like to see him get what's coming to him, but I won't have the blackmail case fall over because of police coercion. Kelly, take a constable with you as a witness. Let's all remember that we need evidence before we even think of arresting him. Until that time, you'll treat Tulloch as a potential victim and witness. Am I clear?"

"Crystal clear, sir," Charlie said. "Come and meet the pups when you have a moment to spare. Once the twins arrive, our lives will be chaotic." More chaotic, he meant. He hoped the blackmail case would be over by then, or he'd have to leave it in Declan Kelly's capable hands.

"How is Grace?" Wallace said. "Sorry. Should have asked after her first, not the pups."

"Unbelievably huge. Coping with her usual good humour, but it's not easy. She'd welcome a visit, now that her examinations are over."

"Will do. Wish her well from me." Wallace waved a hand and bent over his paperwork, but with a faraway smile that Charlie thought probably harked back to the birth of his own first child, many decades ago. Despite his tough outer shell, Wallace was a doting father and grandfather, and soft as down when it came to children and dogs.

Fifteen minutes later, Declan and Charlie sauntered into the coal yard like a couple of young men with time on their hands and money to enjoy it. The uniformed constable had been told to stay out of sight until he was signalled.

Tulloch took the last bite of greasy meat pie and brushed the pastry flakes from his filthy clothes with a filthy hand. He rose from his seat on a pile of firewood and tipped his hat at them.

Mrs Brown's experience did not predispose Charlie to like the coalman, and first appearances did not improve his opinion. Tulloch was an ox of a man. Not tall, but bulky and muscular, with an unpleasant smirk on his filthy face. In fact, he was a close match to the description of the rough man seen in the church this morning by the cleaning woman. If so, he had the opportunity to empty the hidden compartment of the charity box.

Tulloch looked them up and down, taking their measure. "What can I do for you, sirs? Is it coal and firewood you're after, or something else?"

"Depends on what the something else might be." Charlie glanced around, then slipped him a wink. "Word has it you're a man with fingers in many pies."

"Maybe. Is it moonshine you're after, or does your taste run more to the carnal pleasures?"

"I've heard you can get your hands on certain postcards featuring *artistic* photographs."

"Would it be women you're after?" Tulloch's cold blue eyes assessed the pair of men in front of him, lingering on their freshly starched collars and clean shaves. "Or perhaps it's boys you're wanting."

Charlie saw the curling of Declan's fist and laid a quelling hand on his arm. "How about you show us some girls?"

"Come into my office, gents." Tulloch led the way to a rickety cabin, where boxes of accounts and greasy pie wrappers flowed over every coal-dusted surface. He opened a locked drawer and drew out a folder. "I'll only show you one, mind, or you'll not be parting with your coin."

"Got any pretty young maids?" Charlie asked. "Heard you're a bit of a ladies' man with the maids."

Tulloch gave him a hard stare. "I'm a happily married man."

"Aye, and so are we. It doesn't mean we can't enjoy the merchandise on display." But Charlie had pushed him too far. He could see it from the way Tulloch's leering smirk shut down.

"You're in the wrong place, gents. I sell only coal and firewood." The folder went back into the drawer, which was slammed firmly in place.

Declan retreated to the door, where he had a whispered conversation with the constable, who had followed them in without Tulloch seeing. He returned with a smile on his face and his badge held out.

"Detective Sergeant Kelly, at your service. I'll be having that folder, Mr Tulloch. My constable informs me the crate-shaped lumps under that tarpaulin outside will have to be confiscated too. Possession and sale of objectionable materials and illegal alcohol. What do you reckon, Detective Pyke? I reckon it's enough for a stiff fine and closure of his business. Of course, a prison term isn't off the cards, depending on the contents of that folder and the source of that alcohol."

"I don't know nothing about the booze." Tulloch eyed the police badge as if it carried typhoid. "A fellow I know asked if he could store it in my yard for a day or two. You can't arrest me for doing a favour."

Charlie leaned against the wall, taking a grim satisfaction from Tulloch's reaction. "Prison, I'd say, from the way Mr Tulloch is quivering like a jellyfish." He left a couple of beats before adding, "although I expect we might show some leniency under the right conditions."

Tulloch opened his cash box. "Take it all. If you don't say a word, I swear I'll never sell the pictures again."

Declan removed a pair of handcuffs from his pocket. "Attempting to bribe an officer of the law. Definitely prison, I'd say."

Tulloch gaped at them. "But you said …"

"I said leniency under the right conditions," Charlie said. "By which I meant information, not a bribe. But if you are not willing to cooperate, Detective Sergeant Kelly here will be delighted to arrest you and remove your sordid little enterprise from our fair streets."

Tulloch's eyes narrowed as Declan retrieved the folder and flicked through the first few photographs, before handing them to the constable. Declan's disgust told Charlie that the photographs were even worse than he'd expected.

Tulloch saw it too, and he knew that no amount of bluster would dig him out of the hole. "What information would you be wanting, officer? Naturally, I'd be happy to oblige in any way I can."

"I'd like to know whether you put money in the charity box at church on Sunday." Charlie noted Tulloch's flinch. The question had taken him by surprise.

"I put a shilling in the box for a good cause. Business is good, and I can afford to be generous. Is it a crime to give to charity now?"

"Shall I be more specific, Mr Tulloch?" Charlie said. "Were you being blackmailed?"

Tulloch hesitated, no doubt deciding what lie to spin. "Got a note accusing me of selling underweight. Darndest thing, because whoever sent the note didn't want me to make it right, only to give a shilling to charity. No accounting for folks, eh? Still, no harm in making a donation, although I pride myself on providing customers with an exact measure."

"You're right, I do find that hard to believe," Charlie said. "Now, if you'd told me you'd been accused of abusing a young maid, I'd have believed that no problem. Word on the street is that you've been at it for at least a quarter of a century."

"How the hell did you —" Tulloch clamped his jaw shut. His skin gleamed a sickly white under streaks of coal dust, with sweat creating runnels in the dust as it ran down his forehead. "The blackmailer got it wrong. I never abused Bess. I only did what I was told and took her to the railway station."

This time it was Charlie who was caught by surprise. Bess was the other maid who worked for Mrs Carmichael while Mrs Brown was there – the maid who had supposedly run away with Hugh Brown. And Tulloch had just admitted he was being blackmailed over what he did to Bess, not what he did to Mrs Brown, or Evie as she was then.

However, he had Tulloch on the back foot now that the coalman seemed convinced Charlie knew why he was being blackmailed. He pressed his advantage while it lasted. "Who told you to take Bess to the station?"

The coalman shuffled backwards, his eyes on the entrance to the shed.

Charlie stepped forward, towering over him. "Who told you to take her?"

His eyes flicked sideways again, but Declan and the constable had moved to block his escape. Tulloch did what came naturally to him – he passed the blame. "It was Mrs Carmichael. She wanted Bess out of the house. Didn't hold with having no fallen girls under her roof." Tulloch paused, his thick lips curving into a knowing smirk. "Right little tart our Bess was."

The comment was the final straw. Every primitive instinct in his body urged Charlie to punch that smirk off his face. Instead, he recalled Wallace's warning and thrust his face within inches of the suspect to ensure he saw the anger ready to explode. "If I find out you laid a hand on that girl, I'll make you wish you were dead."

The coalman clawed at Charlie's chest to push himself away. "Get off me, copper. I never touched the maid. Wasn't me what knocked her up. And I reckon Bess never got on that train neither. She must have sneaked back to find that lusty little lad from the fishmonger's shop, because I heard they ran off together."

"What about the other maid who was there at the same time as Bess?" Charlie said. "A young woman called Evie?"

"What about her?" Tulloch replied. "As far as I know, she was given the heave-ho after Mrs Carmichael caught her in a wicked lie. Had nothing to do with her myself, except to eat her scones when I got the chance. Right good little cook she was, but a cold fish who wouldn't give you the time of day, not like Bess."

Charlie stepped away before his anger got the better of him. The interview had veered wildly off course. He'd been sure Tulloch was the blackmailer, but his story supported the conversation overheard by Johnny Todd before the church service, which suggested Tulloch was the victim of blackmail. That he deserved it was not relevant, legally speaking. The problem Charlie now faced was the same one he'd had throughout this investigation. Everyone had a reason to lie, both suspects and victims. To a man like Tulloch, lying would be as natural as breathing. After all, what better way to cover his role as a blackmailer than to pretend to be a victim?

What they needed was hard evidence or a confession. The woman cleaning the church said she wouldn't be able to identify the rough-looking man seen near the charity box, but it was worth a try. "You were seen at the First Church early on Monday morning, Tulloch. Care to explain?"

"What? I never was! I was here, shovelling coal for delivery while the birds were still snoring, like I am every day but Sunday."

Tulloch's reaction had been instant, outraged, frustratingly genuine. Without eyewitness testimony, they had no hope of pinning the removal of the blackmail payments from the charity box on him. "We'll be checking with your customers," Charlie said.

"Go ahead. I ain't got nothing to hide." Tulloch backed away to the desk and retrieved his order book. A grubby finger flicked it open. "Here it is, this morning's delivery schedule. Knock yourself out checking that lot." He handed the order book to Charlie. "I'll want it back, mind, copper."

Charlie exchanged a glance with Declan, who stepped forward and snapped handcuffs around Tulloch's wrists. "You're under arrest for the possession and sale of objectionable materials and illegal alcohol. Perhaps a spell behind bars might convince you to tell the truth, in which case I might turn a blind eye to your attempted bribery of an officer of the law. We'll be searching your house and the coal yard from top to toe, so you'd better be straight with us."

Charlie watched Declan haul the protesting coalman away in handcuffs. A partial success, in terms of getting a lowlife off the streets for a while. He could only hope that an experienced detective like Declan Kelly would get a confession out of Tulloch, especially with the leverage of the indecency charge to get him talking. If not, their best hope lay in a search of his home and business premises for evidence of wrongdoing.

The worst of it was that he was inclined to believe that Tulloch was telling the truth about being a victim of blackmail. Charlie had as much sympathy for him as he had for a cockroach in a sugar bowl, but it didn't make him feel any better. He felt a stab of guilt, knowing his determination to nail Tulloch for blackmail showed a concerning lack of objectivity.

All he could do was plod on with the investigation, hoping for a crucial piece of evidence. Where next? Mr and Mrs Carmichael seemed the most obvious next port of call, but Charlie knew he would be a fool to face them before he calmed down. What he needed was a reminder of the good in this dark world. His wife, the babies, Blaze and her pups, his happy home.

Besides, he was eager to share the news of Tulloch's arrest with Mrs Brown.

An Unwelcome Visitor

After Charlie left to confront the coalman, Grace forced down the rest of her lunch.

The rage in Charlie's gold-flecked green eyes when he left had been terrifying to behold. The thought of him accosting a foul lecher like Tulloch turned her stomach, but she trusted Charlie would be safe with Detective Sergeant Declan Kelly by his side. Their intimidating size alone would deter most criminals, especially a bully like Tulloch, who preyed on defenceless young women. Although Evie had proved far from defenceless, since she had escaped Tulloch with a well-placed knee. His humiliation would not be readily forgotten, just as Mrs Brown would never forget his catastrophic effect on her life.

Her husband wasn't the only one furious at what Mrs Brown had suffered, but Grace meant what she said about resting. She was in no state to go storming off to berate Mrs Carmichael for throwing Evie out of the house with neither her wages nor a reference. And she certainly wasn't going anywhere near Tulloch's nasty wife, the former cook, even if they could track her down after all these years.

Instead, Grace went to the drawing room and attempted to settle down for a nap. Although she felt physically drained, mental agitation made sleep impossible. She could only hope Tulloch was the blackmailer, putting a quick end to this distressing investigation. She could bask in the euphoria of completing her medical degree and savour the freedom to rest and prepare for the birth at the end of the month. She closed her eyes and tried to imagine what their children would be like.

The doorbell rang.

Grace jerked upright, before dropping back onto the sofa cushions with a groan. What now? A sudden longing to have her mother by her side overwhelmed her. Had her mother's famous intuition told her she was needed in Dunedin? She listened for the familiar laugh, for Mrs Brown's delighted cry of surprise at Mrs Penrose's arrival, but it wasn't to be.

Mrs Brown entered the drawing room, her face a sickly hue. "Mrs Carmichael to see you, Mrs Penrose Pyke," she announced in a fragile voice. "If you feel up to it."

Mrs Carmichael didn't give Grace a chance to refuse. She pushed past Mrs Brown without a second glance, clearly not recognising her as Evie. The old harridan probably hadn't given Evie a second thought after she ejected her from the house, other than to curse her disgraceful behaviour and disloyalty. Grace would have to ask Mrs Brown about their guest's initial reaction when she answered the door. If Mrs Carmichael really was ignorant of Mrs Brown's identity, she could not be Mrs Brown's blackmailer.

On the other hand, it was also possible she was pretending not to recognise Evie. Grace had no experience of blackmailers, but her gut told her such a callous breed of criminal must have a heart of ice and exceptional skill at deception. Mrs Carmichael was definitely selfish and obsessed with status, but Grace struggled to see her as evil. And to be fair to her, Evie's dismissal was not entirely unreasonable given the lies the cook had told about Evie.

The visitor was glaring at her, presumably because she had not yet been welcomed with appropriate pleasantries. Keep a civil tongue, Grace reminded herself. They needed the truth from this woman, no matter how badly she had treated Mrs Brown in the past.

"Good afternoon, Mrs Carmichael." Grace dredged up a faint smile and waved vaguely at her bulging belly. "Please, take a seat. I hope you'll excuse me if I don't get up. It's been a trying morning."

Mrs Carmichael sat. "I understand perfectly, Mrs Penrose Pyke. I know what you are suffering because my firstborn was two weeks overdue. Indeed, I must apologise for calling unannounced, especially given your condition."

Grace nodded encouragingly, hoping to get a straightforward confession for once rather than a frustrating meander around the unpleasant truth.

Her visitor glanced around, as if expecting eavesdroppers behind the furniture. "It's a matter of some delicacy, you see. One feels a reluctance to discuss such matters with anyone who doesn't share a … a mutual bond of understanding between ladies of a certain class."

"Of course, Mrs Carmichael. You honour me with your trust. What did you wish to talk to me about?" Grace fixed her smile in place. She wanted to strangle her visitor with her awful marigold-coloured shawl, which clashed horribly with the crimson trim of her hat. But she didn't. Her testimony was sufficiently vital to overcome Grace's desire to lambast her.

Grace held up a hand at the sound of an approaching tea tray. After a discreet knock on the drawing-room door, Mrs Brown entered. Grace waved a hand at the side table. "Leave the tea tray, Mrs Brown. We'll serve ourselves."

"Yes, ma'am. Will there be anything else, ma'am?"

Grace fixed her lips into a haughty pout to stop herself laughing at the transformation of Mrs Brown's vowels to a plummy tone worthy of Buckingham Palace. "Perhaps you could go upstairs and take down those dreadful curtains in the nursery. They really must be replaced before the babies are born."

Their housekeeper did as she was told with a subservience never before seen in the household. An atypically heavy tread was soon evident on the stairs. Mrs Carmichael's tension deflated. Grace asked if she would mind pouring the tea, hoping the clatter of cups would cover the sound of Mrs Brown creeping back down to listen in to the conversation, if that was what she wanted to do. The curtains in the nursery were new and gorgeous, and their housekeeper was wily enough to take the hint to make herself scarce in the far reaches of the house. Or, at least, to give the appearance of having done so.

Mrs Carmichael placed a cup on the table next to Grace with nervous fingers, slopping tea into the saucer. "I see we understand each other, Mrs Penrose Pyke. Servants can be such dreadful gossips." She added sugar to her cup and stirred with agonising slowness before she spoke again. "I need your husband to find the blackmailer with all haste. I will pay whatever you ask."

Tempting as it was to extract a pound of flesh, Grace waved her offer away. The last thing they needed was to be beholden to a suspect. "My husband already has a client and fully intends to catch this scoundrel as soon as he can. However, it would be a great assistance to his investigation if we could have a frank discussion. Perhaps there were details of the blackmail note you did not wish your husband to be aware of?"

The rattling of her cup on the saucer became so pronounced that Mrs Carmichael put it down. "Yes, that is it exactly. I am not in the habit of lying to my husband, you understand, but I could not bear to admit the true horror of the blackmail demand in front of him. So cruel an accusation. So much money. My husband is a good man, but he has a truly fierce temper when his family is threatened."

"Tell me what you recall of the note." Grace saw an extra flicker of tension in her visitor's tight lips. "Or perhaps you very sensibly kept the note after all."

"I wanted to burn it, but I hadn't yet decided what to do." Mrs Carmichael reached into her reticule.

Grace leaned forward eagerly as her visitor handed her the blackmail note she claimed to have burned. The note read: *Your cruelty to a maid killed her baby. Put £50 in the church charity box before the morning service on Sunday, or everyone will hear of your evil deed. I hope you die in the flames of Hell.*

She stifled a gasp at the shocking words. This was a far cry from the other blackmail notes in all ways: the seriousness of the accusation, the venom of the words, and the massive sum demanded.

"It's a foul lie," Mrs Carmichael said. "I would never be cruel to a woman carrying a child. In fact, I have never hit any of my servants, no matter how much they deserved it. If this vile slander spreads, my reputation will be in tatters."

Her reputation seemed a secondary matter to Grace, compared to the welfare of the maid, but it appeared Mrs Carmichael had other thoughts foremost in her mind.

"Fifty pounds is unthinkable. Even if I paid, what proof would I have that the blackmailer would stop?"

"Could you afford such a sum?" Grace asked.

"Absolutely not. We don't have that kind of money available, even if I dared risk my husband's wrath by asking for it. If only he'd sell the house. I've pleaded with him time and again. The house is far too big for us now the children are gone, and it's far too much work for one maid. If we sold, we could move to a smaller home in a more fashionable neighbourhood. But men hate change, don't they? My husband says he's got his garden just how he likes it, and besides, it's close to the shop so he can work

135

alongside his son. He might not mind gardening and working until he drops dead, but I don't want to end my life toiling over a mop and bucket because we cannot afford more servants."

There was a petulance to Mrs Carmichael's attitude that angered Grace. It was as if she expected to be looked after in grand style with no effort on her part. Her husband's fortune had dwindled since the heady days of the gold rush, but he was far from the only man in such circumstances. Mrs Carmichael still had more than most women, who toiled their whole lives without ever having wealth and a grand house to live in. And she had failed in her one responsibility – to ensure the well-being of those who did the real work within her household.

Once again, Grace wondered if Mrs Carmichael was the innocent, distressed victim she played so well. Had she written the blackmail note to force her husband into giving her the money she felt she deserved, or to divert suspicion from herself? She was well placed to be the blackmailer, as a regular churchgoer who would know the gossip. Her husband's hardware business could have supplied the tools needed to rig the charity box, and her suspicious fumbling as she tripped beside the box had given her the opportunity to trigger the false bottom mechanism. Above all, she had the oldest motive of all, greed, and the selfish character to put her needs above the suffering of others.

For all of Grace's desire to challenge the suspect, she knew a soft approach would be better to gather the information they needed to make a case. "I sympathise with your situation, Mrs Carmichael, and I promise you we are doing everything we can to find the blackmailer. However, to achieve that end, I must ask you some personal questions about the accusation and your household."

"I expect the scoundrel simply made up lies to extort money from me." Mrs Carmichael's jaw thrust out in a failed attempt to pretend there was no truth to the blackmail demand. The fact that she was here told Grace otherwise.

"That's certainly a possibility," Grace said. "Am I to assume that you put nothing in the charity box?"

"Only a shilling. I pretended to stumble so nobody could see how much I put in. Whatever minor act of so-called cruelty this person thinks I am responsible for, it cannot be worth so very much."

Grace nodded, but privately she was wondering how Mrs Carmichael thought a shilling would fool the blackmailer, since he or she would know that the collection was short by the massive sum of £50. "The note accused you of cruelty to a maid, resulting in the death of her baby. Have any of your maids fallen pregnant?"

"How can anyone be certain until they show? Girls will get themselves into trouble occasionally with their foolish dalliances. In such cases, the maid could not expect to stay in employment. Losing a maid is such a nuisance, since we only have a maid-of-all-work these days. In the past, we've had two maids and a cook, but not anymore."

Was that a yes or a no? Grace gritted her teeth and tried a different tack. "Have you ever had a maid leave unexpectedly?"

Her visitor's jaw quivered. "The two maids we hired when we first arrived in Dunedin both left us suddenly, which caused a great deal of disruption. But that was twenty-five years ago. Far too long ago to come to the notice of a blackmailer, surely. I wasn't aware that either of them was with child. Certainly, I had noticed no indication of it. I was a great deal more cautious with my maids after that. No more going out at night or talking to male callers. We've had many maids come and go over the years, but all the rest at least did me the courtesy of giving notice. As you know, it is extremely difficult to keep them for any length of time. Most vexing."

Grace didn't know any such thing. In her experience, maids stayed as long as possible if they were treated with respect and paid appropriately. Resignations usually followed a marriage proposal from a respectable young man. Mrs Carmichael's assertion that the blackmailer wouldn't know of long-ago events was also incorrect. The depth of the blackmailer's memory was clear from the blackmail demand sent to Miss Mackenzie, which accused her of being the daughter of a red-headed boarder. Interestingly, that accusation was also founded on an event from about a quarter of a century ago.

"The note's accusation, that your cruelty to a maid killed her baby, was very specific, Mrs Carmichael. What made those two maids leave suddenly?" Grace already knew why Evie left, of course, just as she knew Evie had not been pregnant when she left. However, she wanted to hear Mrs Carmichael's version of events, especially in relation to the other maid, Bess.

"Who knows? Girls are fickle beings. To be honest, I had my suspicions about one maid. She up and left without so much as a by your leave to elope with a local lad, which does rather suggest a hasty marriage was necessary. I assure you she cannot have any claim against me. I swear I never laid a finger on her. For all her flirtatious ways, Bess was an excellent maid."

Grace hoped Mrs Brown wasn't listening. She should have sent her out on an errand. It must be devastating to know the man you loved had run away with another girl. Presumably, Hugh Brown had played the field, pretending to love them both to get them into bed, before choosing Bess over Evie.

She hesitated, but they had to know if Mrs Carmichael knew what happened to Evie. "What about the other maid?"

"Goodness, I cannot even recall her name, it was so long ago. Enid, Ellie? Something like that. She seemed a nice girl, always polite and obedient, never a complaint. But Cook told me she saw a man coming out of her room while my husband and I were out one night, so naturally I had no option but to dismiss her on the spot. I was shocked, I can tell you. She did not strike me as that type of girl. Never for an instant did I think Enid was with child."

"Never a single complaint?" Grace said, with a sharpness that brought a startled look from her visitor.

"Not that I heard. We missed her dreadfully after she left, because the standard of cooking plummeted overnight. She was supposed to be the downstairs maid, but she must have been doing most of the cooking as well. To be honest, once I calmed down, I wondered if Cook had taken against her and made up the story about the man in her room. I left the management of the maids to her. She was a housekeeper-cook really, but it soon became clear who did all the work when the girls left. The place fell apart. I did ask around about the maid I dismissed, but nobody had seen her, so I presumed she went back to her family."

Mrs Carmichael appeared to be telling the truth about Evie, which meant the cook had not passed on Evie's complaints about the coalman. However, Grace believed she had not yet uncovered the whole truth about the other maid, Bess.

"You said you did not know Bess was pregnant before she left, Mrs Carmichael. May I ask if you had any suspicions about Bess after her departure, aside from the haste of her elopement?"

"I cannot say I would be entirely surprised if she was with child," Mrs Carmichael said, with a disapproving sniff. "Bess was a pretty, lively girl, and didn't she know it. She'd flirt with any man between fifteen and fifty, that one. When she left so hastily, Cook admitted she had her suspicions, because she had noticed that Bess had put on weight and seemed to be sick a lot. It was no surprise to her when the maid ran away with the fishmonger's boy. A shame, because Bess was a dab hand at dressing my hair and looked after my gowns to perfection, never scorching them with the iron and always fixing any little tears before they ran. Not like my last maid, who ripped my best shawl and didn't lift a finger to fix it. And Bess was always polite and attentive to me and my husband, not like maids these days."

Grace didn't want to listen to another litany of complaints about recent maids, so she diverted the discussion back to the past. "How did you know Bess ran away with the fishmonger's son?"

"One evening she was there, the next morning she had gone, without a word of apology to me or Cook, let alone giving proper notice. But Cook knew the fishmonger's wife, who told her what happened. Apparently, the fishmonger's son left his parents a note to say he was running away to marry Bess. I vowed never again to employ pretty young maids, I can tell you. More trouble than they are worth."

Grace recalled Mr Carmichael lamenting the lack of pretty maids, probably not knowing it was a deliberate choice on his wife's part. However, employing ugly maids clearly hadn't made retaining staff any easier for Mrs Carmichael, which confirmed she was a difficult woman to work for.

Not that it would be easy to work for their own household either. Grace was ever thankful to have the marvellous Mrs Brown. She hoped they would find a new maid who had the right character for the job. It wouldn't be easy, with babies, dogs, detecting, and doctoring adding disruption to their lives. She dragged her attention back to Mrs Carmichael, whose tirade against servants was continuing unabated. Grace had the feeling her visitor could go on for hours if left unchecked.

"… and blow me down, I had to dismiss Cook shortly after Bess flitted off with her lover. I caught her fornicating with the coalman. Servants! I ask you. No moral standards at all."

"The coalman?" Grace queried.

"Tulloch, his name was. Rough fellow and abominably arrogant. He was terribly rude to me once. Quite above his station. Seemed to think himself my equal, just because my husband was civil enough to pass the time of day with him. I heard Cook married him after I dismissed her. I suppose she was grateful for any man to take notice of her, but, really, a coalman!"

No wonder the cook lied for Tulloch, Grace thought. The point was a crucial one, so she wanted to be sure of the facts. "Let me be sure I understand you, Mrs Carmichael. After one maid was dismissed and the other maid left suddenly, you had to dismiss your cook for unseemly behaviour with the coalman, Mr Tulloch. The cook then married Tulloch?"

"Quite so. I was left entirely without servants. Most aggravating. We had only recently arrived in Dunedin, so perhaps I didn't conduct the rigorous checks on their characters that I should have before employing them. A mistake I never repeated, you can be assured."

"And you relied on the cook's word about the maid's indiscretions."

"Naturally," Mrs Carmichael said. "Cook was a mature woman, not a silly girl. However, considering Cook's appalling behaviour afterward, I concede that I may have misjudged the situation. The maid I dismissed on Cook's word did try to tell me that Tulloch was to blame, but I doubted her story at the time. Who ever heard of a coalman daring to enter a gentleman's house while he was out? And then to have the gall to drink his port? It seemed too ludicrous to be true."

Grace didn't respond, because she was thrown by what sounded like genuine regret for Evie's dismissal.

Mrs Carmichael was silent for a moment, too, her brow furrowed. "Gracious me, I see what you must be thinking, Mrs Penrose Pyke. Why didn't I think of it sooner! That dreadful coalman and the cook could be the blackmailers, just because I dismissed the cook without notice and ensured that no other household would employ her. Well, I expect you're right. What a cheek blackmailing me for cruelty to the maid, when it was more likely Cook who abused the girls. She was the one in charge of them, after all."

Grace couldn't let her leave and spread gossip about her suspicions. "Please, Mrs Carmichael, we cannot leap to conclusions without evidence. I urge you to stay silent on the matter until the investigation is complete." She could sense reluctance from the rebellious pinching of Mrs Carmichael's lips. "I mean it. Not a word. You wouldn't wish to alert the blackmailer to our line of inquiry. The person or persons behind this are dangerous."

The puff went out of her visitor, replaced with smug satisfaction. "I promise. Just make sure you bring that pair of scoundrels to justice for me."

Mrs Carmichael took her leave, looking far less agitated than when she had arrived. There was nothing like having one's problems solved discreetly at no cost to oneself.

For the sake of her unborn babies, Grace needed to restore her calm. She retrieved Blaze and her pups from the outside pen and brought them into the house. Charlie had told her the first step in training the pups was to handle them and gain their trust. A pleasant half-hour of hugging adorable little fur balls was exactly what she needed after her encounter with Mrs Carmichael.

Mrs Brown had probably listened in on their conversation. It must have shaken her to the core to hear that Bess was probably pregnant when she eloped with Hugh Brown. Two to three months pregnant, judging by the signs the cook had noticed, which meant Hugh had bedded Bess before he met Evie. What a dilemma he must have faced. Hugh loved Evie, but he would have seen that marrying the maid he got pregnant was the honourable thing to do, especially if someone had assured him that Evie had been with another man.

What a mess. Mrs Brown could use a dose of puppy therapy too.

The Ironmonger

Charlie arrived home to the unexpected sight of Grace and Mrs Brown sitting on the floor of the drawing room, cradling a pup each, and laughing merrily as they threw a ball to the other two pups. Blaze sat watching, her tongue lolling, the matriarch guarding her pack.

His heart melted at the joyful scene after his unpleasant encounter with the coalman. If he had his life to live over, Charlie couldn't imagine anything better than the family he had right here. A sudden jolt of longing for his parents caught him by surprise. They were coming for Christmas, but that seemed a long time to wait, although it was only six weeks away.

Grace put the pup down and lifted her arms for Charlie to help her up. "We've been training the pups while you were out."

He helped his wife onto the sofa, plumping the cushions for her back. "I'm delighted you kept your promise not to do anything rash." Her eyes darted sideways, suggesting her time had not been entirely spent throwing balls to Spark and Sage.

"What happened with Tulloch?" Mrs Brown asked. "Is he as repulsive now as he was when I knew him?"

"I'm afraid so. You'll be pleased to know that Declan arrested him for possession of lewd photographs and illegal alcohol. Unfortunately, we've not yet found any evidence of his involvement in blackmail. Declan has taken him away in handcuffs for a formal interview, but I got the impression he was a victim, not the blackmailer."

"Are you sure, Charlie?" Grace said. "Mrs Brown and I have discussed it, and we're both sure the coalman and his wife must be behind the blackmail notes."

"His wife?" Charlie picked up Sage for a pat and tried to recall if Tulloch had mentioned a wife.

"Tulloch married the Carmichaels' cook after Mrs Carmichael caught them fornicating and dismissed the cook on the spot." Grace's gaze flicked to Mrs Brown. "This happened after Evie was wrongfully dismissed and the other maid, Bess, ran away."

"Mrs Carmichael said Hugh ran away with Bess because she was with child," Mrs Brown said. "In a way, it's a relief to know he chose her for an honourable reason."

Charlie's fingers stopped stroking silky ears, causing Sage to butt his hand for more. "How did you come by this information, Grace?"

"Mrs Carmichael visited me, uninvited, to urge us to find the blackmailer. She hadn't told the full truth at our first meeting, as we suspected. The blackmail note accused her of cruelty, causing the death of a maid's baby, and demanded £50 or all would be revealed." Grace handed him the blackmail note, which Mrs Carmichael had been glad to leave behind. "Look at the vindictiveness of the words. *I hope you die in the flames of Hell.*"

"Cook must have hated Mrs Carmichael after she was caught in a compromising position with the coalman and dismissed," Mrs Brown said. "Tulloch's an evil man too. Who else but those two could be the blackmailers? Nobody else knew about my situation. Mrs Carmichael didn't appear to know the truth about Tulloch's abuse of me. She could have lied, I suppose, but I am certain she didn't recognise me when I opened the door to her."

"Mrs Carmichael couldn't even recall Evie's name," Grace added. "She appeared genuinely sorry to lose Evie, whom she held in high regard until the cook told the lie about Evie having a man in her room. I got the impression Mrs Carmichael had little idea about what went on in her house, as long as her needs were met."

Charlie wasn't sure about any of them. The coalman's denial of being the blackmailer had seemed the only sincere part of his interview, but he undoubtedly had years of experience in deceit. However, Charlie trusted the police to get to the bottom of the coalman's dodgy dealings.

"Declan will get Tulloch to talk, and a thorough search of his premises might provide the evidence we need. We'll have to interview Mrs Tulloch as well. It's conceivable that she might be working on her own regarding the blackmail, leaving the other sordid business dealings to her husband. What a pair!"

"The cook has a lot to answer for, if you ask me," Grace said. "Mrs Carmichael denied any cruelty to Bess. According to her, Bess ran away without saying a word to her. It was only through her cook knowing Hugh's mother that she heard about Bess eloping with Hugh. She didn't suspect Bess of being pregnant until after she left, when the cook mentioned it."

"That's not what Mr Tulloch told me," Charlie said. "He swore Mrs Carmichael asked him to remove Bess from the house because she refused to have a fallen girl under her roof. Tulloch said he took Bess to the railway station. One of them is lying, or both."

Grace heaved a frustrated sigh. "As far as I can see, every single person is lying about something – or everything – because of their shame at being blackmailed or to cover their despicable behaviour."

"Cook was no better than that foul brute she married," Mrs Brown said. "I trusted her to keep me and Bess safe, but she never told Mrs Carmichael about Tulloch's appalling behaviour. Instead, she ensured I was thrown out without a reference. Without Anne Drummond, I could have died on the street. I still have nightmares about sitting on that street corner in tears, being harassed by men and ignored by women passersby. There were times I almost wished I were dead."

Charlie felt her pain as a deep ache. He'd had rough patches in his life as well, but never anything as awful as Mrs Brown had faced.

Grace turned to him with a fierce look. "Charlie will bring them to justice, Mrs Brown. He's already put Tulloch behind bars, which is a fine start. He'll squeeze the truth out of Mrs Tulloch, don't you worry."

Charlie knew a hint when he heard it. He set the pup down and rose, wishing he could return to the moment he had entered the drawing room and witnessed joyful laughter.

"Time for me to get back to work," he said, "but I'll let Mrs Tulloch stew while Declan deals with her husband. She sounds like a tough character, which means it would be best to gather as much evidence as we can first." Charlie pulled on his jacket. "However, there is one other person who may know what happened all those years ago, and that's Mr Carmichael. I shouldn't be long. Don't get into any trouble while I'm out."

He made his way down High Street to Princes Street, expecting to find Mr Carmichael at his shop. While he doubted Mr Carmichael had any knowledge of what happened to the two maids a quarter of a century ago, at least it would be a relief to talk to an ordinary, straight-speaking working man. And Mr Carmichael was as close to an independent witness as he was likely to get. He hadn't had a blackmail letter, and he hadn't known about the letter sent to his wife. Nor did he have any personal contact with the First Church, apart from through his wife, which made him an unlikely suspect as the blackmailer.

Of all the people in this investigation, Mr Carmichael seemed the most content with his life, having made a success of his business beyond what most shopkeepers could hope for. If he was less successful now that he was older, he seemed to have found ample solace in having a son and three daughters to be proud of. A man happy to be passing the business to his son, so he could potter in his garden. Charlie could understand that, even if he didn't approve of the man's old-fashioned attitudes toward women.

As he walked, Charlie reflected on the new information Grace had learned from Mr Carmichael's wife. The enormous sum demanded and the vitriol of the blackmail note put Mrs Carmichael at the bullseye of the blackmailer's target. The accusation, that she had caused the death of a maid's baby, was shocking – but was it true? Mrs Carmichael denied knowing Bess was pregnant and said the maid had left without telling her, but she could be lying. And Charlie wouldn't put it past either of the Tullochs to have made up the worst allegation they could imagine in order to demand a higher blackmail payment from the woman who threw them out of her house.

However, if the accusation in the blackmail note was true, the dead baby's parents had the strongest motive for revenge. Bess and Hugh had run away together, but did they really leave New Zealand, as Hugh said in his note to his parents? Hugh's note seemed to be one of the few solid pieces of evidence they had. Hugh had no reason to lie about going away. Anne had talked to his parents, who believed the note had been left by Hugh because it was on the paper used in the fishmonger's shop and was left on their kitchen table.

This case was giving Charlie a headache. There was still so much he needed to find out to make sense of the conflicting accounts, not least the question of why the blackmailer would wait a quarter of a century for revenge. A specific event must have triggered it – something the blackmailer found out that he or she didn't know before. Unless it was simply that the blackmailer urgently needed money and used their knowledge of past scandals to get it.

Charlie's head was pounding by the time he stood outside Mr Carmichael's ironmongery shop. Or rather, Carmichael & Son, according to the freshly painted sign above the door.

A bell jangled when he pushed the door open. The shop smelled of dust and oil. He was the only customer, as far as he could see, although his line of sight was much diminished by the piles of wares stacked high on rows of shelves. There wasn't much made of iron that one couldn't purchase here. Everything from adzes to anvils, braziers to buckles, fire irons to firearms, mangles to mirrors, spades to spoons, and possibly the odd xylophone and yoke. The firearms were locked away behind the counter in a glass-fronted cabinet that a child could break into. Such laxity was not uncommon in a country where shotguns and rifles were seen by some sectors of society as ordinary household items, necessary for putting meat on the table or a stag's head above the mantelpiece.

Mr Carmichael's son, Donald, sat at the counter, looking glum despite the arrival of a potential customer. Charlie saw a spark of recognition as he approached, but Donald's bunched eyebrows told him he couldn't recall where they'd met.

Charlie nodded a greeting. "We met briefly at your parents' home on Sunday afternoon. It's your father I was hoping to speak to. Is he in?"

Donald's frown cleared as he put a name to the face, perhaps thinking Charlie was a friend of his parents. "Ah yes, Mr Penrose Pyke. I'm afraid you have missed him. Father didn't come back to the shop after his midday meal. I expect my mother has put him to work on the house. She's encouraging him to tart up the grand old homestead in order to sell it, but she has more hope of moving a mountain than moving my father from that place."

"Your father has good reason to be proud of it. He must have made a great success of his business to have bought such a magnificent home for his family."

"Father was astute enough to tap into the glory days of the gold rush. If you ask me, the future is in engineering and machinery, not shovels and pickaxes, but don't tell my father that. He wants me to take over the shop."

Charlie heard the despair behind the words. "You know, I spent years believing my father wanted me to follow in his footsteps, but it turned out I was wrong. Fathers only want the best for their children. Deep down, they know a young man must make his own way in the world."

"Father has just had a Carmichael & Son sign painted." Donald sighed. "But I suppose I must summon the courage to talk to him, or I'll be stuck with this dreary shop forever. Not that I'm ungrateful for all he has done for me. I've had a fine life, and I truly want to make him proud."

Charlie wished Donald well and went on his way. He arrived at the Carmichaels' house a few minutes later, where he found the man of the house leaning on a spade, contemplating an apple tree, with his shoulders slumped as if they carried the weight of the world.

Mr Carmichael turned at the sound of Charlie's greeting. His initial shock at being disturbed from his reverie quickly turned to resignation. "Mr Penrose Pyke. I thought you might be along. My wife told me about visiting your wife."

"Shall we go inside to talk?"

"Er … perhaps not. Vera and I had a blazing row. My wife had no right to talk to anyone without consulting me, especially about such an important matter."

"My wife was surprised by her visit too," Charlie said. "Did Mrs Carmichael tell you about the blackmail note?"

Carmichael's jaw tightened. "I had to insist. She had no right to keep it from me in the first place. Whoever wrote that note must be deranged. My wife can be rather strict about the standards she wishes to maintain, but she never, ever abuses servants physically. As for causing the death of a maid's baby, it's utterly preposterous. And £50! The blackmailer must be a certifiable lunatic to think we could pay such a ridiculous sum."

Charlie sympathised with his anger at the blackmailer and his support for his wife, but he wondered if there was an undercurrent of something other than anger. He struggled to put his finger on it, but there was a pinch of worry in the crow's feet around Mr Carmichael's eyes, as if he didn't entirely believe in his wife's innocence.

"I can't help but wonder where this person got the idea for such a claim against her," Mr Carmichael said. "But, more than that, I'm worried for my wife that this appalling allegation will be shared with other members of her church community. Vera is a sensitive soul. She would be mortified to be the subject of gossip. Not like me. I couldn't give a damn what people say about me. I am who I am, and proud of it."

"Could there be an element of truth in the allegation?" Charlie put up his hand to halt Carmichael's angry retort. "All I meant was that if a maid was dismissed after falling pregnant, the girl might believe the dismissal contributed to a subsequent loss of her child, even if her belief was unwarranted. People always seek someone else to blame for their troubles. From what I understand, you did have a pregnant maid in your household long ago, didn't you?"

"Apparently so. The first I heard of it was when my wife told me when she got home today. I leave servant business to her. I've got enough on my plate without worrying about girls who go silly over lads. The girl ran off with her young Romeo, so I hear. All's well that ends well."

"Not if their child died," Charlie said.

Carmichael waved the comment aside. "Infants die every day. Terribly sad, naturally, but the pair of them probably have a dozen brats by now. Anyway, that was half a lifetime ago. Why would the maid create a fuss now?"

An excellent point. That very issue had been vexing Charlie since the start of the investigation. "Your guess is as good as mine, Mr Carmichael. A simmering resentment reemerging, perhaps. Grudges have long memories, I suppose."

"Balderdash. You mark my words, it's nothing more than some nasty piece of work out for easy money, muckraking by making up ludicrous lies." Carmichael's knuckles turned white as his grip on the spade tightened with every word. "If I get my hands on him, he'll be sorry. Nobody threatens my family and gets away with it."

"You could be right, but I must insist you leave the blackmailer to me and the police." The last thing Charlie needed was an angry victim with itchy fists. He didn't agree with the easy money comment either, because blackmail was a barbed weapon, not an easy way to make a little extra income. It was a dangerous game, risking a prison term and the wrath of aggrieved victims, as Carmichael's words demonstrated all too well.

"I suppose you're right." Carmichael wrenched his spade from the ground, signalling that the interview was over.

But Charlie was far from done with him. "Did you know that the coalman, Tulloch, abused your maids around the time the pregnant maid left?"

Carmichael was shocked speechless.

"You didn't know?"

"No! Absolutely not. When you say abused, what exactly do you mean? Teased them? Exchanged cross words with them?"

"Far worse than that, Mr Carmichael. He pressed himself against them and made lewd suggestions. He threatened one of them in a very nasty manner when the girl found him where he had no right to be."

"I'm shocked." Carmichael frowned as the revelation sank in. "Although I suppose I'm not wholly surprised about the lewd comments. Tulloch was a man with … robust appetites."

"You would know, since you purchased lewd photographs from him."

A flush of red flared on Carmichael's cheeks, but he shrugged it off. "Nothing wrong with looking at the odd racy picture. That's entirely different from taking advantage of a vulnerable girl. Why didn't the maids complain?"

"They did. They complained to the cook, who promised to pass the information to your wife."

"I'm sorry to hear it. My wife never mentioned anything of the sort to me. With her strong religious beliefs, she would never tolerate inappropriate behaviour, let alone anything as appalling as this. I can only imagine the cook must have failed to pass the information on. Come to think of it, my wife had to dismiss the cook after she found Tulloch humping her in the pantry. Maybe the cook turned a blind eye to his behaviour to win his favour. I believe they got married after she left."

Carmichael sank into grim silence, leaning heavily on his spade again.

"Have you had any contact with Mr or Mrs Tulloch since then?" Charlie asked.

"I haven't. We changed coal merchants immediately, of course. To be honest, we were glad to see the back of them, although we were desperately short of servants at the time. My wife still sees the Tullochs at church every Sunday, but naturally she never talks to them. She was incensed by the cook's wanton behaviour, as you can imagine. Tulloch used to be friendly enough, but I always felt he had a dark side. One to hold a grudge, I imagine. Could he be the one who is blackmailing my wife?"

"The possibility had occurred to me," Charlie said, "but there is no evidence to support that theory yet. I'd ask you not to share your speculations with anyone at this point in the inquiry."

"You may be assured that I cannot bear to think about it, let alone talk of it. I'm sixty-four years old, Mr Penrose Pyke, and all I want to do is enjoy my garden and help my son succeed in the business he will inherit. Is a little peace and quiet too much to ask?"

"We can dream, Mr Carmichael, but fate is not always on our side. As for our children, perhaps it is best to let them choose their own paths in life."

Carmichael sighed. "Wise words, but not always easy words for a father to accept. My son assured me he was content to work in the shop, but I've had a feeling for a while that Donald has another future in mind. He's a marvel with mechanical devices, and his future father-in-law can offer him better prospects than I can. I would not wish to stand in the way of his success."

He held out his hand, surprising Charlie with the firmness of his handshake. "Will you promise me one favour, Mr Penrose Pyke?"

"If it's within my power."

"I'm very worried about my wife. She's dreadfully upset by this blackmail outrage. Will you let me know the moment you make any progress in the investigation? I won't rest easy until my wife feels safe again." Carmichael didn't release his hand until he'd finished his plea.

Charlie didn't doubt the man's sincerity. The throbbing of his hand would have confirmed it, even if the intensity of the plea hadn't. He felt for the poor man. If somebody were blackmailing Grace, Charlie would have felt exactly the same. However, he could not promise to divulge details of the investigation.

Instead, he gave a noncommittal nod and left Carmichael contemplating his beloved garden intently, as if his problems might vanish if he stared long enough and hard enough at the apple tree.

The Cook

Grace could tell from the dragging footsteps in the hallway that Charlie's meeting with Mr Carmichael had yielded no fresh leads.

He took her in his arms and held her silently for a time before speaking. "I told Carmichael more than he told me. I checked in at the police station on the way back. Declan had no luck either, despite using every trick in the book to get Tulloch to admit he was the blackmailer. He's having Tulloch's home and business pulled apart to search for evidence, but it's not looking hopeful. The police have also tracked down most of the people Johnny identified as potential victims. They either denied being a victim or said the accusation made in the blackmail demand was absurd. So far, the police have uncovered no obvious links between the victims. If this investigation drags on much longer, I'll have to turn it over to the police entirely."

"It's only been a week since Miss Mackenzie came to us, and already you have made significant progress. You've had seemingly impossible cases before, Charlie. All it takes is one loose thread. One clue to lever the truth out of its hiding place. Why don't you give that brain of yours a rest for a while?"

Charlie kissed her forehead and went upstairs. Grace heard the nursery door open and close. Her husband had taken to sitting in there when he wished to retreat to a peaceful spot for reflection.

She didn't disturb him until it was time for dinner. Mrs Brown, perceptive as ever, plied Charlie with a large helping of delicious beef stew. The meal passed with a two-way conversation between Grace and Mrs Brown about the joys of finishing examinations and having the birth and Christmas festivities to look forward to.

Nobody mentioned blackmail, but it hung in the air like a rancid odour all the same.

The stew worked its magic on his empty stomach, and Charlie's residual gloom evaporated at the sight of apple pie and custard for pudding. By the time he was settled in his favourite armchair with a glass of whiskey in his hand and his dogs asleep at his feet, he was back to his normal self, if rather quieter than usual.

Grace could see that this investigation weighed as heavily on her husband's shoulders as on her own. They were making progress in uncovering past events, but the identity of the blackmailer was still tantalisingly out of reach, at least by the standards of proof required by a court of law. She still favoured Mr or Mrs Tulloch, or both. As the Carmichaels' former cook, Mrs Tulloch was their last hope to uncover critical evidence. It would be a relief to leave her interview in Charlie's capable hands, because Grace had no desire to meet the woman who ignored the maids' pleas for help.

With Charlie distracted and showing no signs of wishing to talk, Grace changed into her loosest nightgown and covered it with a blessedly comfortable dressing gown. She resumed her position on the sofa, tossing up between reading a novel or having an early night after a gruelling day. The book had great appeal – goodness, when was the last time she had read a book for pleasure rather than for study? – but her heavy eyelids seemed determined to vote for sleep.

The doorbell rang.

Charlie jerked out of his musing. He hurried to the door, perhaps hoping that Declan had made a breakthrough after all.

A strident female voice echoed down the hallway, shouting abuse at Charlie. If Grace had been more agile, she would have escaped up the stairs to avoid the second unwanted caller of the day. But it was too late. The voice came closer, still shrieking abuse as she barged into the drawing room. Blaze sprang to her feet, putting herself between Grace and the threat. Four pups followed on ungainly paws, lining up beside their mother with their sharp little teeth bared.

The stout, middle-aged woman behind the voice came to a dead halt at the sight of the dogs and an enormously pregnant woman. Grace's arms instinctively went around her belly to protect her babies from this harpy. Mrs Tulloch, she presumed. If so, she was mighty glad Charlie and Blaze were there to protect her.

Charlie forced his way around the woman and joined Blaze and her pups in forming a barrier.

Despite the wall of angry muscle and snarling canines in front of her, the woman cast a defiant eye over her hosts. She paused, making Grace wonder if she was about to apologise for the rudeness of her intrusion into their home at such a late hour.

But then Mrs Tulloch's broad jaw thrust forward. "Call yer mangy mutts off or I'll squash the little runts under my heel. How dare you lock up my husband and spread nasty lies about his business?"

"How dare you intrude on my family and threaten us?" Charlie countered. If sparks could fly from a man's eyes, they would have fried their unwelcome visitor in her clogs.

"Only what you deserve, you filthy little Oriental half-blood. I've had coppers swarming all over the house like cockroaches and customers cancelling coal and firewood orders right, left and centre. You'll ruin us. If you don't –"

"Mrs Tulloch," Grace said, in a voice commanding enough to stop a platoon at fifty paces. "If you wish to talk to us, you may take a seat like a civilised person. However, I warn you that I will set our well-trained purebred collie on you if you cannot show some respect to my husband, who is neither filthy nor little, and is rightly proud of his Chinese heritage."

Grace patted the seat beside her to get her husband to sit, because she feared he was on the verge of losing his temper – an extremely rare and terrifying event. Charlie hesitated a moment before sitting. Blaze took her place at his feet, still bristling. The pups sat, one by one, their eyes bright with excitement at their first encounter with an intruder.

Mrs Tulloch waited until she was the last one standing before perching her ample posterior on the edge of an armchair, poised for action. "Your fancy ways don't impress me. I demand you release my man immediately."

Grace placed a restraining hand on her husband's knee. "Demand? A strong word, Mrs Tulloch. As is your use of the word Oriental in such a derogatory tone of voice. Few people would guess from his looks alone that my husband has a Chinese grandfather. You must have been exceptionally inquisitive to find out."

She raised a hand to stop their visitor's interruption. "You see, Mrs Tulloch, we are hunting a blackmailer who is very adept at prying into other people's lives and demanding money under threat. Someone who fits your character precisely. In fact, somebody who has such specific knowledge of past events that you and your husband are on a very, very short list of suspects. Wouldn't you agree, Detective Pyke?"

Charlie leaned forward. "Should I have her arrested, my dear? Since I have no intention of asking the police to release her husband, it might be a kindness to throw her in a cell alongside the scoundrel to whom she is so devoted."

Mrs Tulloch's fingertips dug into the armrests, but she restrained her anger. The low hiss that emerged from her mouth was even more alarming than her shouts. "How dare you accuse me? Call yourself a detective. More like a hapless oaf, if you ask me. You've got the wrong end of the stick. Me and Tulloch ain't the blackmailers. My husband is a victim of this rogue, and you coppers are treating him like a criminal."

Charlie leaned back, letting his disbelief show with a raised eyebrow. "I'll believe your husband is a victim when you show me the blackmail note."

"Can't, can I? Tulloch burnt it. Bunch o' lies, anyway."

"Don't you get weary of covering for your husband's misdeeds?" Grace asked. "Selling compromising photographs of women. Forcing himself on servant girls. Doing the Carmichaels' dirty work by getting rid of the girls when they get pregnant."

Grace paused after each statement to gauge the cook's reaction. The lewd photographs yielded no more than a slight shrug, while the accusation of Tulloch's physical abuse resulted in an angry pout. But the last accusation hit a nerve. Mrs Tulloch pulled a handkerchief from her sleeve and held it to her eyes to cover her reaction, but it was too late.

She dabbed the handkerchief at dry eyes. "There's no call to blackmail a man who only did what he was paid to do. It's Mrs Carmichael you should be badgering for sending that girl away to the convent. Only what she deserved, mind you. Sent to do soiled laundry, like the dirty little harlot that she was."

Grace felt Charlie tense beside her. She was struggling to rein in her own fury, but they couldn't let emotion get in the way of uncovering a crucial piece of the puzzle. "Perhaps you could ask our housekeeper to bring tea and cake, my dear. We ladies have women's matters to discuss."

Charlie shot her a glare, but he quickly realised she was asking him to bring Mrs Brown into the room to see Mrs Tulloch's reaction. If this repellent woman was the blackmailer, she must know Mrs Brown used to be Evie. He rose and left, but not before ordering Blaze to stay on guard.

"You were saying about Bess being sent to a convent, Mrs Tulloch," Grace said, as calmly as she could, given the extreme aggravation this woman was causing. "The Sisters of the Guiding Star, was it?"

As far as Grace knew, there was only one convent that took in fallen and troublesome girls to do laundry as penance for their perceived sins. Girls who had been taken advantage of by unscrupulous men, girls whose circumstances gave them no option other than to work on the street, or even girls who were guilty of nothing more than being disrespectful to their employer by demanding better working conditions.

Mrs Tulloch didn't answer, but it was clear to Grace that the answer was yes. And that she, as Bess's supervisor, did nothing to stop the maid being taken away against her will to a horrible fate.

Belatedly, their guest realised she had been provoked into saying too much. "It's time I left. I expect my husband to be released first thing tomorrow, cos he ain't done nothing wrong."

As Mrs Tulloch pushed herself off the seat, little Spark bumbled forward, heading for their visitor's ankles with bared teeth. Blaze was quicker than Grace, heading her pup off. Spark nipped under the chair where her mother couldn't follow, while Blaze resumed her watchful pose by Grace, ready to defend her mistress if necessary.

Grace stroked the faithful collie's head. "Won't you stay for tea and cake, Mrs Tulloch? We have the best cook in Dunedin. Perhaps you've heard of her reputation."

"Look, missus, I'm sorry for getting cross over Tulloch being thrown in the lock-up, but I've no mind to sit down to a tea party no matter how good your damned cook is. Tell your husband to let my husband go, or he'll be sorry."

Mrs Tulloch stalked to the door, stopping only to let Mrs Brown come into the room with a tray. She glanced at the housekeeper's face but showed no sign of recognising her as Evie.

When Mrs Tulloch exited the drawing room, Charlie followed close on her heels to make sure she left the premises without setting fire to the place with her dragon breath. To Grace's dismay, the argument continued at the front door. A sharp slap of a hand on flesh prompted Blaze to race into the hall, followed by her four little black and white shadows, all growling.

The front door slammed, shaking the lamps. Grace exchanged grimaces with their housekeeper.

Mrs Brown put the tray down before her shaking hands dropped it. "Dreadful woman."

A gross understatement, in Grace's opinion. The thought of that woman being in charge of two vulnerable maids turned her stomach.

Charlie returned to the drawing room, sporting a red mark on his cheek.

"I cannot believe she assaulted you," Grace said. "By all that's holy, Mrs Tulloch is a braver woman than most."

"She slapped me for telling her what I thought of her appalling treatment of the young maids under her care. To be fair to her, I did not mince my words. It was worth it to see her reaction to being called the most contemptible, vindictive, scheming human who ever existed on God's green earth. There may have been a few other choice adjectives used, but I won't sully your ladylike ears with them."

Mrs Brown's grin lit up her face. "Thank you for your support, Charlie. I wish I had been there to witness it. I'm sure she wasn't *quite* so bad when I worked under her. That said, I have to say I don't believe the old tyrant recognised me. A great shame, because I fancied her as the blackmailer."

"I agree," Charlie said. "After she slapped me, I said: 'I hope you die in the flames of Hell.' The exact words used in the blackmail note sent to Mrs Carmichael. She didn't so much as blink at the phrase, although she did answer me back in terms I would not care to repeat. Right before she slammed the door an inch from my nose. I'm starting to feel sorry for Mr Tulloch."

Grace contemplated whether to share what Mrs Tulloch had told her while they were out of the room, but Charlie needed to know, and it wouldn't be fair to Mrs Brown to shield her from the truth.

"Perhaps you should take a seat, Mrs Brown," Grace said. "It seems Mrs Carmichael might have been lying when she said she didn't know what happened to Bess. I'm afraid that it was far worse than just taking her to the railway station. Mrs Tulloch said Mrs Carmichael paid Tulloch to take Bess to the laundry run by the Sisters of the Guiding Star. Her penance for falling pregnant under Mrs Carmichael's devout care."

Mrs Brown sat ominously still, which meant she must know what awaited girls who were sent to the convent laundry. "Poor Bess. I dread to think what she suffered, slaving all hours under atrocious conditions. No wonder her baby didn't survive. If Mrs Carmichael ever dares enter this house again, I swear I won't be held accountable for my actions."

Grace knew all too well what Bess must have gone through. Anne Drummond had fought against the establishment of a convent laundry ever since it was set up as an offshoot of the many similar institutions in Britain. However, it was allowed to continue because the state had no desire to interfere in church business.

They had visited four years ago, as part of an inquiry into the working conditions of women. Anne had taken Grace with her to inspect other workplaces around Dunedin too. The investigation had opened her eyes to what women suffered to make a few shillings a week doing factory work. But, for all women suffered in paid work, it was nothing compared to the slave labour the girls were forced to do for free in the laundry.

The findings of the commission of inquiry had prompted significant improvements to labour conditions since then, but, tragically, they could do nothing about the convent laundries. They operated outside the law as a religious institution, not a workplace. They held themselves up as a place of reform, but they were a place of punishment. Little different from prison labour, but without the justice system passing fair judgement on innocence or guilt prior to sentencing.

"If it's true, then Bess never ran away with Hugh after all," Mrs Brown whispered. Tears ran down her cheeks. "Hugh deserted both of us when we needed him most."

Grace knew Mrs Brown was weeping for Bess and her lost baby, but also for the loss of the man she had loved, who hadn't loved either maid enough to help them. She held Mrs Brown until her tears ran their course before speaking again. "Charlie and I will go to the convent tomorrow. We'll do what we can to find out what happened to Bess and her baby, but it's a long time ago."

She only wished she could add a promise to hold Mrs Carmichael to account, but there was no law against sending a maid away. Disgrace in front of her peers was the best that could be hoped for. Perhaps that was what the blackmailer wanted too.

Dirty Laundry

Charlie rose early the next morning. His wife, of course, had insisted on going with him to the convent laundry, arguing that the nuns would be more willing to answer questions posed by a pregnant lady than a male detective. She was probably right. Thus, he was heading down to the local stables to hire a gig rather than the horse he had planned on.

Mrs Brown stopped him before he got past the kitchen. She smiled sweetly, but there was nothing sweet about the way she crossed her arms over the front of her apron, heedless of the flour she was spreading onto her sleeve. "I'm coming too, Charlie. The nuns cannot refuse to answer the questions if they are posed by a close friend of Bess. I can say our former mistress confessed her fate on her deathbed if we are asked why we are interested after so long."

"Subterfuge, Mrs Brown? I fear we are teaching you bad habits."

Her lips quirked, but the arms stayed firmly crossed.

Charlie recognised a steely determination that he knew all too well from his wife. A steely determination that seemed to afflict all the women in his life, for that matter. He had long since learned there was no point in resisting. "In that case, I'd better hire a larger conveyance."

"Splendid. I shall have breakfast waiting for you when you return. I've got a nice bit of gammon, and we have plenty of fresh eggs and last night's leftover potatoes to fry up. Can't go into battle on an empty stomach."

Charlie's stomach rumbled. "My dear Mrs Brown, it's as if you were planning a feast to butter me up."

She gave him a wan smile. "The feast was planned as a celebration of the end of Grace's medical training. It will have to do as a hearty start to a challenging day instead."

An hour later, Charlie helped Grace into the hired carriage with Mrs Brown's help. Once the two ladies were seated, he climbed onto the driving seat. With Grace looking charming in her new green gown and Mrs Brown in her Sunday best, he felt like a coachman taking a pair of ladies on an outing. Unfortunately, this would be no picnic in the park.

The journey passed pleasantly with the usual discussion of criminal and household matters. By the time they pulled into the convent driveway a little over an hour later, they'd agreed on a strategy for discovering Bess's fate, as well as the menu for Christmas dinner, the best way of squeezing the truth out of their suspects, Grace's plan for the birth, and how to keep Spark out of the pantry.

Charlie nodded and smiled at appropriate intervals, but privately he doubted whether any of these challenging issues would be resolved in the agreed-upon manner. Most of all, he hoped Grace would get her wish for an easy, serene birth at home with Anne Drummond as her midwife. He crossed his fingers. His wife had attended enough births to know that the odds weren't in her favour, especially with twins. Frankly, acid rose from his stomach every time he thought of it. Whatever was in store for her, he prayed it would not be as awful as what Bess went through when she gave birth in the convent laundry.

Grace's forced cheerfulness dissipated as soon as clouds of steam and smoke came into view further up the valley. Last night, she'd warned him that he would see sights to upset even the toughest of men. Young girls forced to plunge soiled linen into boiling coppers amidst clouds of steam from dawn to dusk, while others rubbed their knuckles bare on washboards. Girls with scars from scalding water and caustic soda, girls with terrible injuries from getting their hair or limbs caught in the mangles.

On this fine day, the rows of flapping white linen on the outdoor lines looked benign enough. Almost festive, like a row of white banners heralding their arrival. Further on, long lines of starched aprons and caps hung so stiffly that they swayed rather than flapped in the breeze. As they got closer, the sharp tang of bleach joined the scent of wood smoke. The forbidding walls and belching chimneys only added to his disquiet, as did the sobering sight of graves in the field beyond.

Charlie pulled the horses to a halt in front of a massive arched door set in an unwelcoming wall of dark stone. He jumped down to hitch the horses beside a trough. Grace and Mrs Brown made no move to dismount.

"Perhaps it would be best if you waited outside," Charlie said. "Hopefully, their records will answer our questions without delay."

Grace closed her eyes, as if bolstering her courage, then she held out her hand to be helped down. She wore a broad-brimmed hat to shade her from the sun, and from his scrutiny. Mrs Brown climbed down after her, taking Grace's arm. They had agreed to appeal to the sympathy of the nuns by playing a mother and her heavily pregnant daughter. Not a great stretch of their acting skills.

Mrs Brown stopped in front of the door. "Before we go in, I want you to know that Bess was not the wanton hussy the Tullochs made her out to be. She was a friend to me in a house with no other friendly faces. Her lively spirits made her flirtatious, but she was a good girl and a hard-working maid. Although we quarrelled over

Hugh Brown, she did not deserve to end up here, just as I did not deserve to end up alone on the streets of Dunedin. Hugh duped us both into thinking we were in love, foolish, naive girls that we were. All these years I've blamed Bess for taking the love of my life from me, never knowing the truth. I wish they had run away together after all, now that I know what really happened to her."

Mrs Brown thrust out her dainty chin and rapped on the solid wood of the door with a heavy iron knocker. She stepped back as they waited. "I must admit, it crossed my mind to wonder if Tulloch took advantage of Bess, like he tried to do with me. However, after reflecting on the matter last night, I doubt Tulloch was the father of her child. He might have leered at her pretty smile and shapely figure, but Bess stood up to him more than I did. She even slapped him once when he got too free with his hands. He tried to punch her back, but she was quick on her feet and screamed for Mr Carmichael to help. Tulloch never bothered her after that."

Charlie wished it were so for Bess's sake, because he couldn't bear the thought of Tulloch forcing himself on Bess. Mrs Brown's statement was at odds with Mr Carmichael's claim that he did not know about Tulloch's abuse of the maids, which had seemed genuine. Perhaps Carmichael believed it to be a trivial matter of a misinterpreted hand in the wrong place. Bess might have been too ashamed to be explicit, because all too often it was the woman who was blamed for leading the man astray – perhaps especially a pretty, flirtatious young woman of eighteen or nineteen.

Footsteps approached from inside. The door opened to reveal a sour face, reddened by steam and wrinkled from her work. A kerchief held grey strands of hair off her sweating brow, but the unrumpled state of her faded grey dress and starched apron told Charlie that she no longer worked the scrubbing board. He had expected a nun, but it seemed they employed lay supervisors for the laundry operation.

Mrs Brown stepped forward. "Good morning. We are here on urgent business with the person in charge of the laundry."

The woman opened the door a little further but made no move to step aside. "I supervise the girls. We have no time to spare for visitors when there's a mountain of dirty linen waiting."

"It is the person who keeps the records we wish to see," Mrs Brown said, ignoring the sourness in the woman's voice, which perfectly matched the sourness of her countenance.

"Sister Julieta is a busy woman too. Do you have an appointment?"

Mrs Brown looked up at the woman on the top step with pleading eyes and hands pressed together in prayer. "It is very important."

The woman turned and stomped back along the flagstone corridor, her displeasure at having her time wasted echoing off stone walls. Since she hadn't closed the door on them, they took it as an invitation to follow her. At the intersection of two corridors, she turned right, away from the sound of clanging and bustling, past empty dormitories with close-packed rows of beds, storage rooms, and a kitchen, until they reached an office.

The laundry supervisor motioned for them to stay outside while she went in, but she left the door ajar and they could hear her rasping voice.

"Do you have a minute to speak to visitors, Sister Julieta?"

They couldn't hear the response, but the laundress returned to beckon them inside, before hurrying off about her business.

Charlie had hoped for an elderly informant, who might remember a girl from a quarter of a century ago. In a place like this, it was a forlorn hope, now dashed by the sight of a nun with pursed lips and an unlined face. She'd paused in her task of writing in a ledger, but her hand hovered near the pen, signalling the interruption was unwelcome and liable to be brief.

"I am Sister Julieta. How may I help you?"

"My name is Mrs Brown, and this is my daughter and son-in-law. I have recently received the most unexpected and concerning news from a lady on her deathbed. My best friend, Bess, disappeared from her household, where she was a maid, and has not been seen since. We were told that she had run away with a young man, but now I am informed she was sent here. I wish to find out what happened to her."

"Bess was with child," Grace added, with one hand holding a handkerchief to tear-filled eyes and the other resting on the round of her belly. "Now that my own baby is due, I simply must know what happened to her and her child. She was as close as a sister to my dear mother."

Sister Julieta's hand moved away from her pen. Her brow wrinkled in concern, although Charlie couldn't tell if it was sympathy for their plight or anxiety for the convent's reputation.

"How long ago was this?" Sister Julieta asked.

"Twenty-five years ago." Mrs Brown said.

"Twenty-five years? Oh, dearie me." The nun looked to heaven for guidance, but evidently she got no response. "I'm not sure you appreciate how many girls we have cared for in that time."

"Do you not keep records?" Charlie said, waving a hand at the shelves of ledgers arrayed around the room in such numbers that the space was scarcely large enough to hold the desk and four people.

Sister Julieta switched her impassive gaze to him. "We cannot search by the girl's birth name. In order to protect our girls, we assign them a new name as soon as they arrive. A saint's name to give them a new start under the eyes of God, giving them a chance to wash away their sinful pasts."

"Bess wasn't wicked," Mrs Brown said, quietly but with a hint of steel.

Sister Julieta regarded her with pity, but her reply was firm. "She was unmarried and with child, you said. A fallen girl."

Charlie rested a hand on Mrs Brown's arm to halt her retort. "Please, Sister Julieta. It would mean the world to my wife and her mother to know that Bess and her child left your charitable care to return to a better life after seeing the error of her ways. We had hoped that the child's father might have come in search of her. Knowing that would lift a burden from our minds before our own child is born. We have an approximate date for her arrival here, which will narrow down the options considerably."

Grace pressed her hands together and crumpled her face into a plea. "A few minutes of your time, and then we will be gone."

The hint that it would be quicker to accede than argue seemed to tip the scales. Sister Julieta rose and went to the registers' section. When Mrs Brown gave the date range of Bess's likely admission to the convent laundry, it was the work of seconds for the nun to select the register for the correct year.

She took it back to her desk and flipped through the pages to the likely dates.

Fortunately, Charlie was adept at reading upside down. "That one," he said, placing a finger next to a woman of nineteen who was listed under the name Ursula. The person who admitted her was listed as Mr W. Tulloch. He couldn't read the small print that followed, but it was no more than a few sentences.

Sister Julieta looked up with genuine sadness in her eyes. "I'm sorry about your friend, Mrs Brown. It seems the father of her child did not return for them after all. Many girls are left in such circumstances." She closed the register with firm finality.

"However, the splendid news is that Ursula must have made a success of her time here, because she left our care a little over a year later to take up employment."

"Are you able to tell us who employed her, Sister?" Charlie asked.

"That was not recorded. Many of our benefactors prefer to remain anonymous, as it helps the girls make a fresh start."

"Did Bess take her baby with her when she left?" Mrs Brown asked.

A flash of pity crossed the nun's face. "It is not in the girl's best interests to keep their babies. It's easier if the baby is removed as soon as it is born."

Easier for whom, Charlie wanted to ask. A baby was not an inert mass inside a woman's body – it was a living, kicking being. This ridiculous notion that attachment only occurred after the baby was put into its mother's arms could only have been concocted by someone who had never had a child or any exposure to a pregnant mother. A single man – or a nun.

Grace squeezed his hand. "What happens to the babies, Sister Julieta?"

"The infants who live are sent to an orphanage if they cannot be adopted by relatives. Now, if that is all, I must bid you good day, as I have accounts to attend to." Sister Julieta picked up her pen, signalling the end of the discussion.

Charlie noted her failure to mention the babies who did not live. The tiny souls who now inhabited the disturbingly large graveyard he had glimpsed through the trees. Although he did not relish the reminder of the high death rate of newborns and their mothers, the question had to be asked. "I presume you keep a register of deaths."

The nun's grip on the pen tightened. "That register is not for public viewing out of respect for the sensitive nature of the information. Many of the deaths occur before term or are stillbirths, and all are born out of wedlock. They are buried in unmarked graves, naturally. I am sorry, but the rules do not allow me to say more. I can see you mean well."

"Does Ursula's entry in the register record the fate of her child?" Grace persisted. "Please, it would be such a great kindness for us to know the truth."

The nun sighed, but Charlie could see the plea had moved her. She opened the register again.

"Since it was so long ago, I suppose there's no harm in telling you that no adoption was recorded against her name, and the baby was not sent to an orphanage."

That sounded ominously like a roundabout way of confirming that the baby had died. They had suspected it anyway, after the blackmail note to Mrs Carmichael accused her of causing the death of a maid's baby. Charlie wondered if the convent reported the deaths to the authorities, or indeed whether they were required to, since infant death was so common. He drew out his wallet and opened it to display a small wad of banknotes. "We appreciate your assistance, Sister. Perhaps the convent is open to donations to support its fine work in sheltering the girls and preparing them for service?" Slavery followed by more servitude.

Sister Julieta pushed a donation box across the desk with an angelic smile, oblivious to the undercurrent of irony in his voice.

Charlie slotted in an overly generous pound note, keeping his wallet open. "Is there anybody who worked here back then, who might have known what happened to Bess? The woman who showed us to your office, perhaps?" He'd estimated her age at around sixty, although the years had likely fallen hard on her.

"The only woman we have here aged over fifty is the supervisor of the pressing room. She is *extremely* busy."

Charlie slotted an encouraging banknote into the collection box.

Either the donation tipped the balance, or Sister Julieta realised she wouldn't get rid of them any other way. She pulled a bell-cord labelled Pressing Room. "You may wait for her in the corridor."

Having stood as close as possible to the nun's desk to read the register, Charlie had not seen the effect of the interview on Grace and Mrs Brown, although he had heard the strain in their voices. When he turned to escort them out, he saw that Mrs Brown had aged ten years. Her usual perfect posture and imperturbable smile had vanished, to be replaced by sagging shoulders and a sickly hue. He took her arm and helped her out of the office, taking her to a bench seat further down the hall.

Mrs Brown sank onto the seat, her head hanging. "It's hopeless, isn't it? Whatever we are told will be spun with euphemisms and white lies to make it seem as if it was for the good of the girls and their babies. The truth is that they stripped unwilling victims of their identity and rights and robbed them of the joy of motherhood. Who's to say that 'left for unspecified employment' does not simply mean dead and buried like her sweet child? I wish we'd never come to this awful place."

Silver Lining

Grace put her arm around Mrs Brown's slumped shoulders. "I promise you we are not leaving here until we have achieved something, no matter how small. Even if it is only information about conditions in the laundry to take a further case to the Inspector of Labour."

"They're never going to let us see inside the laundry, Grace," Mrs Brown said.

"We'll see about that." Grace rose at the sound of shuffling footsteps and rasping lungs coming in their direction.

A thin, stooped woman came towards them, clad in the same uniform as the woman who'd met them at the front door. Unlike the first woman, her tread was not an angry stomp but a grim drag of one foot after the other. Grace had seen the same lack of both life and hope amongst the old diggers of the goldfields who'd watched their comrades strike riches while their own pans turned only gravel. Like the diggers, the woman had scars on her face, although her scars were from burns or scalding water, while the gold diggers were scarred by rocks and frostbite. No doubt there were worse scars on the inside.

The woman gave them an incurious glance and disappeared into Sister Julieta's office after giving the briefest of knocks. A minute later she was out again, eyeing them up like a trio of hornets sent to make her hellish life that much worse. With a jerk of her head, she gestured for them to follow her. They did so in silence, taking the second corridor towards the noise of the laundry.

She took them into an alcove, where she looked them over with dull eyes. "You want to know about a girl called Ursula who was here so long ago I cannot recall what I myself was like back then."

"Her real name was Bess," Mrs Brown said. "She was clever and lively, with brown hair."

"Clever don't count for nothing here, Missus. And none of our girls are lively for long. Tis a hard life at the tubs."

"A hard life for you, too," Grace said. "May I ask your name?"

"They named me Magdalene. The girls in the pressing room call me Magda."

Grace wanted to ask her real name, but she didn't want to upset their informant. "The girl we're looking for used to be a maid, Magda. We believe her baby may have died."

The supervisor of the pressing room cast a grim glance at Grace's swollen belly, softening her tone. "Many babies die here. The heavy lifting does for them, most often sooner rather than later. For most, tis a blessing to lose the babe early."

Mrs Brown faltered, searching for a way to spark recognition. "Bess loved to sing, and she could darn so neatly you'd never know the item had been mended."

"There's no singing allowed. No talking either."

But Grace saw a moment's hesitation. She put her hand on the woman's arm. "I think you do recall a girl like that, Magda. Please, we need to know what happened to Bess, or Ursula as you would have known her."

Magda's gaze drifted to the row of hooks on the wall as she cast her mind back. "There are two types of girls who come here. The sensible ones knuckle down and do what they're told to avoid a beating. I knew from the start I would never escape this place, so I set out to make the best of it. With exemplary conduct and hard work, I rose from boiling and scrubbing, to pressing and sewing, before becoming a supervisor after I'd done my first decade of penance. It takes a tough soul to work the laundry girls, so I was put in charge of the girls pressing the linen and sewing the buttons and lace back on."

Grace saw Magda falter, as if she had forgotten her train of thought. "You said there were two types of girls," she prompted.

"The other, less sensible, type of girl refuses to buckle under the yoke. I recall the laundry supervisor talking about a particularly stubborn girl called Ursula, who refused to answer to her assigned name. She kept saying her name was Bess, and it was all a terrible mistake. We've had a few like that, who persist in believing that the father of their child will come to their rescue. They soon learn to shut up, after a beating or two. Ursula lasted longer than most, from what I heard."

Mrs Brown seized Magda's arm. "I beg you, tell us what happened to her."

Grace wished she'd never insisted on persevering with a hopeless quest. The last thing she wanted was to add a fresh scar to their housekeeper's heart.

"Ursula gave in to the inevitable, as they all do in the end," Magda said. "The pregnant girls move into my work area when they grow too large for the back-breaking labour of washing and scrubbing. Pressing is easier, but hard enough at that late stage. Ursula was one of those girls. She proved a dab hand at sewing and darning, just as you said, Missus. She had no spirit left in her by then."

"Did she have the baby?" Grace asked.

"She did. I feared for her, because she was in no condition to give birth when the pains started. It was a fiercely hot spell in the middle of February, and the heat in the pressing room was worse than anything the Devil would punish sinners with. But she came back alive after delivering the child. Alive, but with no life in her. She said her baby died."

"Is that what they tell all the women?" Grace asked. "To stop them demanding to see the child?"

Magda closed her eyes. "I don't know. My baby never made it that far. I suspect they tell the girls whatever they want to hear. They told me to be joyful that my baby was safe in heaven. I know other girls were told their baby went to a lovely home with the best of parents."

"And Bess, or Ursula, as you knew her?"

"She faded away in front of my eyes. I asked to see the Sister in charge to share my concerns about her state of mind. A few weeks later, Ursula was gone. They said she had secured employment on the outside. I hoped in my heart that it was true, but I fear she simply gave up. You must think me callous, but there are many such stories to haunt my sleep. I do what I can, though it's little enough."

Mrs Brown gathered the long-suffering laundress into her arms. "Would you leave if you could?" she whispered.

Magda allowed herself a moment of human warmth before pulling away. "I'm too old to cope with life on the outside now, but I thank you for your kindness, Missus."

Grace felt Charlie's arms wrapping around her. In truth, he seemed as much in need of comfort as she was. She'd warned him about conditions in the laundry, but nothing could have prepared him for the reality of pregnant women doing such heavy, dangerous work. It was a miracle any of them made it to full term.

As she drew comfort from his strength, a radical plan sprang fully formed into her brain as if by divine inspiration. Or desperation for a miracle.

"Charlie," Grace whispered, in the tentative voice she used for something she thought he wouldn't like. "I plan to discuss the situation here with Auntie Anne. If anyone can press for action to improve conditions, it is Anne."

"Of course, Grace. And?" He raised an eyebrow, instinctively knowing there was more to come.

"And I wonder if you would agree to take on one of the young women here as a maid. I know that rescuing one soul amongst many is a small step, but …"

He squeezed her shoulders. "… but one saved soul is better than none."

Magda must have overheard, because she shook her head doubtfully. "These girls would not be suited to a household of ladies and gentlemen. There are few like Ursula, who are decent girls who've been abused by men. Most come from poor homes or off the streets, and not always because they are with child. The police don't want pickpockets and beggars about town, nor in the gaols, so they end up here too."

"Are there none you can think of who might be suitable for household duties and caring for babies?" Grace asked. "We are a kind household, but somewhat eccentric. A clever young woman with the ability to cope in unusual circumstances would be ideal, no matter her background. Mrs Brown – my mother – would provide all the training required."

"One of my girls in the pressing room told me she came from a large family," Magda said. "She's a nice, quiet girl, who wouldn't give any trouble. I never asked how she came to be in the family way, but I suspect it was not her fault because she's as timid as a mouse."

"Can we meet her? I should like to see her in her workplace." If nothing else, Grace thought, seeing inside would give them first-hand information to take to the Labour Inspector.

"Visitors are not allowed in the workrooms." Magda must have seen the plea in Grace's eyes because she relented. "I suppose just this once won't hurt. Don't touch anything. There would be hell to pay if you got burned by a hot iron."

The humidity of the pressing room hit Grace the moment the door opened, causing her to sway as if she'd walked into an operating theatre laced with ether. The room was so full of drying linen that it was difficult to see the workers at first. She ducked under stiff white sheets, still shimmering with bluing agent and starch. Beyond, a row of young women created a steady rhythm of clunk and hiss, as they took heated irons off the stove and clapped them onto whatever item they were pressing.

Grace would have lasted a few minutes at most, but she suspected the women had already been at work for hours and likely had many more hours ahead that day.

Magda pointed to the young woman second from the end, who didn't look strong enough to pick up an iron. The scorch marks on her hands made Grace want to whisk her to safety immediately. When Magda called her over, the woman froze in place like a child about to be punished for misbehaving. She crept towards them, averting her gaze from the unexpected, broad-shouldered man in the room.

Charlie recognised her fear and took a sudden interest in the starchiness of a sheet hung near the door. Mrs Brown, her spine now straight and her expression determined, took charge of the interview. She took the young woman aside with a kindly smile, asking her name and reassuring her they meant no harm. The interview was over in seconds. The woman was terrified of men and dogs. So much so that she hurried back to her irons as if returning to a sanctuary. They followed Magda back out of the pressing room, sighing in relief when they met the cool air of the corridor.

"I'll ask at the laundry proper," Magda said. She had a determined tilt to her jaw now that she saw a chance to rescue one of the girls. "You'll have to wait at the door. It's not safe for you to enter."

Peeking through the open door, Grace could see what she meant about it being unsafe for visitors. Vast coppers sent up billows of steam from boiling water. The *double, double toil and trouble; fire burn and cauldron bubble* from Macbeth paled beside the malevolence of this scene.

The cauldrons were tended not by witches, but by weary young women in drenched aprons, with their hair bound by rags. They fed their coppers with armloads of linen and the contents of tins – presumably soaps, bleaches, washing soda, and other additives to ensure no stain was left untouched for the wealthy customers to complain about. Once the linen was soaked, the workers took up laundry paddles to churn and pound the wash until it was clean, only to empty out the sodden washing, which must have weighed a ton, to begin the rinsing process. In the far corner, mangles creaked as the water was squeezed out between giant rollers.

Backbreaking work, fraught with danger. Grace recalled throwing a shirtwaist into the laundry basket that morning, oblivious to the work needed to get it clean. She'd have a word with Mrs Brown later about the conditions at the laundry they used, although she was sure their housekeeper would only choose the best-run laundry, not this hellscape.

As she watched, a painfully thin girl slipped in a pool of soapy water on her way to the mangle and dropped a bundle of rinsed-clean laundry. The sour woman who had opened the front door to them was quick off the mark. She stomped over with a spare laundry paddle at the ready and gave the offender a whack on the rear that Grace could hear over the noise in the room. None of the other workers dared to turn their heads.

Magda came back from her discussion with another mature woman, who was supervising the counting-in of newly arrived bags of laundry. "The girl she recommended is called Beatrice. To be honest, I suspect the recommendation says more about their eagerness to rid themselves of a troublemaker than her skills for the maid position."

"Which one is she, Magda?" Mrs Brown asked.

"The girl with the newly tanned hide."

"Can we talk to her?" Grace asked.

Magda gained permission from the sour woman to remove Beatrice from her work. The sourpuss was grinning, presumably at the prospect of getting rid of the troublesome girl. Grace felt a twinge of anxiety. The last thing they needed in their lives was more trouble.

The meeting convened in the alcove. Magda gave the girl a reassuring pat on the shoulder and went back to her work. If Beatrice felt nervous at being hauled away from work to meet three strangers, she hid it beneath a mask of mistrust. Charlie hovered on the outskirts of the group, but the presence of an intimidating man seemed not to bother her.

Mrs Brown put on her best motherly smile as she introduced them, before asking Beatrice her real name.

Beatrice hesitated, as if she had not been asked the question for so long that it disconcerted her. "My name was Matilda, but everyone called me Tilly." Her eyes narrowed, and her fists remained firmly on her bony hips. "What do you want from me?"

"There's no need to be alarmed, Tilly," Mrs Brown said. "Mr and Mrs Penrose Pyke are looking for a maid to help with their babies and general duties about the house."

"Pull the other one, Missus. That lot in there aren't going to recommend me for a sweet position like that. They think I'm trouble because I stand up for my rights."

"I expect that's why they want to get rid of you," Mrs Brown said. "However, we need a girl with a bit of backbone. If you are interested in the position, perhaps you could tell me about your life before arriving at the convent laundry."

Tilly inspected them suspiciously but saw only encouragement. Her fists fell from her hips. "My father was a shepherd in the high country. After he drowned in a flooded river, we had to leave because the farm cottage we lived in came with the job. My mother took the younger children to her sister's house, but she didn't have room for the older ones. My older brothers got farming work, and I was sent to Dunedin to be a maid. The household had young children, so I was happy there at first, pretending we were a family."

"You like children," Grace said.

"Practically raised my little sisters and brothers, what with my ma so busy cooking for the shepherds and shearers, and cleaning the Big House."

"What brought you here, Tilly?" Grace asked gently.

"It was my own stupid fault. A lady came around asking if we'd sign a petition to give women the right to vote. All of us women, not just the lady of the house. Only I couldn't sign because I was only nineteen then. The mistress overheard me encouraging the housekeeper to sign and dismissed me without a reference."

Nausea rose in Grace's oesophagus. It might have been her who came to the door seeking signatures for the petition, causing this young woman's downfall.

"I never did anything bad, honestly," Tilly said. "I never lay with a man or stole anything. All I wanted was the train fare to get back to my family, but I was arrested for begging."

"Begging for a coin or two is hardly a crime worthy of sending you here," Mrs Brown said.

"Well, it probably didn't help that I kicked the copper when he tried to take me away. Only a wee tap on the shins mind, but he called it grievous bodily harm against an officer of the law."

"Do you have a particular dislike of policemen?" Grace asked.

Tilly grinned. "Only that one. Mind you, I've never met any others."

Grace thought it was about time she laid the truth before Tilly before Mrs Brown abducted her and smothered her with kindness. "As a maid, you would work under this lady, Mrs Brown, who is our housekeeper. You won't find a kinder woman or a better cook than her. However, our household is a little unconventional. My husband's work as a private detective brings with it a few complications, such as late-night forays and occasional danger. I am expecting twins soon, but I will begin work as a medical doctor in a few months' time. Like my husband, I may have desperate visitors at all hours."

Tilly clapped her chafed red hands to her mouth, but not from shock at the idea of dangerous detecting work. "You're a doctor? A *woman* doctor?"

"And a suffragist," Grace said. "I'm truly sorry your dismissal was for championing our petition. Will the odd hours be a problem? We shan't disturb you too much."

"My pa was out at all hours during lambing. Me too, for that matter. I loved lambing season."

Charlie stepped forward, smiling. "We have a border collie too, who has recently given birth to four pups, which rather adds to the state of chaos, I'm afraid."

Tilly's eyes lit up. "I adore dogs, and sheepdogs best of all."

Grace was delighted to see Charlie's satisfied nod. Just one more deal-breaker to go. "Our friends and family are somewhat unusual, too. My husband's grandfather was Chinese."

"Takes all sorts to make the world go around, as my pa used to say." Tilly glanced between them, her suspicion long since turned to desperate hope. "I'm not a bad person, honestly. It's only that I hate it here, and I don't see why I should be nice to people who are not nice to me."

"Sounds like a perfectly reasonable attitude to me," Grace said. "We'll do our best to be kind, but we also expect anyone living in our household to show respect for others, including troublesome visitors, even when we may wish to kick them in the shins."

Tilly seized Grace's arm. "Please take me. Please, please, please. I'll work until I drop for free and never cause you a moment's bother, I promise."

"You'll do nothing of the sort," Mrs Brown said. "Proper wages and fair hours. A room of your own and a uniform. If you don't like the work, we'll give you the fare home to your family. How does that sound?"

Tilly nodded so vigorously that the wrapping fell from around her head, letting loose a brutally cut mop of lank brown hair.

Mrs Brown was already clucking like a broody hen around her new helper, asking her if she had any possessions she wanted to take or anyone she wished to farewell, and assuring Tilly they would take good care of her.

Charlie took out his wallet again. "I expect a donation will be in order to expedite the paperwork. Why don't you inform the supervisors and collect Tilly's possessions. I'll join you at the carriage as soon as I have settled matters with Sister Julieta."

After seeing the way her husband charmed the Sister earlier, Grace had every faith Tilly would soon be safe. She reached out to clasp his hand. "Thank you for agreeing to my mad rescue plan."

He brushed a damp strand of hair from her face. "What are husbands for if not to do their wives' bidding?"

"I'll remind you of that the next time I suggest a foolhardy scheme." Grace linked her fingers with his and felt like the luckiest woman alive. "It will be a relief to leave this place having achieved a minor victory, even if we have made little progress in the investigation."

"Hardly a minor victory, Grace. Tilly has a new life, you have a new maid to help with the twins, and Mrs Brown has a worthy project to divert her mind from the horrors of the past." He paused to wiggle his eyebrows. "And, far from making no progress on the investigation, I believe we just might have cracked the case."

"You do?"

Her maddening husband wiggled his eyebrows again, and then set off with a determined stride, humming to himself. She started after him, before deciding there was no way she was going to beg him to explain what he meant. He had spotted a clue somewhere in this steamy hellhole, and Grace would not rest until she had worked out what it was.

A Dropped Stitch

Charlie exited the office, his wallet lighter, but with Tilly's release secured. He hurried back down the corridor, eager to be out of this place.

Harrowing as it had been having his eyes opened to the fiery underworld of the laundry, the visit had achieved more than he had hoped. Although they had no definitive answer regarding the fate of the Carmichaels' maid, Bess, the clues were now lined up to swivel his internal compass in a very particular direction. Unfortunately, the direction he had in mind led to a dark and thorny path. If the blackmailer was the person he had in mind, he wasn't at all sure which side of the scales of justice he was on.

He closed the front door of the convent laundry behind him with a satisfying thud. Even if nothing came of his new hunch, they were leaving this place with more than one soul in a better state. He had a good feeling about Tilly, although he hoped she didn't make a habit of kicking policemen and calling his border collie a sheepdog. Blaze considered sheep to be unworthy of her attention; she was a crime-fighting tracking dog.

Across the courtyard, their new maid was gently heaving Grace onto the front seat of the carriage. Slight of build she might be, but Tilly showed unexpected strength. Or perhaps not so unexpected, as there could be few tasks more muscle-building than lugging sodden piles of linen all day. The thought of pregnant girls doing that work made his blood boil, but that was a battle for another day.

By the time Charlie reached them, Tilly had unhitched the horses, given each of them a friendly rub on the nose, and turned the carriage into the driveway. His heart lightened further at the sight, because kindness to animals and work ethic were excellent indicators of character in his mind. Her eagerness to prove her worth boded well too.

He took the reins from her. "All done. You're coming home with us, Tilly, if you haven't changed your mind."

"Home," she sighed, then gave a little laugh and sprang up onto the rear seat, settling next to Mrs Brown with a grin all the way up to her eyes.

Charlie mounted the front seat, noting the bag beside Tilly, presumably carrying all her worldly possessions. The bag was smaller than many ladies took on an outing to the park. He took up the reins and clicked his tongue to set the horses moving. They needed little encouragement, since they were heading toward home. He knew how they felt about going home, although his feelings were mixed about how to proceed from there. Grace's arm slipped around his waist and held him close; she knew his moods all too well.

Tilly and Mrs Brown were soon chattering away like old acquaintances. By the time they reached the outskirts of the city, Mrs Brown had answered a hundred questions about the household and assured her that their priority would be to contact Tilly's family, so her loved ones knew she was safe.

When the spire of the First Church came into view, Grace leaned closer to him. "Will we be making a stop on Dowling Street on the way home, Charlie?"

"I will go after I take you home and return the carriage."

Charlie wasn't surprised that Grace had picked up the same clues as he had once she diverted her brain from rescuing Tilly. From her expression, she shared the same mixed feelings about the suspect. He worked through the clues again in his mind, looking for the flaw in his theory.

Point one: the blackmailer knew that the maid, Bess, had not fled to Australia with her lover as most people believed, and that she suffered the tragic loss of a baby. The note sent to Mrs Carmichael made that clear.

Point two: after their visit to the convent laundry, they knew that the fate of the babies born there was never revealed to the outside world. That narrowed the suspect list to one probable candidate, Bess herself, although he couldn't discount the possibility that the blackmailer was a person Bess had confided in.

Point three: of all the suspects, Bess had the most reason to feel the depth of rage needed to spark revenge. From Magda's description, Bess had undergone a downward spiral from lively maid to rebellious laundry slave, and finally to a pit of despair after the death of her baby. There was little doubt that she must harbour a deep resentment against Mrs Carmichael and the Tullochs, who had caused her downfall. What better punishment than to make them pay dearly for their cruelty?

The problem for Charlie was that his sympathies lay partly with Bess, because of what she had suffered, although he could not condone her actions in resorting to blackmail to punish them.

Grace's arm tightened around his waist. "Will you be taking Declan with you to Dowling Street?"

And that was the nub of it. Did Charlie want the blackmailer to be arrested and thrown into a police cell, awaiting one-sided justice? How could that be a just outcome for a woman who had not wallowed in her misery but had set herself to making a success of her life and used her success to rescue other women who had suffered? Which brought him back to point four, the list of clues directing his attention to a clear suspect.

Bess, presumably short for Elizabeth, was now middle-aged and adept with a needle and thread, and likely physically scarred by her year in Hell. He could not be sure, but the fit to Eliza Harper, the dressmaker, was impossible to ignore. The heavy powder to cover her facial scars, her rise from a difficult past, her intimate knowledge of gossip. And then there was her ready access to the First Church and the witness statement that she was seen in the church during the period in which the charity box was emptied of the blackmail money.

"Charlie?" Grace prompted.

"I'll go alone. I cannot condone a dreadful crime like blackmail, but I want to hear Mrs Harper's side of the story before I involve the police."

Grace sighed into his chest. "I really wanted it to be the repulsive Tulloch and his vile wife. Why did Bess wait so long for her revenge, I wonder? And why target Mrs Brown?"

"Bess must have been angry at Hugh for not rescuing her and blamed his new love, Evie. She probably never knew that Evie had been abandoned too. As far as the world knew, Mrs Brown had married before she had Sadie, and only then suffered the tragic loss of her husband. Perhaps Bess's resentments were reignited when she met Mrs Brown again after all these years, while fitting a wedding gown for a beloved daughter."

"The Carmichaels' son is getting married too," Grace said. "If his fiancée also purchased a wedding gown from Mrs Harper, it would be a doubly barbed reminder of her own loss. How aggravating it must have been to see Mrs Carmichael and the Tullochs attending church all those years and never recognising the young girl they abandoned at the convent laundry."

"Don't forget that Bess was very much changed by her year in the laundry. It must have taken years of quiet dedication to work her way up from being employed out of charity, to owning a dressmaking business." Charlie suddenly registered the silence behind him. Had Mrs Brown heard her own name being whispered? Their housekeeper was no fool. If they could put the clues together, so could she.

Grace carried on, oblivious to listening ears. "I admit I struggle to see it, even now. Eliza Harper has such a good heart and a caring manner. Could she really be seething with inner resentment when she has been so successful at overcoming a tough start in life? Clever as her hands are, would she have the skills to construct the hidden compartment in the charity box?"

Mrs Brown leaned forward, her voice low. "Your train of thought has brought an old memory to mind. When I first met Bess, all those years ago, she told me her father was a carpenter. She had happy memories of working beside him before he died, doing the intricate details of woodwork her father's big hands couldn't manage. It never crossed my mind to consider her a suspect, because, until last night, I thought she was far away in Australia. However, I believe you are wrong about Eliza Harper. I agree with Grace. She is a good woman, dedicated to helping others."

"Her philanthropy is directed at helping women like her," Charlie said. "Women with sewing skills but pasts that might prevent them from finding employment elsewhere. One has to wonder where the money came from to set up her business. If she is the blackmailer, perhaps she justifies it as taking money from the unworthy to help those in need."

Charlie was playing Devil's advocate, because he too struggled to see Mrs Harper as a criminal. However, there was no doubt that she was clever and ambitious, and his long experience of criminals warned him never to underestimate a person's ability to project goodness despite having a streak of darkness deep in their heart, especially when that darkness was driven by a powerful motive.

"Mrs Harper is not like the Bess I recall," Mrs Brown said.

"Are you sure, Mrs Brown?" Charlie asked. "It is a quarter of a century since you last saw Bess, and a year in the convent laundry would age a person beyond recognition."

"But it does not change the shape of the nose. I'm sure Bess had a snub nose, because it seemed to suit her round cheeks and merry character so well."

"I pray you are right, Mrs Brown," Charlie replied, "but I'll still have to talk to Mrs Harper. The sooner this investigation is laid to rest, the better."

His stop at home was a brief but pleasant reminder of the good side of life. Charlie gulped a bowl of soup from the pot always simmering on the stove to the sound of Tilly's squeals of delight at seeing her room. Blaze had given their new maid her seal of approval by allowing her to stroke the pups on short acquaintance.

By the time Charlie let himself out of the house, Grace was rifling through her old, slim-fitting garments so Tilly could cast off her laundry smock, while Mrs Brown plied her new helper with food and attention. He left, knowing the scales of natural justice were a little more in balance than they had been this morning.

After returning the hired horses and carriage, he walked the short distance to the dressmaker's salon. He half-hoped that Eliza Harper would be absent, but she was behind the counter, discussing an order for fabric with a slim woman in spectacles. When their conversation ended, the slim woman disappeared into a back room with the order form. An employee then, not a customer.

Nobody else was waiting, so Mrs Harper turned her pleasant smile on Charlie. Her nose could not be described as snub, but nor was it hooked or sharp.

"Good afternoon, Mr Penrose Pyke. Does your wife's gown need adjusting?"

"It is perfect as it is, Mrs Harper. I am most thankful to you for rescuing my wife from her sartorial crisis. Indeed, I hear that rescuing women in need is something you are renowned for. Your workers, as well as your customers, I mean."

"That is kind of you to say, sir. Those of us who are successful are duty-bound to help others, don't you think?"

"Quite so. Is your charity inspired by your own background, Mrs Harper?" Charlie asked.

The dressmaker looked up sharply, no doubt wondering where the conversation was heading. "It is. My mother worked all hours as a seamstress for appalling wages until she dropped from exhaustion. Fifty-one years old she was when she died – the same age that I am now – but my poor mama had the hunched back and poor eyesight of a woman twice her age. I'd worked at the same factory as her since I was fourteen, and I vowed not to end up in her shoes."

Terrible as her story was, a seamstress position in a factory was a far cry from the convent laundry, if she was telling the truth. And Bess would be around forty-four or forty-five years old now, not fifty-one. Charlie eased out a held breath, hoping he had misread the clues pointing to her. After all, many women were skilled sewers, and Elizabeth was a common name.

"You have certainly made a success of your career, Mrs Harper."

She waved a dismissive hand, but her smile was back. "I was far more fortunate than most. Mr Harper, a talented and kind local tailor, took pity on a skinny young woman with chickenpox scars and a determination to succeed. He trained me, treated me well, and eventually became my husband. But you do not wish to hear my rags to riches story. What can I do for you, Mr Penrose Pyke?"

"I am investigating several incidents of blackmail targeted at members of the First Church congregation."

The dressmaker's pleasant smile remained, but now it seemed distinctly forced. "I am aware of the rumours. How can I assist?"

"Did you go to the church this past Monday morning to inspect the fallen vase for damage? The vase beside the charity box."

"Briefly. The vase had a tiny chip in the rim, but nothing worth fretting over." Mrs Harper spoke without guile, although she was obviously puzzled by his interest in a vase when he was investigating a blackmailer.

"Did you use your key to open the church?"

"There was no need. Miss Kerr was already cleaning the lobby when I arrived, and I believe Miss Rudd had arrived before her."

Charlie tried to recall the words of her assistant, Miss Rudd, who had left him with the impression that it was Mrs Harper who had arrived first. Miss Rudd also told him about a rough man who'd been in the church when she arrived. Her description had directed him to Mr Tulloch, but the coalman had an alibi for that time.

"Did you see a man in the church that morning, Mrs Harper? A rough sleeper? Or anyone else?"

Mrs Harper's reply came quickly and with certainty. "Nobody other than my assistants. I was only there for a couple of minutes."

While the man's description had been general enough to fit many men, Charlie began to wonder if Miss Rudd's aim had been purposeful misdirection to distract him from the fact that it was she who had been alone in the church, with ample opportunity to empty the charity box. Miss Rudd was about the right age for Bess.

Mrs Harper was still looking puzzled. "Was there a problem with the vase?"

"Not at all," Charlie said. "I see now that it was a distraction. Tell me about your assistant, Miss Rudd. Was she one of your rescued ladies, Mrs Harper?"

Her smile returned. "Yes indeed. She came from the convent laundry. I wrote to the Labour Inspector about that awful place, but he claimed he could take no action because the church is exempt from labour laws. Would you like to speak to Bess?"

"I would." The tangle of uncertainty cleared, leaving Charlie's pulse pounding at the scent of a chase nearing the end.

Mrs Harper called the woman in spectacles back to the counter. "Could you ask Miss Rudd to come down, please?" She turned back to Charlie. "Poor Bess was gravely disfigured by scars from the laundry work. She has repaid my rescue of her tenfold. Her exquisite embroidery is something to behold. Stitches so fine, no machine could replicate them. She would make a fine dressmaker in her own right if she could only cultivate the confidence to overcome her dreadful past. She lost a child there. A terrible tragedy, which I fear has left her understandably bitter. People say time heals, but that is not always so when the pain runs deep."

Footsteps coming down the stairs announced the arrival of Bess Rudd. As soon as her face came into view – a scarred face with a snub nose – she saw Charlie and fled back upstairs. He ran after her, but she was devilishly quick on her feet. Bess might be middle-aged, but she was all wiry sinew and muscle, with not an ounce of excess fat to slow her down.

Gasps of outrage met his arrival in the fitting area at the top of the stairs. Charlie ignored the scandalised glares of half-dressed ladies. "Which way did Bess Rudd go?"

It was the helpful Miss Kerr who answered. "Upstairs to our living quarters, but you cannot go up there."

Charlie was already halfway up the stairs before she finished her sentence. Unfortunately, another of the workers was coming down, wiping crumbs from her face. A dashed inconvenient time for a meal break, but her glare told him she was not about to stand aside to let a man up the narrow staircase to their private living quarters. He couldn't push past her without squashing her, which left him with no option but to waste precious seconds by retreating.

When the worker reached the base of the stairs, she stopped to bar his way. "Miss Rudd said you required my help urgently, Miss Kerr."

Charlie had to give Bess credit for her quick thinking in blocking his way so effectively, but he didn't dwell on it. He spotted a gap wide enough to push past the woman without toppling her and took it at a sprint, leaving her spluttering furiously behind him. The next floor buzzed with the noise of sewing machines, so he carried on upwards.

At the top of the stairs, a narrow hall ran the length of the building under a sloping roof. An attic space with doors off it at frequent intervals. Two of the doors were open. In the first room, he glimpsed an abandoned slice of bread spread with cheese and pickles. In the second room, a pair of slender legs were wriggling their way out of an impossibly narrow dormer window, accompanied by the clink of coins in a bag.

His first thought was frustration at failing to secure the blackmailer. The second was how on earth Bess could escape out of a window so high up the building. In the second it took to cross the small room, by jumping over a mattress that had been upended on the floor, the slender legs vanished.

The answer was obvious as soon as he reached the window. The steepness of Dowling Street meant the buildings stepped down in roof height with the gradient of the street. Miss Bess Rudd had slithered straight out onto the roof and slid the short distance to the roof of the adjacent building. The roof next door was longer than this building, running some fifty yards to the next street over, which ran upwards along the bank on which the First Church sat. The steep rise of the hill meant the building was only a single storey at the far end. Bess could escape along the roof until she reached the far side, where she could scramble down to street level.

He raced along the inside of the building, looking for a window big enough to squeeze his bulk through, catching glimpses of her floundering her way along the length of the adjacent rooftop as he checked each window. Charlie kept pace with her until he reached the end of the building, only to find he was looking out onto a drop into a courtyard, with no way out and no way down. He flung the narrow window open anyway.

"Bess, stop," Charlie shouted, knowing it was pointless. Why would she stop, fearing that she would end her days in prison? After her time in the convent laundry, she would look upon incarceration with justified dread.

Bess turned at the sound of his voice, losing her balance. Her arms cartwheeled as her feet slid from under her. Charlie could do nothing to help as he watched her slide down the pitched roof towards the deadly drop on the high side of the building. Bess's fingers clawed at the roof until she arrested her slide, stopping with her feet dangling over the edge. Even in her precarious state, she still gripped the bag of blackmail money.

She was back on her feet within seconds, not sparing Charlie a glance. Ten seconds later, the dressmaker's assistant dropped out of sight, over the ridge of the roof and down to the building below.

Charlie's only option was to retreat down the stairs. He could run back down to the front entrance and up the alley to the next street, but by the time he got there she would be long gone. She could flee up the road to Moray Place, from where she could escape in multiple directions into the bustling heart of the city. Or she could go down towards the railway station, where even now a plume of rising steam indicated a train waiting. He doubted she would ever be seen again.

He banged the window shut, helpless and frustrated by his failure.

There was no point in attempting to chase her. Instead, he made his way back to her room. He could only hope she had left a clue to her escape plan, such as a labelled steamer trunk or the address of a relative with whom she might make contact.

It took only a few minutes to search her spartan quarters. The overturned mattress had a hole in the bottom where she had hidden the bag of blackmail proceeds. He felt inside, but there was nothing else in the hole. The rest of Bess Rudd's meagre possessions fitted into a single, battered, unlabelled trunk. Not a very large trunk at that.

On top of the low drawer beside the bed sat a tattered copy of a novel called *Jane Eyre*, which Charlie knew to be the story of an unwanted girl who had struggled to make her way in a harsh world before finding happiness with her beloved. An unsurprising choice for an abandoned woman. Blackmail could never be condoned, of course, but he wished with all his heart that Bess's life had had a happier ending. Although Mrs Harper had done her best by her workers, it must still have been hard for Bess to spend her days serving ladies who could afford to spend the equivalent of a month's or even a year's wages on a gown for a single ball or wedding.

The drawer beside her bed contained a well-thumbed Bible, a small vial of cheap perfume, assorted brushes and hair accessories, and a pretty box that had once contained an expensive pair of kid gloves. Inside the box was a pair of baby bootees, never worn. Charlie lifted out the bootees, which fitted easily into the palm of his hand. He stroked the soft wool, a poignant reminder of a life never lived. How often had Bess sat here after work, weeping for the child who died at birth and fuming at those she held responsible for the death?

A wave of guilt washed over him at the thought of the many pairs of bootees he and Grace had been given, and the beautifully decorated nursery their own children would grow up in, filled with books and toys and love. Despite all the gifts, Grace was determined to knit garments for their children herself, as if it was a rite of passage to motherhood. For a woman who could stitch a wound closed with deft strokes, Grace's knitting skills left something to be desired. Charlie suspected Mrs Brown of unpicking sections overnight to fix the dropped stitches.

The bootees in his hand had been expertly made, as befitted the sewing skills of the mother-to-be. Charlie placed the tiny items back in the box. He had allowed himself to become distracted. Bess was the dropped stitch he ought to be focused on, since his incautious approach to summoning her had led to her escape.

He resumed his search. Where would Bess hide something that she didn't want found, such as a list of addresses of places she might hide from the police? He ran his hand around and under the drawer, finding a notebook wedged behind the back of it. He flipped the pages, finding irrefutable proof that Bess was the blackmailer. It was a record of conversations overheard, written in the blackmailer's handwriting.

On the third page, a passage read: *Measured up a wedding gown for a pretty young woman with golden hair. When she left, I overheard Mrs Anderson tell her companion that Miss Mackenzie was marrying above her station, despite her decidedly dubious origins. "She's no daughter of Robert Mackenzie with hair like that", Mrs A said. "Her father must be the fire-headed boarder who used to live in the Mackenzie house, right under Robert's nose. I've a good mind to tell young Dougal Matheson the truth."*

The book was full of similar notes. Charlie's sympathy for Bess ebbed at the sheer number of potential victims and the callousness of her use of these overheard motes of unsubstantiated gossip for her own gain. He sighed. No point in castigating himself for letting her get away. He tucked the notebook into his pocket to study later.

His first duty was to inform Detective Inspector Wallace and Detective Sergeant Kelly of developments.

They weren't at the police station, so he left a note with the duty officer to alert them to the blackmailer's escape, promising them a full report within the hour. Meanwhile, he would take the opportunity to check on his much-neglected wife and dogs. He longed for the comfort of his wife's embrace and the silky pleasure of warm dog fur against his palm.

The Notebook

Grace woke up from her nap to the sound of frantic yapping. Mrs Brown had taken Tilly down to the shops and market, ostensibly to show her around the places she would need to know. Grace would be very surprised indeed if Tilly returned without a new bonnet or combs and ribbons for her hair. A good thing, too, after suffering a deficient of affection for so long. Meanwhile, Grace was alone, and the dogs were going crazy.

She waddled down the stairs with a fire iron in her hand, in case it was an intruder, but found her husband submerged under a joyful pile of black and white bodies. His jacket was hanging off the arm of a chair. Spark seized the dangling cuff and dragged the jacket across the floor to her. Grace had to tickle the pup to get it to release the cuff. Their teeth might be little, but they were sharp already. Grace felt sorry for Blaze, who would be relieved when the pups were fully weaned.

Charlie emerged from the pile of dogs, grinning. "Sorry to wake you, my love. I wanted to check you were well before I returned to the police station."

"Does that mean you are now sure Eliza Harper is the blackmailer?" Grace sat in her armchair. The growl of an over-excited pup wrestling with an object came from underneath her seat. One of her shoes, probably. They really must begin training the little devils before their possessions were reduced to shreds.

"Not Mrs Harper. The blackmailer is one of her assistants, a woman called Bess Rudd. She's a quiet one, who keeps her face and secrets well-hidden. Mrs Harper told me she lost a baby at the convent laundry, but I was too slow to react. Bess got away by squeezing through a narrow upstairs window. Pity you weren't with me."

Grace laughed. "I think you'll find my days of squeezing my thin body through narrow gaps are long past. Last time I tried to do it, it did not end well."

Charlie's smile grew wider as he recalled the occasion. "Sorry. Sometimes I forget that I'm the slim one in our marriage now. It's a novel experience for me."

"Not for much longer, Pyke." Grace thought back to her recent visit to the dressmaker's salon. "I think I recall Miss Rudd, but the name Bess was never mentioned. She was the assistant who brought out the fabrics. I wish I'd paid more attention."

"That goes for me too. Right from the start, you told me that a dressmaking salon was a hive of gossip." Charlie picked off three overexcited pups and put them into their pen, before standing and brushing dog hair and drool off his trousers. "I must go and report to Wallace and his team. I'll be home as soon as I can."

He took his jacket from Grace and patted the pocket. "Darn it, I had Bess's notebook. She recorded all her blackmail targets in it. Where can it have gone?"

Grace was sitting in the armchair he had flung his jacket on. Spark was underneath it, still wrestling with something. When she called her name, the pup emerged, dragging her prize with her. After a short tug-of-war, Grace won the notebook back by distracting Spark with the dangling tassel of a curtain-tie.

"Looks like Spark has a nose for clues," she said. "Are you taking the notebook to Inspector Wallace?"

"I wanted to look at it myself first. In fact, if you have the time, perhaps you could read it. A woman's perspective might help, and I need to brief Wallace on developments. Bess had ample time to flee, but we'll still have to go through the process of attempting to find her. Make a note of any personal information she may have recorded about friends or family members who might shelter her. After that, it'll be up to the police to find her and arrest her."

Grace was already flipping open the notebook, eager to satisfy her curiosity. "I'd like to confirm what set Bess on the path of blackmail and revenge against the people who wronged her after all these years. One would think that she would be reconciled to her fate by now. I still feel there is too much we don't know."

Charlie pulled another chair up to hers and took her hand. "I sense you have something on your mind."

"I've been thinking about Hugh Brown," Grace said. "If Bess didn't run away with him, as we were led to believe, what happened to him?"

Charlie's soft breath tickled her ear as he leaned close. "It's not uncommon for young men to flee their responsibilities. When Bess discovered she was pregnant, she would have pressured Hugh to make an honest woman of her. He would have been left with a terrible dilemma, having switched his professed love to Evie, whom he had also bedded. Perhaps he ran away because he couldn't face what he would see as his duty to marry Bess. I suspect we'll never know. Unless you have another theory."

"I think we should try to find Hugh Brown's parents, to ask if they ever heard from him after he left. It would be astonishing if he didn't contact them as soon as he was settled elsewhere to assure them that he was safe and well."

"Good point, Grace. I'll ask Declan to get a constable to check on them. His parents would be elderly now, if they are still alive. If Hugh was the kind man Mrs Brown thinks he was, he would want to stay in touch with them. However, I fear his actions indicate a man who shirks his responsibilities."

"I've been wondering if Hugh did more than contact his parents," Grace said. "This is pure speculation, but he might have returned to Dunedin so he could be near them in their old age. If —

and it's a big if – Bess saw Hugh Brown in Dunedin and recognised him, she might also have blackmailed him for deserting her in her hour of need."

Grace sensed the sudden tension in her husband's muscles and the narrowing of his eyes that indicated a brain hard at work.

"That's not the only possibility if you're right," Charlie said. "If Bess knew Hugh was back, she might have told him what had happened to her. Assuming he didn't know she had been taken to the convent laundry, which seems likely, Bess could not blame him for failing to rescue her. Remember that Hugh lost a child too. If he finally found out what happened all those years ago, his anger might have been the trigger for revenge."

"Are you thinking that Bess and Hugh could have plotted it together?" When Grace thought about it, having two conspirators would make the blackmail easier and safer than one alone. "It's not impossible."

"Unlikely, maybe, but worth considering, especially as Bess has to take shelter somewhere now that she is on the run from the police, if she hasn't already left town. Has Mrs Brown described Hugh to you?"

Grace thought back to the various conversations she'd had with their housekeeper. "As far as I recall, she described him as being of slight build and about her height, with a mop of sand-coloured hair and a kind temperament that drew people to him. The overwhelming feeling she gave was that she was still in love with him. Love at first sight, she said. Oh, and she also said Hugh was clever and a good businessman. But twenty-five years is a long time. Hugh could be fat, bald, and bad-tempered these days. He could go by a different name to make him less recognisable and thus to avoid the shame of what he did to the two maids."

She could see that her husband was practically quivering with excitement. "You're thinking of someone in particular, aren't you, Charlie?"

"The man who counted the money from the charity box was about Mrs Brown's height. He also had the slim wrists of a person of slight build, despite running to plumpness around the middle. He'd be about the right age for Hugh, and he returned to Dunedin a few years ago to take up a bookkeeping position. Also, he is said to be sociable and the type of man people go to with their problems. Mr Landsburgh by name. He is grey-haired and has bushy whiskers, but the grey is the whitish shade that is typical of pale-haired people as they age. What better person for Bess to conspire with than a man who could ensure the secret of the charity box remained hidden?"

"If Landsburgh is Hugh," Grace said, "the whiskers and paunch would make him difficult to recognise as the slim young man who fled Dunedin a quarter of a century ago. The same could be said of Bess, who is far from the pretty, lively maid of the past."

"I agree it is highly unlikely that most people would recognise either of them. But remember that Bess and Hugh knew each other intimately, and she was a volunteer at the First Church, as Landsburgh was. But therein lies another problem. Wasn't Hugh Brown a Catholic rather than a Presbyterian?"

Again, Grace had to search her memory, which seemed to be functioning at half speed these past few weeks. "I think you're right. It was one reason Hugh's parents didn't approve of their match, because Mrs Brown is Anglican. I suppose it's possible that attending the First Church rather than a Catholic church might have been part of his attempt to disguise his past. A fateful choice if Bess also worshipped and volunteered there."

"Indeed. Still, I feel we are stretching the bow very tight on this, because it's no more than wild conjecture based on the vaguest of similarities between Hugh and Landsburgh. However, we are running short on leads. There's certainly no harm in asking Wallace's team to visit Landsburgh's house and investigate his past. They can search for Bess while they are there."

Charlie reached over to give her a fleeting kiss, and then he was gone.

Grace suspected the sad eyes the puppies were casting at the door were mirrored by her own. Although she was sorry for Bess Rudd's tragic life, it would be an enormous relief when this investigation was over, leaving her and her husband to focus on their last days as a couple before they became parents.

She settled back into the cushions and opened the notebook. As Charlie had said, it was a record of Bess's blackmailing activities written in diary form. Pages and pages of gossip, with dates and details. Dozens and dozens of potential victims. No wonder Bess had needed a central collection point like the church charity box.

The first entry read: *Mrs Gilchrist is a horrid cow. She refused to let me serve her because my scarred face upsets her delicate constitution. Delicate! Gilchrist is as fat and ugly as the pug dog she carries around with her like a baby. I wanted to steal from her fat purse, but I can't afford to lose my position. She owes me, and I won't forget it.*

There were more entries in this vein, expressing anger and resentment at rich women who looked down on her. For a bright, flirty girl like Bess, losing her attractiveness must have been a bitter blow. But nowhere near as bitter as the loss of her freedom and her baby.

The notebook soon turned into a more meticulous account of observations and overheard conversations. The supposed sins ran from minor (*Miss W wears wispy silk underwear under her dowdy grey gown*), to embarrassing (*Mr M cheats at cards*), to shocking (*Mrs O beats her servants*), to reputation destroying (*Master J has been seen embracing young men in the pleasure gardens of Jubilee Park*).

Grace took a second look at the man who cheated at cards, since that was what Johnny suspected Mr Landsburgh's colleague of doing. The notebook entry read: *Mrs Abbott was whispering about a respectable banker who was caught cheating at cards. She had it from her lady's maid's cousin, who is married to a man who works at his club. It sounds like Mr Morton, who is entrusted with the church's money. What a scandal if it turns out to be true.*

She flicked through the pages of the notebook but found no mention of Mr Landsburgh as a blackmail victim, and no sign that Landsburgh, or anyone else, was in any way connected with Hugh Brown. Hardly surprising. As Charlie had said, it was an extremely long shot. Grace wished she hadn't mentioned it, because Charlie would send the police on a wild-goose chase after Landsburgh when their time could be better used searching for Bess. That was always the problem – when clues were scarce, the investigation was like unravelling multiple balls of entangled string, where only one strand led anywhere useful.

Grace read on. Mostly, the notes were detailed summaries of gossip that could be used for blackmail, albeit with threads of jealousy and vitriol. However, towards the end of the notebook, she came across an entry so venomous that the pen nib had gone through the page. The entry was dated three weeks previously.

The note read: *A young woman full of her own importance came in for a wedding gown fitting today. Her mother tried to convince her that an ironmonger's son wasn't good enough for her, but the girl was having none of it. She said her Donald was handsome and loving, with fine career prospects. His father made a fortune in the gold rush and had a huge house on Maitland Street. I was so shocked, I jabbed her with a pin. It must be the Carmichaels she was talking about. If Mrs C ever came in here, I'd stab her with every pin in my tin. That witch ought to be burned at the stake for sending me to the convent just for fluttering my eyelashes in the wrong direction. She caused my baby's death by her cruelty, just as much as if she had smothered the poor mite with her bare hands.*

Grace flipped to the next page, dated two days later, where her gaze came to a sudden halt at seeing the name Evie Brown. Bess had underscored the name and added two exclamation marks.

Another wedding gown. This one was a young woman called Sadie Brown, who came in with her mother and Mrs Drummond. Because it was Mrs D, Harper fussed over her and tended to her personally. Hearing the name Brown made me think of Hugh, my first love, stolen from me by a maid I'd thought of as my friend. When I made an excuse to leave my customer to spy on them, I could not believe my eyes.

The mother is Evie, I'm sure of it, because she hardly looks any different, unlike me. Mrs Evie Brown!! She didn't look at me, of course, because her eyes were glowing with pride at her beautiful daughter. Hugh's daughter, I'm sure of it from the look of her. Evie really landed on her feet. She thanked Mrs Drummond several times for gifting the expensive gown to Sadie. Some women have all the luck. If Hugh had stayed with me, it might have been my child in there being pampered and feted, instead of lying cold and dead in an unmarked grave, with me not even knowing if I had a daughter or a son.

Mrs D told Sadie that twenty-five was the perfect age to marry. I suspect that I now have an answer as to why Hugh left me for mousy little Evie. I'll bet she lured him away by bedding him in the hope of trapping him into marrying her. What a sneaky little tart she turned out to be. The daughter said she wished her father had lived to see this day. I'm sure Evie and Mrs D exchanged a guilty look. What is she hiding?

Resentment sizzled from the page. This was why Mrs Brown had been blackmailed – out of spite for Evie taking Hugh from Bess, and out of bitterness that Evie's daughter lived, while Bess's child died. It must have been a terrible blow to Bess to see Evie Brown again, looking so happy, within two days of hearing that Mrs Carmichael had the joy of a son's wedding to look forward to. They need look no further for the reason Bess turned her small-time money-making scheme into a vicious new plan for revenge by blackmail.

Grace reached the last pages of the notebook, finding a list of names, addresses, amounts, and the wording used for each blackmail note. The first victim was Mrs Gilchrist, who received her note a full two months after refusing to be served by Bess Rudd, indicating that the idea for revenge through blackmail took a while to crystalise. Either that, or Bess had played a clever hand, waiting long enough that the victims would not make the link between the blackmail threat and their visit to the dressmaker weeks before.

The sums of money demanded mostly ranged from a shilling to a pound. Presumably, the different amounts were based on a scale of the victim's perceived sins and their ability to pay. The amounts were by no means crippling, but not trivial either.

It was a fiendishly clever scheme, setting an amount that was not enough to provoke outright refusal and a complaint to the police. Those who were innocent victims of ill-informed gossip would probably ignore their notes as a nasty prank or case of mistaken identity, while the guilty would think the easiest option was to pay up and hope it never happened again. With so many victims, the combined payments would represent a fortune to an assistant dressmaker who might be paid as little as twenty shillings a week plus lodgings.

Three sums stood out for their disproportionate size, each targeted at people from Bess's time as a maid in the Carmichael household. She had demanded £5 from Mrs Brown, £20 from Mr Tulloch, and £50 from Mrs Carmichael. A sliding scale based on the perceived level of blame. The lowest amount to Evie out of jealousy for her success in life. A larger sum for Tulloch's complicity in taking Bess to the convent. And a massive demand from the woman who issued the command to take her away, leading to Bess's suffering and her baby's death.

Mrs Tulloch was not mentioned in the notebook. Presumably Bess thought she had no role in removing her from the Carmichaels' house.

Grace had already seen the blackmail notes to Mrs Brown and Mrs Carmichael. The note Bess sent to Mr Tulloch read: *You dragged a pregnant maid away from all she knew and took her to a house of horror. Black-hearted scoundrel that you are, you even tried to take advantage of her by offering to take her to the railway station instead if she lay with you. As if she would, after your vile behaviour left young girls in fear for their safety. Repent your sins by putting £20 in the church charity box before the morning service on Sunday.*

The note laid bare the depths of Tulloch's cruelty. It was no surprise to discover that he lied about his admission that he was only being blackmailed for a shilling for underweight coal. However, the wording of the note suggested that Tulloch was not the father of Bess's baby. Had he taken advantage of her in that way, he would surely have been blackmailed for it. That tallied with the information given by Magda at the convent laundry. Bess had loved the father of her child and clung to the belief that he would return to rescue her.

Hugh Brown, loved by both maids, had a great deal to answer for in Grace's view, wherever he was. She wondered if Bess was so furious at Evie because Bess herself had tried the tactic that she accused Evie of – bedding her suitor to trap him into marriage – only to find Hugh chose Evie.

Grace went back over the dates of the blackmail demands. Bess had sent out a slew of demands leading up to last Sunday's church service. The unexpected encounters with Mrs Carmichael's future daughter-in-law and Mrs Brown had triggered a fury that set her carefully managed scheme aside in favour of a single substantial payoff. She'd targeted the former Carmichael household but had the good sense to obscure her motives within a flood of lesser demands.

She was surprised Bess hadn't taken the money and run when she could, but perhaps the plan was to keep making demands of her hated victims until they were squeezed dry. Excessive greed was a temptation every blackmailer fell into. Until today, Bess would not have had the least inkling that they suspected her, so she must have felt safe even though she knew that the blackmail was being investigated.

Grace rested her eyes for a moment to think through what she had read.

The sound of Mrs Brown and Tilly arriving home roused her from an unintended nap an hour later. Charlie was with them too. When Grace stretched her legs, a low growl came from under her chair.

"Spark? Are you up to mischief again, you little devil?"

Spark slunk from under the chair with a piece of paper in her mouth. Grace had to gently prise open the pup's jaw to remove it. Mrs Carmichael's blackmail note. She'd been wondering where that had disappeared to. Grace was busy pushing the chair aside when Charlie walked in.

He was across the room in seconds. "Grace, Doctor Harvey insisted you do no heavy lifting."

"It's just an armchair, Charlie, and I was pushing it, not lifting it. It appears our smallest detective dog has been hiding clues underneath." Grace picked up Spark and put her back in the pen.

Charlie moved the chair. "One of your slippers, a handkerchief, a hairbrush, and sundry other items. Our smallest detective dog needs some serious training in how to spot relevant clues."

"Spark dragged Mrs Carmichael's blackmail note under there, too, and Bess's notebook. I suspect she has a better nose for clues than you give her credit for."

"A nose for trouble, more likely." Charlie took Grace to the sofa, where he helped her to sit. "Wallace sent me home to see if you have read Bess's notebook. I can't stay long."

"It's disturbing reading." Grace patted the sofa for him to join her. They might as well make use of the moment of calm to enjoy each other's company. "You may wish to wear gloves to prevent the poison dripping off the page."

"That bad?"

Grace grimaced. "There's little doubt that the weddings of Sadie Brown and Donald Carmichael turned Bess's cunning blackmail scheme into a full-scale revenge plot. I was wondering why Bess didn't flee with her ill-gotten gains earlier, until Spark's little hoard reminded me that Mrs Carmichael did not comply with the blackmail demand for £50 for lack of funds. And Tulloch only put a shilling in, rather than the £20 demanded."

"Excellent point, Grace. Bess would not want to leave town without exacting her pound of flesh from her most hated victims. I had better warn the police. You know how dangerous people can be when they are desperate."

"I'll warn Mrs Brown. I know she feels guilty that her own life has been blessed when it could so easily have been her who ended up in the convent laundry. She needs to know that Bess is no longer the sweet maid she knew from the past, but a bitter and twisted woman bent on revenge."

"Was there anything in the notebook about Landsburgh or Hugh Brown?" Charlie asked.

"No mention of Landsburgh, which suggests he was not a blackmail victim. Hugh was only mentioned in the notes about Mrs Brown. Bess recognised Mrs Brown as Evie and knew that Sadie was Hugh's daughter from her looks."

Grace showed him the notebook entry. "It's unclear whether Bess believed Hugh had stayed and married Evie, as opposed to leaving Evie in the lurch after making her pregnant. Bess was certainly suspicious of Mrs Brown's reaction to Sadie saying her father was dead. Bess would know that unwed mothers often pretend to have a deceased husband, and I'll bet she didn't rest until she discovered the truth."

"Hm. I'll still get Declan to check into Landsburgh's background because we cannot afford to discount any possibility. Did Bess's notebook give any hint about her escape plan?"

"Not that I found."

Charlie took the notebook and left her with a lingering kiss. "I'd better deliver this proof of the blackmailer's identity to Wallace. I'll be back as soon as I can." He paused at the door. "Tell Mrs Brown and Tilly not to let anyone into the house without me here."

And then Grace was alone again, wishing she could be curled up beside him, where she felt secure and loved.

A few minutes later, a gentle knock on the drawing-room door roused Grace from her wool-gathering. "Come in."

Mrs Brown entered with a tea tray. In the background, a sweet voice sang in the bathtub. Grace smiled. She wondered how long it had been since Tilly had enjoyed a long, hot bath, or a song for that matter. As if the work at the laundry wasn't harsh enough without forcing the girls to work in silence as well. After all, the girls were not nuns who had chosen that way of life.

"I made tea," Mrs Brown said. "Has Charlie left again?"

"You know what he's like when he gets his teeth into an investigation. I will be happy to have his share of tea, though." Grace tipped her head towards the singing. "Tilly seems to be settling in."

Mrs Brown smiled. "Like a duck to water."

"Did you buy anything nice at the shops?" Grace asked.

"A lovely piece of mutton and a hat for Tilly." Mrs Brown's hands went to her hips. "We cannot have her disgracing the household by wearing rags, can we?"

"No, indeed. I'll make sure we increase the housekeeping money now that we have another mouth to feed. She'll need shoes and such like too. Oh, and Mrs Brown? Perhaps we can put Tilly to work this afternoon."

"As you wish," Mrs Brown said, although her tone made it clear that she really meant, *what, so soon, when the poor mite has barely settled in?*

"I thought it might be jolly if we put up a few Christmas decorations to brighten up the house. We'll all be too busy once the little ones arrive. We can get a Christmas tree later, just before our parents arrive."

Mrs Brown's frown turned to a beaming smile. "Splendid idea, Grace. The poor wee mite sobbed at being given a room and a hat. I fear she will be quite overcome by sparkly tinsel and baubles."

By the time Charlie came home late that afternoon, the drawing room smelled of pinecones and cinnamon biscuits, and sparkled red, silver and gold. Grace put a finger to her lips and pointed to the corner, where a pile of black-and-white bodies lay sleeping the deep sleep of the young and exhausted. They too sparkled, because even the quick-on-her-feet Tilly couldn't prevent the pups rampaging through the tinsel before it could be put up out of harm's way.

"What a charming domestic scene," Charlie whispered. "One might think it was December rather than November. Mrs Brown and Tilly seem to be enjoying themselves in the kitchen. I'm not sure which of them is happier with the new arrangement."

"We're all delighted. What about you, Charlie? What news?"

"The police have put out a warrant for Bess's arrest, but we've had no luck in finding her. Wallace told me to go home and let the police handle it from here. I confess I was happy to oblige. Now that we know Bess is the blackmailer, Mr Tulloch has been released from the police cells on bail, pending his appearance in court on the indecent publications and illegal alcohol charges."

"I'm sorry to hear it," Grace said. "Tulloch deserves to be in prison, but I suppose the charges are not sufficiently serious."

Charlie lifted her swollen feet into his lap and rubbed them with powerful strokes. "I have to admit it feels like an anticlimax, although I am glad that I can turn my attention to more important matters."

The doorbell rang, as it always seemed to when Grace wished to be alone with her husband. They heard Mrs Brown opening and closing the front door. She poked her nose into the drawing room to tell them it was only a messenger boy delivering a note for her. After asking them when they would like dinner, she returned to the kitchen.

Grace let out a huff of held breath. "Thank goodness. I've had quite enough excitement for one day. We won't hear anything more from Declan tonight, I expect. Now, where were we? Oh yes, massaging my poor, swollen feet. I think an early night is in order, don't you, dearest?"

Charlie gave her one of those long, slow smiles that always made her heart flutter. "An early night is always a delightful prospect. We'd better make the most of our time alone before the twins turn our lives upside down."

Grave Developments

The next morning, Charlie was awakened by a shout from downstairs. Grace's voice, shrill with panic. He lurched out of bed and ran down the stairs, two at a time.

Despite her hints about an early night, Grace had fallen asleep on the sofa straight after supper, no doubt worn out by a taxing journey to the convent laundry and a surfeit of Christmas-inspired cheer. Charlie hadn't wanted to wake her to take her upstairs, so he'd covered her with a blanket and left her to sleep.

He leaped over the final three steps and flew down the hall.

Grace was standing by the open front door, outlined by weak pre-dawn light. "I heard someone moving around downstairs. Mrs Brown has disappeared. I found this on her dresser. It must be the message that came late yesterday afternoon."

Charlie took the note she handed him. *I'm sorry I misjudged you, Evie. You were always good to me, and I could see Hugh loved you with all his heart. I know I deserve no sympathy, but I am begging for your help. I need money to get away from here and start again. Meet me at sunrise at his grave. Please come. I need you. Don't tell anyone, because I'd rather die than go to prison.*

Grace clung to his forearm, her fingernails digging into the flesh. "You can't let Mrs Brown meet Bess, Charlie. She may be deranged. The note pretends to be sympathetic, but I'm sure that's just a trick to get Mrs Brown to help her."

He didn't need any convincing. Charlie dashed upstairs to throw some clothes on, then sprinted out the door with buttons undone and shirttail flapping. He took the Maitland Street route, judging it to be quicker. The route took him past the Carmichaels' house, where the upper storey remained dark but a flicker of light lit what he presumed to be the kitchen.

He raced onward, passing a beat constable, who gave him a hard stare to see from what or whom he was running. Charlie ignored him, his lungs burning as he redoubled his efforts, desperate to get there before Mrs Brown confronted her blackmailer. In another minute or two he would be at the main entrance to the cemetery on the south road.

A gunshot cracked through the still morning air, coming from the direction of the cemetery. Behind him, Charlie heard the constable's whistle, but he didn't stop. When he passed the sexton's cottage, the sexton was at the open door, the braces of his trousers dangling as he tucked his nightshirt in.

The gunshot still rang in Charlie's ears, warning him he might be too late, but he ran on, fearing another shot. The Brown grave was at the far side of the cemetery, up a steep path, which forced him to slow his pace. Two pairs of boots thundered behind him, but Charlie could only think of Mrs Brown, alone and unarmed, confronting a woman bent on revenge for past wrongs. He pushed his burning limbs to go faster, hoping he might yet save her life.

As he puffed up the hill to the grave, a nightmarish scene came into view. A body, deathly still, and Mrs Brown kneeling over it with blood-red hands.

Charlie got to her first. Mrs Brown was rigid with shock but did not appear to be injured. He helped her up. "Are you hurt?"

Mrs Brown stared at him, unblinking. "She's dead, Charlie. Bess is dead. She must have shot herself just before I got to her."

The constable and the sexton converged on them, both scarlet-faced and breathing heavily.

"There's blood on her hands," the sexton said, through racking gasps for air. He seized Mrs Brown's arms and pinned them behind her back, while the constable frisked her for a weapon.

"I didn't kill her." Shock stripped all emotion from Mrs Brown's voice. "I have never fired a gun in my life."

"This woman is not a killer, Constable," Charlie said.

"We caught her red-handed," the sexton said. "Hey. I know you. You are the lover I caught with this woman on Sunday night. Don't listen to him, Constable. I expect the woman shot a jealous rival for her young fancy man."

Charlie cursed his luck. He reached into his pocket for the letter he always carried, which gave him the authority to act on behalf of the police in criminal matters. The letter was in his other coat, but he did find a card, which he handed to the constable, a man he didn't recognise.

"As you can see, my name is Charles Penrose Pyke. I am a private detective, and I have been working with Detective Inspector Wallace to apprehend a blackmailer. This woman." He pointed at the body. "Miss Bess Rudd. She escaped from me yesterday before I could have her arrested."

The constable straightened at the mention of Inspector Wallace's name. Still, he eyed Charlie dubiously. "The other woman has blood on her hands."

"You don't get blood on your hands from shooting someone, only from trying to help them," Charlie said. "Look at her clothes. There is no spatter of blood as you would get from shooting someone at close range."

"Who's to say she was shot at close range?" the sexton said.

Charlie ignored him. "Look at the victim's head, Constable. The entry wound is a neat hole with burns around it, indicating the firearm was held against her head."

The constable looked, but he was young and inexperienced. From his sickly expression, it was likely his first suspicious death.

"And who is this woman?" the constable asked, pointing at Mrs Brown.

"I can vouch for her. She is my housekeeper, Mrs Brown. She came here this morning to help this woman, not to murder her."

"I arrived after the gunshot," Mrs Brown said. She was shaking now, as shock took its toll. "I was too late to save her."

Charlie inspected the body. "Small calibre. Instantaneous death, I imagine. The weapon should be nearby if it was suicide."

He had his doubts about suicide. The calluses on the victim's right hand showed she was right-handed. The entry point of the bullet was high on the temple on the left-hand side of the head, and the exit wound showed it had been fired at a downward angle, which would have been extremely awkward to achieve for a right-handed person who shot herself. However, Charlie kept his silence for Mrs Brown's sake. He knew he couldn't be involved in the investigation of the death, given his personal link to the prime suspect. He would have to trust Wallace and his team to get to the bottom of it.

"Don't touch anything," the constable said. He snapped handcuffs on Mrs Brown's wrists and left her with the sexton. After fossicking through the grass around the body, he lifted a fold of the victim's skirt and found a pistol. The constable picked it up by the butt and checked the breech, before putting it in his pocket. "Must have fallen on it when she died. Looks like suicide to me."

"Or this murderous she-devil put the pistol there to make it look like suicide," the sexton said.

Charlie wished a sudden onset of lockjaw upon the interfering sexton, but he also knew that arguing wouldn't help.

The constable's eyes swivelled back to Mrs Brown. "I've no choice but to take you in for questioning, ma'am."

Mrs Brown looked at Charlie, not saying a word, but pleading for his help all the same. There was nothing he could do but ensure a fair hearing by an experienced officer.

Charlie moved to Mrs Brown's side and rested his hand on her shoulder. "I understand you are doing your duty, Constable, because I was a detective constable not so long ago. I worked under Detective Inspector Wallace, who is leading the investigation into the shooting victim. Wallace will want to deal with her death personally. Might I suggest you take Mrs Brown to the Central Police Station and tell Wallace the victim is the blackmailer, Bess Rudd? Speak to Detective Sergeant Kelly if Wallace is not there."

The constable stopped short of saluting, but it was obvious he was relieved to have an order to follow. "Sexton, you stay with the body and touch nothing until the police surgeon arrives."

"Upon my honour, Constable, I'll let neither man nor beast near it." The sexton shot another suspicious glare in Charlie's direction, before he settled down on a nearby grave and got his pipe out of his pocket for a smoke.

"Mr Penrose Pyke," the constable said, "I'll need you to come with me to make a statement."

"I've left my wife at home alone," Charlie pleaded. "She's due to give birth to twins any day now. I promise to come to the station as soon as I have found someone to look after her."

The constable wavered, but eventually he nodded. He gestured for Mrs Brown to go ahead down the path. The handcuffs were still in place, but at least he was not hauling her along like a hardened criminal. She stumbled down the path, unsteady on her feet. Charlie called after her that he would send Mr Drummond, but she didn't look back.

With the sexton watching him, Charlie could not conduct a thorough search for clues. He bowed his head, as if in prayer for the lost soul, and scanned the ground in front of him. No signs of a scuffle. No obvious bruises on the victim's face or torn clothes that might indicate a fight between victim and killer. Either she shot herself, which he doubted, or she let someone walk right up to her and put a pistol to her head. Someone she knew and trusted – or, at least, someone she wasn't actively afraid of. Unfortunately, Mrs Brown was the most likely suspect based on those criteria, because Bess would be unlikely to trust any of her other blackmail victims.

It made no sense. Nobody wandered the paths of the Southern Cemetery at dawn by chance, which meant Bess must have invited her killer here, presumably to extract money from them. And yet Bess would have let none of her victims get so close to her. Unless … could it have been Bess who came to the rendezvous with a pistol, thinking she would be safe if she came armed? If so, her intended victim had overwhelmed her with superior force and made her the victim. Mr Tulloch? Or perhaps Mrs Tulloch, who had a fearless, aggressive streak, as Charlie knew all too well.

One thing was certain. If there was a killer on the loose, he or she had to be found as quickly as possible. Murder was an extreme reaction to blackmail, even given the anger the victim must have felt towards the blackmailer. And that was another problem, because none of the victims – even Tulloch and Mrs Carmichael – had been accused of anything so scandalous that they would kill to ensure the blackmailer's silence. In fact, neither of the main targets had been worried enough to pay the first blackmail demand, so why would they react so violently to a second demand?

Charlie had a nagging feeling that there was something he was missing. Could there be another victim they were as yet unaware of, who had a more shocking secret to protect? No one in Bess's notebook, certainly. But perhaps another person with a murderous grievance against Bess?

He turned his thoughts back to the scene. Bess's choice of the Brown grave as a meeting point could not be a coincidence. It made sense as a meeting place to have a quiet discussion with Mrs Brown, but it was also a dangerously secluded spot to meet a less kindly victim, even if she came armed. He couldn't get away from his gut instinct that Bess must have trusted the person who killed her, which left him with another possibility. Had the person been a fellow conspirator rather than a victim?

The name on the grave also reminded Charlie of the other person who had been central to the events of a quarter century ago, Hugh Brown. With a little simple investigating, Bess could easily have uncovered the fiction that the Brown on the grave marker was not Hugh Brown. And a check of marriage records would show no marriage between Evie and Hugh. Perhaps the choice of meeting point was to show Mrs Brown that none of her secrets were safe.

That unwanted thought put Charlie in an even more invidious position. Far too much evidence pointed to Mrs Brown as the most likely murderer. Should he tell Wallace or leave the police to come to their own conclusions? In the end, he decided to wait until the evidence was complete. After all, there was still that nagging thought that he had missed something in the turmoil of the last few days.

The sexton continued to glare at him as he puffed curls of smoke from his nostrils. It was past time for Charlie to leave, but there was one other avenue to consider first. If there had been another person present, he or she had departed the scene quickly. Charlie arrived from the main road within two to three minutes of the gunshot. Mrs Brown cannot have been more than a minute behind the killer, since they had found her kneeling by the body with fresh blood on her hands. Assuming Mrs Brown came down from Eglinton Road, that meant the killer must have escaped through the cemetery, probably via the nearby thicket of bushes to the north of the grave.

Charlie left that way rather than by the road. The probability of suicide took a tumble when he saw broken twigs pointing away from the grave where somebody had departed in haste. The breaks seemed fresh, but there was no way of telling whether it was a midnight reveller or a dawn killer. He backed away, not wanting to disturb the evidence. The one positive was that the person who left this way could not have been Mrs Brown.

He was halfway home, imagining Grace having contractions and screaming for help, when he remembered his wife wasn't alone. Tilly was there. He ought not to have been so comforted by the fact that an unknown girl of possibly dubious origins was with his wife, but he had a good feeling about Tilly. Blaze had taken to her, and that was as good a character reference as he could hope for right now.

Thus, Charlie made a quick detour to visit Kenneth Drummond, because what Mrs Brown needed most was a renowned barrister at her side. Anne Drummond would ensure Grace was looked after while he did his duty by giving a statement to the police.

The Unravelling

Grace paced the kitchen, her stomach churning with fear for Mrs Brown's safety. The babies pressed down inside her, bringing a stab of pain. She rubbed her belly and thought soothing thoughts. *Bess will not harm an old friend. Mrs Brown will not do anything reckless. Charlie will save the day. All will be well.*

And yet, over an hour had passed, and neither of them was home. Fortunately, Tilly had been roused by Grace's shouts to alert Charlie to Mrs Brown's disappearance. Their new maid was now bustling around the kitchen as if she had been with them for months, not hours, making tea and encouraging Grace to eat. She was grateful for it. Experience told her she would need a meal inside her to get through the day ahead.

The front door opened and closed, but it was the tapping of her great-aunt's cane Grace heard.

When Anne Drummond entered the kitchen, Grace threw herself at her, almost knocking her elderly great-aunt off her feet. "What's happened? Is Charlie …"

"Charlie is alive and well," Anne said. "He is at the police station with Kenneth now, because Mrs Brown has been detained for the murder of Bess Rudd."

Grace's gasp was inaudible over the shriek from Tilly. "Don't worry, Tilly," she said. "Mrs Brown wouldn't hurt a fly. I'm sure it is a misunderstanding that will soon be righted by my husband and Mr Drummond, who is a famous barrister. This is his wife, Mrs Anne Drummond, who is also my great-aunt and the owner of this house."

"Hello, Tilly," Anne said. "Charlie told me you'd been hired. Excellent timing, it seems. Is that teapot still warm?"

Anne's calm restored Tilly's composure rather quicker than Grace would have expected for a new maid who was not yet used to the dramas of their household. A promising start to her employment with them.

Anne told them as much as she knew, which wasn't much. Charlie and Kenneth had dashed off to defend Mrs Brown, leaving Anne to attend to the birth pains Charlie had convinced himself Grace would be experiencing.

Grace laughed his concerns away, but she knew it wouldn't be much longer. The babies were sitting lower, causing dull aches and pressure on her bladder, as well as back pain and episodes of mild contractions. Despite having to dash to the water closet at regular intervals, Grace felt only relief that it would be over soon and she hadn't given birth during her examinations.

"Do you mind if I rest on the sofa until Charlie comes home?" Grace needed time to think. The investigation had moved so quickly over the last few days that they had been constantly reacting to each new revelation, without having the time to see the case as a whole. There was something itching at the back of her mind, which she couldn't put her finger on.

What Grace needed was a distraction for her great-aunt. "Auntie Anne, did Charlie tell you we found Tilly at the convent laundry? I think you should talk to her about the conditions there. From what we saw, a fresh approach to the Labour Inspector is warranted."

She left Anne and Tilly at the kitchen table discussing conditions at the laundry while she retreated to the peace of the drawing room. With a pile of cushions propping her up at a comfortable angle – or as comfortable as possible in her overstuffed state – Grace closed her eyes and reviewed everything they knew. The eureka moment came just as she heard voices coming up the path.

Blaze and her four shadows jumped up and raced for the door. Charlie was home, and he had company. Mrs Brown was first through the drawing-room door, with Anne clinging joyfully to her and Kenneth Drummond behind her. Male voices and canine chaos remained in the hall.

Grace held her arms out. "Mrs Brown, come and give me a hug. I'm so glad the police have released you."

Mrs Brown accepted the offer of a hug with obvious relief, which would never have happened a few days ago when she had been a respectable housekeeper with an impeccable past. Her face was grey and drawn from the ordeal of being arrested, but Grace was pleased to see the firm set to her shoulders.

"The police surgeon listened to Charlie's testimony and examined me for blood spatters," Mrs Brown said, with the outward calm of a housekeeper mentioning gravy stains rather than blood. "There was talk of bullet trajectories and whatnot too. I must have passed the test, for which I am profoundly grateful."

"Do the police think it was suicide or murder?" Grace asked.

A gruff voice from the doorway answered. "We're treating it as murder."

"Good morning to you, Detective Inspector Wallace." Grace thought she had heard his voice but couldn't fathom why the city's leading detective would be here, instead of at the police station. "How good of you to escort the suspect home. And Detective Sergeant Kelly, too. We are honoured. Please, take a seat."

Charlie came in with his collie entourage. "We decided that a full review of the evidence was in order before rushing into interviews of the suspects. Your opinion is needed, Grace, so it seemed easier to come here."

Grace patted her protruding belly. "If the mountain can't come to Muhammad, then Muhammad must go to the mountain."

Wallace chuckled. "I would never dare put it like that. However, it seemed as good a time as any to inspect Blaze's litter."

Blaze heard her name and went to sit by Wallace, with whom she enjoyed a mutual admiration. Charlie had promised Wallace the pick of Blaze's litter to train as a tracking dog for his detective team. The inspector's gaze roved the room, taking in the two male pups, who kept their distance.

Spark went to sit by Grace, her bright eyes trained on the two strangers. She was on guard, but without her hackles raised, presumably because Blaze was on such friendly terms with these exceptionally large men. For a pup so young, her instinct to protect seemed extraordinary to Grace. She and Charlie hadn't discussed the pups' futures, but she rather hoped Wallace wouldn't see Spark's obvious potential.

Sage sniffed her way straight up to Wallace and licked his hand. Wallace smiled and extracted a sliver of dried beef from his cuff. He lifted the pup gently and inspected her bright eyes and perfect conformation, before putting her on his lap. Sage sniffed his pockets, unearthing further slivers of beef in seconds. Wallace gave a satisfied nod. Sage inspected his moustache but, fortunately, did not clamp her sharp teeth on it, before settling down to have her ears rubbed.

"I meant what I said, sir," Charlie said. "You can take your pick of the pups. That one's called Sage, but you can change her name if you prefer."

"Sage will do just fine," Wallace said. "I could use more wisdom on my team. Aside from you, I mean, Kelly. One or two of the others seem to have solid brick between their ears."

Grace expected Detective Sergeant Declan Kelly to have something to say about that, but he was on his hands and knees in the corner, tickling Byron's belly.

"Are all the pups spoken for?" Declan asked.

"Afraid so, old friend." Charlie caught Grace's eye and smiled at her. "I cannot bear to part with Spark, who is the one standing by Grace, because my dear wife and our babies will need guarding. The larger male has been promised to the owner of Blaze's mate, who wanted a male pup to replace his aging breeding dog. Unfortunately, the one you're playing with has been set aside as a Christmas present for friends of ours, whose children have been pestering their father for a dog ever since they had Blaze to stay. As long as the parents agree, of course."

Declan beamed. "Reckon they might be persuaded. Moira was saying just the other day that it would be nice to have a dog. Blaze won her over when she stayed with us."

"Byron is more of a dreamer than a detective, but it's early days. He'll be gentle with your children."

"I'm more worried about training the children to be gentle with the dog," Declan said.

Wallace cleared his throat, indicating that the time for pleasant chatter was over.

Kenneth Drummond rose and took his wife's arm. "Time for us to leave, unless we can be of any assistance."

Mrs Brown rose too. "I cannot thank you enough, Mr Drummond, for coming so promptly to my aid."

Kenneth bowed. "It was my pleasure. My dear wife would have flayed me alive if I hadn't set all other matters aside to attend to you. Not that I was needed. We'll leave our buggy outside, in case you have urgent need of transportation."

Mrs Brown saw them to the door, before returning to the drawing room and taking a seat. Wallace looked for a moment as if he was about to query the propriety of having so recent a suspect in the discussion, but Mrs Brown's outthrust jaw stayed his words. Just as well, in Grace's opinion, because their housekeeper deserved to be there after all she had been through.

Oddly, it was Charlie who voiced his doubts. "We must cover all aspects of the case, Mrs Brown. I do not wish to cause you any further distress."

Mrs Brown didn't move. "I won't be left out."

"Very well, then. In that case …" But Wallace was interrupted by Tilly entering the room with a tea tray. She served tea and fruitcake, then hovered in the background hopefully.

"The cupboards in the nursery need dusting, if you would be so kind, Tilly," Grace said, knowing her presence would be a step too far for the policemen and not wishing to corrupt their new maid so early in their acquaintance, despite her apparent willingness to be corrupted. Tilly retreated with good grace.

Wallace waited until he heard her footsteps going upstairs. "I'm sure we'd all agree on several points. The first is that Bess Rudd must have contacted the person who killed her and demanded money so she could make her escape with enough funds to start a new life in comfort. Presumably, Mrs Brown was the backup plan if this person did not show up or refused to supply a sufficient quantity of money."

The inspector paused for a sip of tea, allowing time for alternative views. Nobody spoke, although Grace had the strong impression her husband was holding back.

Wallace continued. "The second point is that Bess chose a secluded spot. The fingerprints on the pistol were too large to belong to her, and she had only a small knife on her person, which suggests she trusted the person not to attack her, at least not with overwhelming force. And the third point is that Bess badly misjudged the killer. He or she must have walked right up to her and fired the pistol before she realised her mistake. Tulloch, the disreputable coalman, would be my pick as a likely murderer, but I cannot see her allowing him that close, or indeed meeting him at all in such a secluded place."

"If you'd met Mrs Tulloch, you'd probably count her out for the same reason," Grace said. "She is very intimidating and has a short temper. Any woman brave enough to slap Charlie is a force to be reckoned with."

"Mrs Carmichael appears to be the primary target of the blackmail attempt," Wallace said. "Do you think the same objections apply to her, Grace?"

Grace took her time to reply because her answer was crucial to solving the case. "Mrs Carmichael can be intimidating too, but she is more ladylike than her former cook, and not a woman to do her own dirty work under normal circumstances. Also, she must be at least sixty years old, and her pampered lifestyle means she would be no match for the younger, stronger Bess. However, if Mrs Carmichael had a pistol, I wouldn't discount her, because I believe she has a very compelling motive."

"You never know what people are capable of when they are pushed to the limit," Declan said. "Anyway, her husband might have done the deed in her stead. Charlie, I can see from your frown that you have something to add."

Charlie choked on a mouthful of cake. "Apologies. Missed breakfast. We ought to consider anyone who might help Bess escape, not just blackmail victims. Which brings me to another possibility, based on the meeting spot chosen. The Brown grave was known to Mrs Brown, and Bess must have figured out its significance, but presumably the grave was unknown to the other suspects."

Mrs Brown leaned forward, alert but frowning. "Bess could have sent the killer a note describing the precise location."

"You're right," Charlie said, "but I hope you will forgive me for raising another possibility."

"Before you continue, Charlie," Declan said, "I must tell you that the suggestion you made yesterday didn't pan out. Mr Landsburgh was employed at the Auckland branch of the bank from when he was old enough to start as an apprentice bookkeeper. He was the son of a staff member and cannot be the man you suspected. And that man's parents haven't heard a word from their son."

Declan was being discreet by not naming names, so as not to upset Mrs Brown by mentioning the possibility that Hugh Brown could be back in Dunedin. Grace was not surprised that Landsburgh had been ruled out, because the remote chance he was Hugh Brown had been based on the flimsiest of similarities. However, her stomach churned at the news that Hugh's parents hadn't heard from him since he ran away. She had hoped that they would, because the alternative was too awful to consider. But consider it she had. And she could see from Charlie's reaction that he was thinking along the same lines, as so often happened.

"Are you absolutely sure the parents were telling the truth?" Grace asked.

"Without a doubt," Declan replied. "They're honest folk and still devastated by the loss of their son. If you could have seen the hope in their expressions when I asked after him, you'd have believed it too."

Charlie clasped his hands together for a moment before continuing. "So, we are left with the question of what really happened to Hugh Brown. And who left the note telling his parents that Hugh and Bess were running away together, which never happened, as we found out yesterday."

Mrs Brown swayed alarmingly. Charlie sprang forward to support her. "I'm so very sorry to mention it, Mrs Brown. It's nothing but speculation, but it is a piece of the puzzle we haven't considered. The fact that Hugh deserted both the women he had courted worries me, especially as he clearly loved you. Even Bess admitted he loved you with all his heart, in her note asking you to meet this morning."

Mrs Brown shrugged off his support. "It's kind of you to say that, Charlie, but I know it is not true. If Hugh truly loved me, he would have stayed with me and not run away when someone told him a lie about me having another man's baby. He wasn't even man enough to marry Bess, when she was pregnant with his child."

Grace pushed herself into a seated position before she was sick.

Charlie cast a worried glance at her before he continued. "I have to agree in one respect. A man in love with all his heart does not leave when someone lies to him about his beloved, especially not when he has a future in his family's shop. But do we know he believed the lie, or even that he was told such a thing? All we know is that Evie came to Hugh in distress, and he responded with kindness and a marriage proposal."

"But Hugh didn't stay with me, Charlie," Mrs Brown said. "He got what he wanted and left me, just as he did to Bess."

"Hear me out, Mrs Brown," Charlie replied. "I asked myself what I would have done, if Grace had come to me in the circumstances Evie found herself in. There could only be one answer to that – an answer any decent man would give. I would have gone to confront the person who caused my loved one to suffer to give them a piece of my mind."

Mrs Brown stared at him for the seconds it took to work through the implications. "The way Hugh vanished without a word always felt inconceivable to me. I convinced myself I was being foolish and naive, especially after I heard that he'd run away with Bess.

But he never did, did he? Hugh went to confront my abuser, just as you would have done, Charlie."

The room fell silent as each person present drew their own conclusions.

It was Mrs Brown who broke the silence. "I can see what you are thinking. Tulloch got the better of him. He's a brutal man, much stronger than my Hugh, who was no fighter. Tulloch must have given my Hugh a fearful beating and told him never to come back. Perhaps he even threatened to do the same to me if Hugh showed his face in Dunedin again. And now he's killed Bess too. If I'd arrived at the cemetery a minute earlier, Tulloch might have killed me as well."

Mrs Brown dissolved into sobs. Charlie put his arms around her and held her tight. Grace caught his eye and knew exactly what he was thinking, because she was thinking it too. She wished she could comfort Mrs Brown, but it was all she could do to remain calm as spasms rippled across her nether regions.

Family Matters

Charlie watched the agony ripple over his wife's face at Mrs Brown's distress. If she suspected what he suspected, the distress was only going to get worse. He could see Grace had something to add, but she was holding back. She caught his eye, and he nodded for her to say what was on her mind. Sometimes the only way forward was to face the worst and cauterise the wounds later.

Grace read his mind, as she so often did. She grimaced and took a deep breath as she formed her words. "Much as I loathe the repulsive Tulloch, I think there might be another explanation. I believe Hugh went to someone else to seek an apology for Evie's mistreatment. Unfortunately, Hugh went without knowing all the facts, which left him vulnerable."

Charlie experienced the dizzying sensation of the pieces of a puzzle coming together as Grace explained her theory. Only his wife would have the knowledge to see what others had not, he thought proudly. When he added his thoughts, she looked equally proud.

Detective Inspector Wallace stood up as soon as they finished. "I expect you'd like to come with us, Pyke, to put this fresh evidence to the suspects."

"Yes, thank you, we'd love to come." Grace rolled her legs off the sofa and levered her body upright awkwardly.

Wallace directed a pointed glance at her belly, before addressing Charlie. "I don't think –"

Grace cut in. "You don't think you have the medical knowledge to put my theory across clearly and precisely? Quite so, which is why I must go, against the better judgement of both you and my husband.”

Mrs Brown took Grace’s arm with the air of steely determination she’d been practicing all week. “Never fear, I shall be there to look after Grace.”

Wallace’s eyes narrowed under slanted eyebrows, but he knew when he was beaten. Charlie felt the same. Unfortunately, they had no option but to take Grace, since the facts were of a complex medical nature. Even Grace admitted she might not have seen it if she hadn’t specifically studied the issue for her recent medical examination.

It was fortunate that Kenneth Drummond had foreseen their need and left his buggy for their use. Detective Inspector Wallace drove Grace and Mrs Brown to the Carmichaels’ house, while Charlie and Declan walked beside the buggy. Although it wasn’t far away in distance, the frisson of anticipation made the journey seem longer.

They found Mr Carmichael at home for his midday meal, reminding Charlie that he had eaten nothing more than three slices of fruitcake since last night. Not that he was hungry. He had far more interesting prey to consider than the cold roast beef and pickle sandwiches on Mr and Mrs Carmichael’s plates.

Mrs Carmichael, naturally, objected to their untimely intrusion during the luncheon hour. However, she could have no objection when Wallace announced he was a detective inspector with the Dunedin police, on the trail of a murderer.

“I’m not sure how we can help, but we are at your service, of course,” Mrs Carmichael said. “Come through to the parlour.”

“Why don’t you take the women into the parlour,” Mr Carmichael said, “while I talk to the police in the family sitting room?”

Mr Carmichael's traditional attitudes to women had annoyed Grace at their first meeting with the Carmichaels. He wasn't doing himself any favours by dismissing the women again, in Charlie's opinion.

"We'll all go through to the largest room," Wallace replied. "Mrs Carmichael's evidence is required, and these two ladies are special advisers to the investigation."

In the family sitting room, Grace spotted a portrait on the wall of the Carmichaels' son, Donald, and his new fiancée. She waddled towards it but changed her mind and took a seat. To Charlie, she didn't look as well as she was pretending, and he wished he hadn't allowed her to come.

However, Grace forced a thin smile at their reluctant hosts as she gestured to the portrait. "What a handsome couple they make. Your son certainly has an eye for fashion. It takes a perceptive person to match colours as boldly as Donald does and yet pull it off to perfection."

Mrs Carmichael practically glowed with pride. "Thank you. I have to agree that our son is exceptionally stylish, and handsome as well, of course. Ambitious too. We are immensely proud of him."

"He is very like his father, I perceive," Grace said. "Indeed, on brief acquaintance, Donald seems to have many fine attributes, except perhaps a slight lack of tact. When we first met, I recall him saying that the décor in the parlour gave him heart palpitations."

"No young man can be perfect," Mrs Carmichael said. "Might we dispense with this irrelevant small talk and get to the matter at hand, Inspector? We would like to return to our meal."

"Oh, but it is relevant," Grace said. "I believe you are colour blind, Mrs Carmichael. Am I correct?"

"What are you talking about? I'm not blind."

"Colour-blind people are not blind, Mrs Carmichael, but they do struggle to distinguish shades of colour, and thus they often wear colours that other people see as clashing." Grace couldn't believe she hadn't seen it earlier, because she had noted the woman's awful colour choices on more than one occasion.

Mrs Carmichael flushed a bright shade of red, ironically matching the garish shade of her shawl. "Perhaps there is some truth to that. Donald has often teased me about my colour choices. However, I do not see why this matters to the police."

"It matters because the trait is inherited," Grace said. "A colour-blind woman always passes the condition to her sons. I'm sorry to have to ask this of you, but Donald is not your son by birth, is he?"

Mr Carmichael caught his wife mid-swoon and helped her to a chair. He stood behind her, gripping the top of her seat with clawed hands. "I protest this outrageous inquisition, Inspector Wallace. Can't you see this woman is upsetting my wife?"

Wallace was unmoved. "You may answer the question on your wife's behalf, Mr Carmichael. Or we can take you both down to the police station for questioning."

After a long pause, as Mr Carmichael weighed up his options, he relented. "If you must know, Donald is our nephew by birth, but our son by all other measures. We have raised him since birth, because my brother died before he was born and his wife could not cope on her own with an infant. We have not told Donald, so I ask that you not repeat what I have just told you outside this room. My brother and I look very alike, fortunately."

"Do you see much of Donald's birth mother, Mrs Carmichael?" Charlie asked.

Mrs Carmichael had recovered the use of her vocal cords, but her face was still deathly white. "I never met her. We had long believed my husband's brother to be dead, as we'd had no word from him since he went to the West Coast to try his luck on the goldfields in the '60s."

"Did you not meet the mother when the infant was handed to you?"

"That's quite enough of these ridiculous questions, Mr Penrose Pyke," Mr Carmichael said. He paused, waiting for an apology that did not come. "If you must know, I had to go to Port Chalmers to retrieve the baby, because my sister-in-law was travelling by ship and it only docked briefly. As I already told you, after her husband died, she did not wish to raise the child alone."

"Do you have her contact details?" Wallace asked.

"No, I don't." The persistent questioning was obviously irking Mr Carmichael, and he struggled to keep his tone civil. "She went back to her family somewhere in the North Island and wanted nothing to do with us or the child. Donald was better off with parents who wanted and loved him."

"I can understand your position, Mr Carmichael," Wallace said. "A man needs a son to continue his legacy, does he not?"

"Quite right, Inspector. Now, if that is all –"

"Not quite all," Charlie said. "Donald was born on Valentine's Day, if I recall our first conversation correctly. Mid-February. He looks about twenty-four in that portrait, which means he will be twenty-five when he marries his sweetheart on his next birthday. Am I correct?"

Mrs Carmichael had recovered from her shock and regained her short temper. "What of it? I've had quite enough of your poking and prying into personal matters that are no concern of yours."

Her husband backed away to the wall, realising what must be coming next. Declan stood in the doorway, poised for action. Charlie kept one eye on Grace, who couldn't seem to get comfortable in her chair, and the other eye on Mr Carmichael.

Grace pushed herself to her feet and slowly paced towards Mrs Carmichael, not seeing Charlie gesturing at her to stay away from the suspects. "Did you know your husband lied about Donald's origins, Mrs Carmichael?" she asked.

"What? Don't be ridiculous. It happened exactly as my husband described. Can't you see Donald looks like his uncle?"

Grace glanced from the portrait of Donald to Mr Carmichael. "I'd say Donald looks more like your husband's son, Mrs Carmichael, not his nephew. Twenty-five years ago, a pregnant maid was dragged from your house and taken to a convent, where she gave birth to a child some six months later in mid-February. She was told her child had died at birth, but I believe the child was really adopted by its father, presumably after a generous donation was paid to the convent for not making a record of the adoption."

Mrs Carmichael looked at Grace as if she were a lunatic. "What are you talking about? Why would you think Donald had been born in a convent, for heaven's sake? He's our nephew, and I won't hear another word of your slander."

"A convent laundry, to be specific, where fallen girls are sent to repent their sins." Grace paused, pacing slowly back and forth, holding her hands low on her hips and breathing heavily. "Mr Tulloch signed her in. Your maid, Bess, gave birth there, exactly as I said. We have witness statements to that effect."

"What nonsense." Mrs Carmichael stood up and crossed her arms defiantly, but she was also glancing over at her husband, even as she continued to deny the accusation. "Bess ran away with the fishmonger's boy. I told you that. I will not have you spreading malicious gossip that my husband had a dalliance with a servant."

Charlie recalled all too well Mrs Carmichael's insistence on ugly maids after Bess and Evie left. She knew what her husband's true nature was, although she clearly still didn't believe – or didn't allow herself to believe – that Donald was Bess's son.

Mrs Carmichael looked again to her husband for reassurance, but the rigidity of his jaw showed he had none to give. Suddenly, the truth struck through her denials, and her face crumpled. "How could you, Richard? You promised me you'd stopped all that when we came to Dunedin. Is that why I was being blackmailed? Because the maid somehow got it into her head that I sent her to the convent? I didn't. I knew nothing of it."

Mr Carmichael stood unblinking and silent, but the conspicuous absence of an outraged denial gave him away. With everyone now looking at him, he belatedly realised that a version of the truth was needed.

"Look, I'll admit I bedded the girl. Bess was more than willing, I assure you. Indeed, she pestered me until she caught me at a weak moment, and I gave in to temptation. I know it was wrong, but I made amends. I paid Tulloch to take her to the convent, where she could give birth in safety. When she bore a son, I took the child off her hands so she could start her life afresh, with no harm done."

Mrs Brown, who had kept in the background to this point, let out a howl and launched herself at Mr Carmichael. She stopped right in front of him with her fists clenched, spitting with fury. "No harm done? You imbecile! Bess was treated like a slave in that vile place. She was told that her child had died. Can you imagine the effect of that news on a mother? You're a foul, despicable fiend for using Bess to bear you a son, then discarding her so cruelly when you had what you wanted."

At first, Mr Carmichael shrank away from her fury, but then he gathered his wits and towered over her, trying to intimidate this woman who dared insult him. "Who are you to say such things to me?"

Mrs Brown didn't cower in the face of his retort. Instead, she thrust her chin forward until she was inches from his face. "I am Evie, the other maid who suffered so atrociously in your household and was cast out onto the streets because of it. I thought I would die, but it turned out I was the lucky one."

Mr Carmichael reeled backwards, bumping his rear into a cabinet. He sat down on it, mouth agape.

"Were you being blackmailed by Bess too, Mr Carmichael?" Charlie asked.

"No, I wasn't," Carmichael replied angrily. "Why would she?"

"Strange, don't you think, when Bess blackmailed everyone else in the household?" Charlie paused to gauge the reaction to his words. "Even stranger that a nice girl and a good maid would allow herself to be seduced by the master of the house – unless you swore to her that you loved her and would look after her. A heartless lie to get what you wanted."

"She seduced me, as I told you." Mr Carmichael was clearly striving to keep his pretence of outraged innocence, but it was wearing thin. Fear showed in the tight lines around his eyes, and his muscles were taut, ready for action.

When Charlie continued, his voice had an even sharper edge than before. "Is that so? Then why did Bess hold on for so long to her belief that you would rescue her, Mr Carmichael? But you never went back for her, did you? It must have been devastating for her. Perhaps Bess thought you didn't know where she was. You were right that she blamed you, Mrs Carmichael, because Tulloch told Bess that it was you who sent her away. I expect Tulloch did as he was told because your husband knew all about his sordid business dealings."

Mrs Carmichael puffed up, her anger now entirely directed at her husband. "What sort of pathetic coward would allow his wife to take the blame for his vile sins? I cannot believe you took her son and left that poor girl to suffer."

Her venom was short-lived as the implications finally came home to roost. Mrs Carmichael deflated, her anger replaced by fear. She dropped into a chair, her eyes on Grace. "Oh, dear Lord, does Bess know about Donald? I can't lose my son. Donald means the world to me. Mrs Penrose Pyke, tell your husband what a child means to a woman."

Grace, who had been standing with her eyes squeezed tightly closed, startled at the sound of her name. "I truly don't believe Bess ever knew about Donald, Mrs Carmichael. She thought her child had died at birth."

"Please, you cannot tell her," Mrs Carmichael pleaded. "Not after all these years. The woman must be quite mad. She should be locked up in prison as a blackmailer."

Grace answered with a sound halfway between a grunt and a groan. It was clear Mrs Carmichael didn't know Bess was dead, and this was not the time to tell her. Charlie had more important issues to pursue, like unravelling her husband's sins. Quickly, so he could get Grace home.

Charlie eased into it with a question that had been troubling him. "Would you have taken the baby if it had been a girl, Mr Carmichael?"

Mr Carmichael didn't reply, but his expression answered for him. He saw their disdain and shrugged. "We already had three daughters. A man needs a son."

Grace made her feelings known with a low, growling grunt.

Charlie flicked another worried glance at his wife, but only briefly, because he couldn't allow himself to be distracted at this critical point. "Did you receive another demand for money yesterday, Mrs Carmichael?"

"No, I didn't. When I heard Mr Tulloch had been arrested, I assumed he was the blackmailer and the distressing episode was at an end."

"Did your household receive any other messages or items by post?" Charlie asked.

Mrs Carmichael took a moment to think about it. "As far as I recall, we had bills from the grocer and butcher by post, and a messenger came with a letter for my husband in the evening."

"It was only a note from a supplier," Mr Carmichael said. "Nothing important. I threw it away."

"It's odd that a supplier would deliver business correspondence to your home by messenger," Charlie said. "What do you think, Detective Inspector Wallace?"

Wallace rubbed his chin thoughtfully. "What I would like to know is where you and your husband were at sunrise this morning, Mrs Carmichael."

"In our beds, of course. Well, I was. We sleep separately because my husband often goes to work early. However, this morning he was at home when I rose around nine o'clock."

"I slept late this morning," Mr Carmichael said. "Not that it is any of your business."

"Did either of you see the other within an hour either way of sunrise?" Wallace asked.

"We just said so, didn't we?" Mrs Carmichael snapped. "Why?"

Wallace kept his eyes on Mr Carmichael as he answered her. "Because Bess Rudd, your former maid and your husband's lover, sent your husband a letter yesterday begging for money to help her. I expect she believed Mr Carmichael would look after her because of the love they once shared. Perhaps she even believed he would want to know their child had died. The meeting was set for this morning around sunrise in the Southern Cemetery."

"Well, Richard," Mrs Carmichael said, "did you pay her or not?"

"Why would I pay that woman a brass farthing? I admit I got a letter, but I ignored it."

"I can confirm he didn't pay her," Wallace said. "Bess was found dead in the cemetery this morning. Your husband has no alibi and every reason to want her dead, both to stop the blackmail and to prevent the scandal of his only son's birth from becoming known. Not only for himself, but to protect the son he loved. Motives don't come any more powerful than that."

"If the woman was that desperate, maybe she killed herself." Mr Carmichael's suggestion might have been more convincing if he hadn't flicked a glance towards the door, where DS Kelly stood guard. "If not, somebody else must have done it, because it wasn't me and you cannot prove otherwise."

"We have the pistol," Charlie said. "You sell pistols at your ironmongery shop, don't you? I expect your son keeps a close eye on stock, as he is required to do by law. If one is missing, it won't look good for you, especially if you have left fingerprints on it. The man who fired the gun was considerably taller than the victim, like you, and fired at close range. Your clothes will show traces of the victim's blood and tissue."

Mr Carmichael kept his mouth firmly shut. Silence was his only ally at this point.

Charlie sensed his suspect was on the verge of breaking, so he tried a new tack. "It must have given you a terrible shock to see Bess standing by a gravestone carved with the name Brown. Perhaps she even mentioned it in her note to pinpoint the meeting place in the Southern Cemetery. Did you panic, Mr Carmichael? Did you think Bess knew your darkest, most shocking, secret?"

"What on earth are you talking about? What secret?"

Charlie saw Carmichael's clawed fists and knew he had him. "That you killed Hugh Brown."

Mr Carmichael turned as white as a convent-laundered sheet. His wife saw it too and let out a strangled gurgling sound, before collapsing in a dead faint.

Mrs Brown froze, but there was fury strung tight in every muscle and sinew in her body.

"Step away from him, Mrs Brown," Charlie said. "Let the police deal with Hugh Brown's murderer."

Mr Carmichael hadn't moved, or admitted the truth, so Charlie threw out his final hunch. "Did you bury Hugh's body in the vegetable garden, Mr Carmichael? No, I'd bet it was under the apple tree, which I've seen you contemplating with such despair. I can see why you never wanted to move from this house."

"I never met the man." Mr Carmichael's terse denial came with an instinctive glance out the window toward the apple tree.

"Hugh Brown came to see you, didn't he," Charlie continued, "to protest at the dreadful way this household treated Evie, the love of his life? Perhaps he even spoke out for both the maids, making you fear your secret liaison with Bess had been discovered."

Carmichael's shoulders sagged. Charlie made the mistake of thinking it was the reaction of a defeated man, when the killer was actually stooping to open a drawer in the cabinet. When Carmichael stood upright again, he was holding a pistol with a disconcertingly steady hand.

"I have access to any number of pistols from my shop, Mr Penrose Pyke. Perhaps you ought to have thought of that before challenging me." Carmichael shifted his aim toward Grace. "I am also an excellent shot. I have no desire to harm your baby, but I can promise you that I will do whatever it takes to walk out of here a free man."

Grace seemed oblivious to the peril she was in. She didn't even look at Mr Carmichael. She just stood, hunched over, breathing in short huffs and moans.

Wallace moved forward. "Do you admit to causing the deaths of Hugh Brown and Bess Rudd, Mr Carmichael?"

"Stop exactly where you are, Inspector," Carmichael ordered. "Anyone who moves in front of Mrs Penrose Pyke will be shot instantly. The bullet might go through you and into her, so I wouldn't try to be a hero if I were you. And, for the record, the death of the fishmonger's boy was an accident of his own making. He forced his way into my home. When he became agitated, I had to fend him off. Unfortunately, he fell backwards onto the sharp edge of the hearth."

"And Bess Rudd?" Wallace said.

Carmichael's shoulders twitched into a slight shrug, conveying his indifference to the fate of his former lover while not compromising his aim. "I thought she must have found out the truth. She could have destroyed me and wrecked Donald's chances of an advantageous marriage."

Charlie had had quite enough of Carmichael's bluster, but he had to keep him talking to give Declan a chance to close in. "If Hugh Brown's death was an accident, why not simply call the police? Why bury his body? And why did you take Hugh's keys from his dead body so you could let yourself into his parents' house to leave a note purporting to be from Hugh? Killing two birds with one stone, if you will pardon the appalling aptness of the expression. Convincing everyone that Hugh and Bess had run away together gave you the perfect excuse to get rid of Bess to the convent before her pregnancy became obvious, while covering up Hugh's death at your hands."

Carmichael swung the pistol in Declan's direction. "You. Back off." When Declan complied, the pistol swung back to Grace. "Mrs Penrose Pyke, walk slowly towards me and don't try any heroics if you want your baby to live. You're coming with me. The rest of you, go to the far side of the room and don't move, or I will shoot."

There was a moment's hesitation, while Charlie worked out the odds of taking Carmichael down before he shot Grace and the twins. But Charlie believed him when he said he was a fine marksman, and the distance and angles were not in his favour. He couldn't risk it, and he saw the same realisation in the two policemen.

Grace let out a deep, wailing moan and clutched her belly. She groped her way towards a chair, bent almost double in agony.

My clever wife, Charlie thought. Pretending to be in labour was certainly a novel solution to avoid being held hostage. He was about to plead for his wife's release in exchange for his own life when she emitted another long, drawn-out groan. Grace was a fine actress, but this groan came from a far deeper place than acting.

In the stunned silence, the sound of liquid hitting the wooden floor was as sharp and shocking as a pistol shot.

"My waters have broken," Grace groaned.

Charlie ran towards her, keeping his body between her and the pistol. He eased her onto the floor and put a cushion under her head. Declan moved to help, but Carmichael swivelled the pistol towards him.

Declan held out his hand. "Give me the pistol, Mr Carmichael. It's over."

The pistol held steady, but Carmichael's focus on Declan was his undoing. Mrs Brown plunged forward with a war cry that would have made Napoleon buckle at the knees.

Carmichael whipped around, firing the pistol as Mrs Brown hurled herself at him. Charlie swore he saw a puff of fabric as the bullet tore the edge of the housekeeper's apron. Then she launched herself at Hugh's killer, chopping his right hand up with her left arm and following through with a splendid right hook. Mrs Brown's many talents never ceased to amaze him, but Charlie had never been more grateful for them than he was now.

Declan dropped to the floor, scrambling to seize the fallen pistol as Mrs Brown's knee whistled past his ear and landed smack in the centre of Mr Carmichael's groin. The men in the room let out a collective gasp, while the murderer went down like a sack of bones.

"That's for robbing my daughter of her father," Mrs Brown snarled. She rubbed her knuckles and stepped aside with a shaky nod to Wallace. "All yours, Inspector."

Wallace shook himself out of his stunned state and fumbled with his handcuffs. "Gorblimey, Mrs B, anytime you want a job with the police force, just let me know."

"Thank you, but no. I am already a member of the best detective team in Dunedin. Now, if you'll excuse me, my mistress calls." The tension in Mrs Brown's voice betrayed her outer appearance of calm. Indeed, she sounded more than a little woozy after taking down Hugh's killer.

While Wallace handcuffed the killer, Charlie turned his attention back to his wife. Mrs Brown's "my mistress calls" was a master of understatement, because Grace was making a noise reminiscent of a cow bellowing. He had read all the books he could on birth and childcare, but every word he'd read fled his mind at the sight of his wife in agony. Fortunately, Mrs Brown took charge. She dropped to the floor beside Grace, ordering him to hold his wife's hand and time the contractions, while she attended to the business end.

"I am not giving birth in this house of evil," Grace wailed, crushing Charlie's hand as the next contraction hit.

"Of course not, my dear Grace," Mrs Brown said. "After the next contraction, Charlie and Sergeant Kelly will carry you out to the buggy. I think, in the circumstances, we should go straight to the hospital."

"I want to give birth at home." Grace panted as the contraction died away. "Only sick and injured people go to hospitals."

Mrs Brown sat back against the armchair, her face pale and sweating. Charlie tore his gaze from Grace, belatedly realising that a red stain was spreading underneath the rip in Mrs Brown's apron. He'd heard of people achieving remarkable feats when they were in shock in the minutes after being shot, before the pain caught up with them, but never anything like this.

"Declan, we need your help over here," Charlie yelled. "Mrs Brown has been shot."

Grace tried to sit up, but Charlie held her down. She squeezed his hand again. "Get Mrs Brown to the hospital first. Don't worry about me. The first birth always takes hours."

Charlie didn't bother to reply, because this was one argument his wife had no chance of winning. He would squeeze them both into the buggy even if he had to ride the horse to the hospital.

Declan stripped off Mrs Brown's apron to improvise a bandage to staunch the bleeding, then he and Charlie carried her out to the buggy on a blanket. Fortunately, she felt nothing because she fainted from the pain when they lifted her. Grace was next. They laid both women on the floor of the buggy, packed tightly together. Charlie propped his rear on the seat and his feet on the front of the buggy.

Declan handed him the reins. "Godspeed, Charlie."

Grace clamped one hand against Mrs Brown's bandaged wound and one hand on her own belly. Between panting and contractions, she gasped out garbled advice, while Charlie whipped the horse into a steady canter.

"Wright is the best surgeon if Mrs Brown needs an operation …

… but tell him to wash his hands first …

… promise you'll stay with me, Charlie …

… and if you have to make a choice, choose the babies over me …

… and for the love of God, tell Beechworth that if chloroform was good enough for the Queen, it's good enough for me."

Homecoming

Four days later, Grace woke up slowly, feeling pathetically weak but determined to go home for the rest of her lying-in period. She would have insisted earlier if she hadn't been in such a daze of exhaustion, pain, relief, bloating, and euphoria. Medically, she knew such symptoms were normal, but it felt as though she was inhabiting a body that was not her own.

The excessive emotions had now subsided into a general state of happiness, tiredness, and mild discomfort. Her eyes teared up every time her little milk vampires latched on, which seemed to be every five minutes, day and night. One green-eyed baby with a healthy appetite and a shock of silky black hair, and one blue-eyed baby with wispy dark brown hair and the wise, wrinkled look of an elderly sage.

Charlie sat in the chair beside her, cradling both babies in one arm. A smile crept across Grace's lips as she watched him staring at them with a dreamy expression of utter contentment. The first time the twins had been placed into his arms, the stare had been rather less dreamy and more the terrified look of a man fearing he might crush or drop an extremely fragile and precious pair of crystal ornaments.

He was dressed in his best black clothes, which meant he had come straight to the hospital after Bess Rudd's funeral. Grace put out a hand to get his attention. "How was the funeral, my love?"

"Moving. I feared I might be the only one there, but Mrs Harper and all her workers attended, along with other people from the First Church congregation. Mrs Carmichael was there too."

"She was?" Grace couldn't imagine Mrs Carmichael emerging from her house at all until the scandal had died down, which probably meant she would have to live out her days as a recluse.

Charlie was momentarily distracted by five teeny-tiny fingers, which he touched with a finger that looked ridiculously huge by comparison. "Look, our daughter is waving at me. She knows her papa. Sorry, what was it you asked, Grace?"

"You said Mrs Carmichael attended the funeral," Grace prompted. "I'm astonished."

"As was I," Charlie said. "Finding out what went on in her household under her nose has shocked her out of her selfish complacency. Mrs Carmichael is a woman transformed, and she is making up for her faults with nothing short of religious fervour."

"I'm glad to hear it."

"You sound doubtful, Grace, but I assure you it is true. Mrs Carmichael didn't just attend the funeral, she paid for it. She even insisted that the baby bootees Bess knitted for her stolen child be buried alongside her. Mrs Carmichael has shown unexpected strength of character since her husband's arrest for murder. The police search uncovered the bag of blackmail money, which Mr Carmichael must have taken from Bess's dead body. Mrs Carmichael insisted that she be the one to hand it to the Minister of the First Church, for return to the blackmail victims."

"After so many of the identified targets refused to acknowledge they were being blackmailed, I imagine it will be difficult for them to claim the money back."

Charlie smiled. "In which case, their donations will be gratefully received by a worthy charity, and the world will be a slightly better place."

A silver lining on a very dark cloud, in Grace's opinion, after all the suffering caused by Mr Carmichael's desire for a son. Bess had caused great harm too, but Grace still felt deeply sorry that she never knew her son had survived.

Charlie anticipated her next question. "Mrs Carmichael has told her son the truth about his birth. Both Donald and his fiancée attended the funeral."

"I'm amazed Donald's fiancée stood by him," Grace said. "She must be an impressive woman to remain true despite the scandal enveloping the Carmichael family. Blackmailers would have slim pickings if everyone followed her example."

If there was one thing their detective work had taught Grace, it was that you could never predict how people would react under pressure. Adversity brought out the best in some people and the worst in others, while many in the middle simply cowered in a corner and looked to others to solve the problem. Grace had every hope that Donald and his wife would have a bright future ahead of them and that Mrs Carmichael's new strength of character would extend to the future treatment of her servants.

Charlie tucked the babies beside her. "I'd better go. I promised to take Mrs Brown home today."

"Charlie, I want to go home too."

"Are you sure you're ready for the journey home, Grace? The doctor said –"

"It's not an expedition into the West Coast wilderness, Charlie." Grace didn't feel much like getting up from the hospital bed, but she yearned for the comfort and peace of her own home. She would manage it somehow, even though the most she had achieved so far had been a slow shuffle along the ward. "By the way, your son has burped up a glob of undigested milk on your shoulder."

Charlie ignored her attempt at distraction. "Grace, you are my dearest love and the mother of the two most beautiful babies in the world, but even you must admit it was a traumatic birth. My nightmares will be haunted for eternity by your screams."

"Piffle. It was a perfectly normal birth, aside from being threatened with a pistol by a murderer." Grace had locked the memory of that long, long day up in a little box in the depths of her brain, leaving only the memory of two tiny bodies being placed into her arms at the end. "Anyway, you exaggerate. I may have uttered a few genteel cries from time to time during the birth, but that is hardly surprising during a sixteen-hour delivery of twins."

"A few genteel cries? Were you actually there, my love? I've witnessed all-out battles between rival gangs of dockworkers that were quieter events than the birth of our babies."

Grace gave her husband The Look. "Mrs Brown and I will return home together."

Charlie let out an overly dramatic sigh, but it didn't disguise the laughter in his eyes. "How fortunate that I anticipated your pig-headedness and hired a carriage big enough for all of us. I'll be back soon. Promise me you won't get up until I return."

"I promise." Grace lay back on the scratchy hospital pillow and counted her blessings. Aside from the twins, the chief blessing was that Mrs Brown hadn't suffered a fatal wound. The bullet had passed through the fleshy edge of her waist, missing vital organs. She was in pain, but the wound had been tended quickly, and there was no sign of that most insidious of killers – infection.

Now that Mrs Brown was recovering, her biggest concern seemed to be that her injury might compromise her ability to cook and clean, especially with Christmas approaching and a houseful of guests coming in a few weeks. However, Grace was not fooled. Their housekeeper's distress went far deeper than concern over whether the mince pies would be baked in time.

Hugh Brown's bones had been dug up from under Mr Carmichael's apple tree, just as Charlie predicted. Grace had talked to Mrs Brown about it late the previous night, when the ward was dark and quiet. Like Grace, Mrs Brown was torn by mixed emotions. Grief at losing the love of her life and the father of her child. Sorrow at the years of wrongly believing Hugh had deserted her. But also relief that her daughter now knew the truth and loved her all the more. Most of all, Grace suspected that Mrs Brown felt an overwhelming sense of peace now that she knew what had happened to Hugh and that he had loved her deeply enough to defend her honour to the end.

Grace curled up under the blankets against the warm, sweet-smelling softness of her two babies and drifted into a doze. Going home was the right choice, because she had loved ones she could depend on to help in times of need. Such as now, with the twins finally on the right side of her body, and their mother trying not to panic about how little she knew about motherhood. Whatever happened, she would muddle through and do everything in her power to keep their children safe.

Before the twins were born, Grace had doubted her resolve to give up hands-on detective work. Now, she knew her vow to stay away from criminals would be kept, at least for the foreseeable future. If she had any spare time, it could be put to good use campaigning for better conditions in the convent laundry.

The next thing she knew, Charlie was shaking her shoulder and lifting her into a bath chair. He wrapped the babies with utmost care and put them in her arms. Mrs Brown walked stiffly alongside them to the hired carriage waiting outside.

Once Charlie had settled them in the carriage, by carefully lifting them one at a time, avoiding their various sore points, Mrs Brown said, "I had an interesting visit from a friend yesterday. She said that Tulloch's coal and firewood business has closed down. Customers refused to use them after hearing of Tulloch's sordid side-businesses. Has he been convicted yet, Charlie?"

"He has. Tulloch received a substantial fine for possession of illegal alcohol and lewd photographs. After investigating his business dealings, Declan arrested him again yesterday on further charges of receiving stolen goods, failure to pay excise tax, and weights and measures offences from selling underweight measures of coal. Declan is confident the coalman will face imprisonment when the full extent of his illegal enterprises is laid before the judge. All his assets have been seized in the meantime, and there is a further investigation underway into whether the women in the photographs were willing participants."

"Good riddance," Mrs Brown said. "Tulloch can rot in prison, as far as I'm concerned."

"I wonder how Mrs Tulloch is coping without her charming husband and his income," Grace said.

"Funny you should mention that." Mrs Brown chuckled. "My friend informed me that Mrs Tulloch has been forced to undertake the only employment she is fit for."

"Not cooking, I hope," Grace said. "She'd curdle milk simply by looking at it."

"Oh no, far better than that. She has been reduced to taking in laundry. Maybe it's uncharitable of me, but it makes my day to think of her bending her back over a washboard scrubbing other people's dirty linen. Now, if you will excuse me, I need to make a list of all the things I need to do."

The rest of the journey home passed in relative silence. Mrs Brown scribbled notes about all the jobs that would need doing before the Penrose and Pyke parents arrived. Grace spent an enjoyable few minutes imagining Mr and Mrs Tulloch's future prospects, then she followed Mrs Brown's example, by making a mental list of all the jobs she had put off, such as buying presents and finding a Christmas tree. Charlie just sat there wearing an inscrutable smile.

Grace tried not to think about the chaos that awaited her at home. With Charlie dashing between the hospital and the police station, their new maid was the only person home to cope with the pups and household chores. Poor Tilly must have felt as though she'd escaped from a boiling laundry copper only to be thrown into the fire. It would be a miracle if she didn't hand in her notice.

Charlie put his arm around her. "Don't fret, Grace. Our parents will be so besotted with their new grandchildren, they won't notice trifles like dust and mince pies."

"Trifles!" Mrs Brown exclaimed, scribbling furiously. "I must order more sherry."

"You're not to do any cooking, Mrs Brown," Grace said. "Stretching and lifting are absolutely forbidden until you have fully healed. We will hire a temporary cook." If they could find one at such a busy time of the year.

"I'll not have another woman in my kitchen," Mrs Brown muttered.

"Before we get home," Charlie said, "I have more news to share. Mrs Brown, you need to know that I went to see Hugh Brown's parents to inform them his body had been found. Naturally, they wanted to know the whole tragic tale. They were devastated at hearing what happened to their son, of course, but they were also deeply shocked that they had believed the lies they were told about you, Mrs Brown. They wish to make amends for the appalling way they treated you. Hugh's funeral has been delayed so you can attend."

"I know," Mrs Brown said. "Apparently, Hugh's parents tried to visit me in hospital and were stopped by my daughter, Sadie. They recognised her as Hugh's daughter instantly. Sadie and I have been talking about it over the past few days, and we have decided to forgive them. To be honest, I think Sadie is as excited at the thought of having grandparents as they are at having a granddaughter. She has already invited them to her wedding. I'm glad. I must admit, it will be nice to have a connection to Hugh through them."

As they neared the house, Grace saw Tilly hopping from foot to foot by the gate.

Charlie waved. "Tilly has been an absolute marvel around the house over the last few days, and she is bursting with excitement to act as a nursemaid to the twins. I know you must be nervous about putting your faith in a maid so new, but she deserves a chance. It would have been so easy for her to abandon us after all that has happened over the last few days."

As soon as the carriage drew to a halt, Tilly offered to take the babies, leaving Charlie to help Grace and Mrs Brown down.

"Oh, they're too gorgeous for words," Tilly cooed. "It looks like they've been fed. If it's all right with you, Doctor Penrose Pyke, I'll take them up to the nursery to change them and put them down for a sleep. I promise I'll take as good care of them as I would my own little brothers and sisters."

How could Grace refuse such a polite offer, especially when being addressed as Doctor added to the warm glow of the welcome home?

"Bring the babies back down after you've changed them, Tilly," Charlie said. "I don't want to let them out of my sight just yet. They'll sleep just as well in my arms."

Grace and Mrs Brown exchanged puzzled glances as they entered the house and smelled the welcome aroma of roasting meat, alongside a spicier waft of warm cinnamon. Sadie Brown came out of the kitchen and ran down the hallway to her mother. An elderly couple followed her at a slower pace.

"Grandma is a marvellous cook, just like you," Sadie said, throwing her arms gently around Mrs Brown. "Come and sit down, Ma. You look like you're about to faint."

"Grandma?" Mrs Brown stammered.

"I got talking to my new grandparents at the hospital," Sadie said, "and they insisted on coming here to make your arrival home as easy as possible."

The elderly couple took turns gently embracing Mrs Brown.

"We only hope you will forgive us for doubting you," Hugh's mother said, wiping tears from her eyes. "We were fools for believing the story about you carrying another man's child and that Hugh ran away because of it. If I hadn't been so stubborn, I'd have sought you out and seen with my own eyes that darling Sadie is every inch Hugh's daughter. Our dear granddaughter."

"Hugh's note was such a bolt from the blue," Hugh's father explained. "Mrs Carmichael's cook came into the shop to warn us against you, too. She told us they had to dismiss you after discovering a man in your room. We had no reason to doubt her, especially knowing you'd been dismissed without a reference. We are so very sorry."

"I do hope you will forgive me and Sadie for taking over your kitchen without permission," Hugh's mother added. "When I heard how badly you were hurt, my dear Mrs Brown, I felt I had to do something to assist in your hour of need."

Mrs Brown gave a start at the use of her married name, which Hugh's parents knew she had no right to. She had to brush a tear away at this admission of her place in their family "Of course you're forgiven," she said. "How kind you have been to us when you must be hurting so deeply."

Grace showed their unexpected guests to the drawing room and left them to a long overdue reconciliation. She and Charlie retreated to the kitchen, where the table was laden with food, a roast was in the oven, and the heavenly scent of mulled wine wafted from a pot on the stovetop. She waved a hand at the feast.

"Hugh's mother cannot have made all of this, even with the help of Sadie and Tilly. There's enough food to feed an army."

"Not quite an army, Grace. We're expecting fourteen for a celebratory meal at midday, but we have many other friends who are champing at the bit to see the twins. Declan and Moira came by with gingerbread, Molly and Rory brought mince pies, Doctor and Mrs Harvey brought a Christmas cake, and Anne and Kenneth Drummond supplied the roast and wine. Even Wallace and his wife came by with a contribution, which included treats for the dogs."

Grace didn't know what to say, so she repeated the obvious. "Fourteen people, you said, coming for a celebration meal. Do we have that many friends able to come on a workday?"

Charlie gave her the sort of smug grin he reserved for his best-kept surprises. "Not friends. Family has priority today."

"Family?" Grace said. Their parents were not due to arrive until mid-December.

"Did you really think our parents would wait until Christmas after I sent them telegrams to say the twins were born early? Lily and Alistair came back too, of course. Everyone arrived late yesterday, but I asked them to wait next door until Mrs Brown had her reunion. Once I give the signal, I suggest you stand back to avoid being trampled in the rush to see the babies."

"All of them? Here? Already?"

Charlie caught up her hand and squeezed. "I tried to tell them not to overwhelm you all at once. On the positive side, they'll help with the twins, leaving you time to rest. You and Mrs Brown won't have to lift a finger. I doubt anyone will even notice if you disappear for a few hours to rest. Or me, for that matter."

"Any more surprises?" Grace asked, although she had already decided it would be easier to sit back and let events take their course. Nod and smile, look serene, don't mention murder and blackmail – how hard could it be? In fact, the more she thought about it, the more wonderful it seemed that both families were here to share this precious moment.

"Only one more minor surprise. Ah, here's Tilly now."

Grace took the infants handed to her, while Tilly rushed ahead into the drawing room. Charlie insisted on covering her eyes as they followed her. When he took his hands away, Grace gasped. The last time she'd seen the drawing room, it had been decorated with a smattering of festive tinsel. Now, there was a fully decorated Christmas tree with a pile of presents underneath.

"Have magic elves paid a midnight visit?" Grace asked.

"Johnny Todd and his lads turned up with a Christmas tree and put it up. And I've been hoarding Christmas presents for weeks. Did you notice Tilly's surprise?" Charlie pointed at the other corner, where Tilly had the pups lined up in a straight row, each with a red bow around the neck.

"They look adorable!" Grace was holding back tears and decided she needed to take a seat before it all became too much.

Tilly let the pups go. Three raced to Charlie, but Spark and Blaze came to inspect Grace and the babies in her arms. Grace could tell from the way they reacted that they would guard the twins with their lives. Charlie came over and kissed her, before taking one of the babies to rock in his arms.

Mrs Brown sat between Hugh's father and Sadie, looking every bit as overwhelmed as Grace felt. Hugh's mother told her she must not lift a finger until she had recovered, before bustling out to the kitchen with Tilly to bring in trays of food and drinks.

With the scene set, Charlie waved an arm out of the window. In less than a minute, there was a commotion at the front door as everyone arrived at once. Grace's parents, George and Louisa Penrose. Charlie's parents, Thomas and Jasmine Pyke. Jasmine's sister, Lily, and her husband, Alistair Stewart. Grace's Great-Aunt Anne and her husband came in last. Anne had assisted Doctor

Beechworth during the birth and thus had been the first to welcome the twins.

"Grace, darling," Louisa Penrose said, making a beeline for her daughter and the blue-eyed, delicate-featured baby she held. "Charlie told us you had a boy and a girl. This must be the little girl."

"Actually," Grace said, "the plump, green-eyed child staring into her father's eyes is the girl."

Charlie held his daughter out for Mrs Penrose to take. "We've called her Louisa Anne. Grace refused to let me call her after Blaze."

"Isn't she simply adorable?" Louisa Penrose cooed. "And so well-behaved. She certainly takes after her father. Grace, I have to say I am impressed that you seem to have everything so well organised, despite your final examinations and the early arrival of the twins. I'm delighted you made it through the pregnancy and birth with no drama, unlike your usual life."

"Mama, dearest, I am the very picture of a tranquil Madonna." Grace exchanged a subtle smirk with Charlie and handed him his son.

Jasmine Pyke darted forward to intercept the baby. "Ooh, isn't he gorgeous? Our first grandson."

Thomas Pyke stroked the baby's tiny cheek with an outsized finger. "What's his name, Charlie?"

"Thomas Alistair."

Behind them, Alistair Stewart smiled and slapped Thomas on the back. "I'll forgive you for being first just this once, old friend. I'm honoured to be included at all."

"I wouldn't be here today without you, Alistair," Charlie said. "With the way my luck was running before I met you and Grace,

I'd have spent the rest of my life trudging through night shifts as a beat constable in some far-flung cesspit."

"You would always have had a place at my side, Charlie," his father said as he got his turn with young Thomas. "But I'm glad it worked out the way it did. We're all so very proud of what both of you have achieved."

George Penrose, who had been watching the excitement with a deeply contented smile, stepped forward to pump his son-in-law's hand and thank him for getting Grace to the hospital in time. As a doctor, he understood all too well the risks of childbirth. Then he turned his attention to his daughter, taking a moment to examine her before kissing her cheek.

"My little girl – the first female doctor in the country and a mother as well. I'm so proud of you, Grace. I'd always hoped that one of my children might become the third Doctor Penrose in the family."

"I'll bet you never imagined it would be your daughter."

"On the contrary," her father said, "I knew it would be you from the moment your pudgy little fingers grabbed my stethoscope and wouldn't let go. I find it harder to get my head around the fact that you are now the mother of twins. Dare I ask …?"

"I'm fine, Papa," Grace said. "Or I soon will be. More to the point, Tom and Louisa are remarkably well, despite being squashed together for the past few months."

"We'll have to have more children because we have so many people to honour," Charlie said. "Grace and I have agreed that the next boy will be George Lee and the next girl will be Jasmine Lily."

"After a suitably long break," Grace muttered.

"And, if we are blessed with another girl, we'd like to call her Evie, after a very special member of our family, who braved a bullet to save the lives of Grace and the twins."

Mrs Brown gave in to another bout of tears, making up for years of being the staunch backbone of everyone else's lives. Fortunately, the older Mrs Brown was there to comfort her.

Charlie perched on the arm of Grace's chair and bent down to whisper in her ear. "Can you imagine a better ending than this, Doctor Penrose the Third? Two adorable, healthy children and our families gathered together to share our joy."

Grace pulled him close for a kiss. "I've truly never been happier, Detective Pyke. Long may the bliss last."

Naturally, little Louisa chose that moment to decide she was tired of being passed around like a rugby ball. The instant she started bawling, Tom joined in. Grace took them both into her arms and rocked them, knowing that happiness takes many forms and seldom comes without hard work and boundless love.

Coming next

Thank You

Thank you for reading this story. If you enjoyed it, I would be very grateful if you would leave a rating or review to help other readers discover it.

And heartfelt thanks, dear readers, for making it this far into the *Penrose & Pyke Mysteries*. Without you, there would be no stories. This feels like the right time for Grace and Charlie to take a much-needed break from peril. As anyone with a newborn (or two) knows, new parents barely have time to sleep, let alone fight crime.

Meanwhile, I am turning my pen to a new writing project. I'd love you to join me on this new adventure. Pre-order now or keep an eye on my website for updates at https://RosePascoe.com

Coming Next

My next book, *A Sleuth's Guide to Murder and Fine Art*, is a contemporary mystery featuring a fresh cast of unconventional characters heading towards retirement – the *Sleuths of a Certain Age*.

As in the *Penrose & Pyke* books, the murder mystery plot will be seasoned with a dash of humour, a dollop of romance, topical social issues, and low levels of violence. The book is set in the stunningly beautiful southern lakes area of New Zealand, where residents rub shoulders with hordes of tourists and outdoor enthusiasts.

Here's the blurb:

A wealthy and very dead art collector was not part of Hazel Bond's life plan. Nor was an accusation of murder. To solve the puzzle of his death, she must set aside her paintbrushes and put her trust in an offbeat band of unlikely allies.

It seems like fate has put a target on her back. A widowed, unemployed art teacher with a bank balance running on empty. Not old enough to retire, too old to start afresh, Hazel retreats to the picture-perfect alpine community of her childhood to pursue her love of painting and the great outdoors.

Unfortunately, peace is hard to come by. A rumoured sale of art and heritage treasures sparks angry protests. Then a rich art enthusiast dies in an apparent accident at a nearby ski field, with Hazel as the only witness. Or, as the police view it, the only suspect.

Her hopes of extricating herself aren't helped when she is drawn deeper into the mystery by two men with their own agendas. Benedict Finlayson is an uptight fish out of water who claims to be an international art expert. Gary Taylor is so laid back that he never left the '70s. Neither man is quite what he seems to be. Luckily, Hazel's eccentric godmother and conventional sister are right behind her, even if that means giving her a helpful shove in the back.

Fuelled by wine, cheese, and pig-headed determination, these sleuths of a certain age are not about to let wealth and power get in the way of justice.

Welcome to a murderous mystery tour of the stunning beauty of southern New Zealand.

Read on for an excerpt from *A Sleuth's Guide to Murder and Fine Art:*

The uniformed constable shoved the classroom door open without knocking, catching Hazel by surprise. Her paintbrush jerked, adding a splotch of paint to her artist's smock. Not that anyone would notice, since her painting style reflected her natural exuberance. A recent series of vibrant sunset landscapes had left the smock splattered with more blood-red paint than an extra in a slasher movie.

The constable froze, his hand dropping to hover near where his gun would be holstered if the New Zealand police carried firearms, which they rarely did. His fingers twitched like a cop longing to say, "Go ahead, make my day."

Hazel held out her hands to show she was armed only with a #12 filbert brush. The bristles trembled in time to her pounding pulse. She wiped the brush and put it in a water jar so she could give the police officer her full attention. He didn't look like one of those lovely community constables who did outreach programmes. None of the junior high school students in her art class seemed like the type to be arrested, and all thirty-one of them were staring wide-eyed at the cop rather than looking guilty.

"Mrs Hazel Bond?" the constable said. "I need you to come with me." After a fleeting pause, he added, "Please."

"Me? What, now? I'm in the middle of a class."

"Now." The straining fabric around the constable's shoulder muscles emphasised that this was an order, not a request.

Hazel stripped off the smock and gathered her coat and bag, her gut churning with fear. Lately, it seemed fate had put a target on her back. As if fate had nothing better to do, like stopping wars and ending poverty.

Thirty-one pairs of eyes lit up at the sight of their art teacher being escorted from the room by a cop. Thirty-one hands instinctively reached for phones. The door closed behind her to a volley of flashes and a burst of excited chatter. It was refreshing to see them taking real-world photographs, Hazel thought. Most young people would rather take selfies than bother pointing the lens at the world to capture truth and beauty. Or worse, they skipped the photo altogether in favour of an AI-generated image. Hazel shuddered. Perhaps fate was right. Maybe she was getting too old for this.

Until being made redundant two months ago, Hazel had been infusing students with the joy of art for almost forty years. Now she was scraping by with relief teaching when she could get it. In a way, it was a godsend to be away from the pressures of modern teaching. The administration, the constant evaluations, the endless, head-against-a-brick-wall debate about the relevance of art in a technological age. And, if she was honest, she relished the chance to pursue her passions for painting and photography. Unfortunately, she also needed the filthy lucre to support her weakness for wine and cheese, and to revive her old love of skiing.

Still, if Hazel had been looking for a sign from above that it was time to quit fighting an uphill battle, she would have preferred it to be a lottery win rather than a constable with a bad-news thrust to his square jaw. It was a cliché to say that cops got younger every year, but this one really was almost young enough to be her grandson.

The assistant principal was waiting outside the classroom. He raised an eyebrow, asking a question to which Hazel had no answer. She gave him a shrug to tell him his guess was as good as hers, adding a puzzled shake of her head to convey that she was an innocent party.

"Take the rest of the day off if you need to," the assistant principal said, but he was not happy about it.

Hazel read in his sour expression that her short stint as a relieving teacher was unlikely to be extended. Not because he disliked her, but because the students would send messages to their parents within seconds, complete with emojis, abbreviations, and a photo of their relieving teacher being taken away. Seconds later, parents would express their outrage with a flurry of messages and social media posts. Within the hour, fake news would circulate with wildly inaccurate conspiracy theories. Guilty until proven innocent these days, with social media playing judge and jury.

The assistant principal pushed past her and through the door, barking out an order to be silent as if the classroom was a parade ground for army recruits. He was an old-school math teacher. Serve the kids right if he forced them to do trigonometry instead of art.

These random thoughts were a distraction. Inwardly, Hazel's stomach was doing flip-flops, because the most likely reason for the constable's visit was that a family member had been in an accident. She crossed her fingers behind her back. Please let it be a burglary or ninety-one-year-old Mrs Murdoch from next door wandering the streets again. Then Hazel felt bad for wishing ill on others. If it came down to it, though, she would make a deal with the devil to save her loved ones from harm. Wouldn't we all?

The constable looked straight ahead and strode towards the car park rather than the staffroom. It must be very bad news. Whatever it was, Hazel had to know. Now, before acid ate away her stomach lining. She hurried after him, pulling on her quilted, autumn-orange coat against the chilly winter air.

"Is it one of my children, officer? Has there been an accident?" Hazel's children were in their thirties, but a mother never stopped worrying.

"Nothing like that," the constable said. "I've been ordered to bring you in to make a statement."

Bring her in? He made it sound as if she were under arrest. "I don't understand. A statement about what? Has there been a burglary in my neighbourhood?"

"No, ma'am. The detective will explain at the station." The constable opened the rear door of the patrol car for her.

Ma'am? Hazel was only fifty-nine years old and in no way part of the twinset and pearls brigade. She ducked into the car before he could do that head pushing down thing that policemen do when a suspect is bundled into a car in movies. Then his second sentence hit home. Detective? Detectives dealt with major crimes, didn't they? Like homicide.

Hazel didn't bother asking for further information. This had to be about the man who died on the ski field two days ago. She was the last person to see him alive and the first to see him dead – a shocking spike on the heart monitor of her otherwise ordinary existence. He had been a nice guy and his death was a terribly tragic accident, but Hazel still felt aggrieved she was being escorted to the police station in a patrol car when she hardly knew the man. She had given a full statement to a police sergeant at the time, of course. Perhaps she had forgotten to sign it. If so, the sergeant could have phoned to ask her to come back in.

Hazel had plenty of time to think about it as they crawled their way through the endless roadworks and traffic that blighted modern Queenstown. Not that thinking did her any good.

When they pulled up outside the police station, Hazel's heart did one of those unsettling jitters. Palpitations, atrial fibrillation, stress flutter – call it what you will, it was another unwanted sign that the manure was about to hit the fan. She didn't know what the manure was, but she had a nasty premonition that she would be the one in front of the fan.

The young constable jumped out to open the door for her. They walked inside in silence. The reception area was utilitarian and bustling, with splashes of colour that looked out of place. Crime-buster posters in stop-sign red and police blue; pamphlets on domestic violence and victim support services in soothing shades of pastel. Miserable people in uncomfortable chairs turned to stare. Hazel wished she could be the lady asking if a purse has been handed in, or even the lank-haired youth with a whopper bruise on his cheek and a missing tooth, dribbling blood onto a Black Sabbath t-shirt.

The constable took her straight through the reception area into a corridor designed to intimidate. The walls seemed closer together than normal, and they were painted a depressing, institutional greyish-green. A delusional paint marketing expert would probably call it Serene Olive or Dusky Sage. The vinyl flooring was even worse. Nobody who had studied art should be subjected to grungy greige, shot with black scuff marks and an erratic line of red blood drops. The pervasive smells of bleach, sweat, and meat pies didn't help.

No wonder they take your belts and shoelaces away when they lock you up, Hazel thought, as they passed a door labelled as Interview Room 1. Benedict Finlayson sat behind the table, opposite a police officer. He was on the wrong side of the table, and he didn't look happy about it. Hazel was not happy about it either, since he was the person who got her into this mess. Although, if she was honest, her innate nosiness and persuasive family probably deserved a larger share of the blame.

Another palpitation shimmied through her heart and circled back for a second and third strike. This felt bad. Very bad. And it was far too late to wind back the clock to a time when an early retirement with a stack of blank canvases and a one-bar heater was her worst-case scenario. Now, that seemed like utter bliss.

The constable opened the door to Interview Room 2 and pointed to a chair. Two long minutes later, a plainclothes officer entered, plopped a file on the table, and took a seat opposite her. He turned on the interview recorder and opened a laptop. Only then did he introduce himself as a detective and ask her to confirm she was Mrs Hazel Bond, widow, aged 59, resident at 6 Lake Vista Street, Queenstown.

Without warning, the detective swivelled the laptop in her direction and hit play on a video clip. In the cold, objective eye of the lens, the scene looked more like a mob than the civilised protest she recalled. A group of mostly grey-haired people waving placards and yelling "traitor, traitor" at a man on the steps above them. The protesters were angry – incensed angry, not just mildly cross.

A tall, white-haired man got out of a black car by the steps. One protester's face turned towards him with an expression that resembled a cobra ready to strike, clearly visible even in the grainy footage from the CCTV camera. Hazel hardly recognised herself, but she couldn't deny it was her.

An improbable series of events had led her from the protest to this interview room. But how was she going to explain that to a detective with the hard stare of a cop who had heard every excuse under the sun?

Historical Notes to *Deadly Demands*

The 1890s were a time of significant improvements in conditions for factory workers, thanks to the strident advocacy of key figures within the church and unions, as highlighted in the first *Penrose & Pyke* mystery. However, servants living and working in households still worked horrendous hours for low pay. Few households could afford more than one or two servants, so the maid-of-all-work had the worst of it. Much depended on the goodwill of the mistress and master, although the difficulty of getting servants in far-flung New Zealand probably helped to shield servants from abuse in most households, or at least provide an easy way out if they wanted to leave.

Conditions were worse still in the convent laundries, as depicted in the story, because they were exempt from labour laws. The laundries existed by the hundreds around the world, mainly during the nineteenth and early twentieth centuries. However, they did not reach New Zealand until the 1880s, with none in Dunedin. Thus, the convent laundry in the story is not only fictional but also before its time. However, it was a terrible era that simply begged to be retold.

My deep gratitude to Heritage New Zealand and all the museums, historical societies, libraries, councils, private individuals and organisations who maintain our heritage on a shoestring. Dunedin is a treasure trove of Victorian style, from the magnificent First Church of Otago to the spooky cemeteries, as well as many fine public and private buildings, parks, farms, factories, and industrial sites. But it is not simply the buildings we must preserve, but the stories that make them come alive. For this,

I applaud the dedication of the people who nurture our heritage and staff our libraries. Thank you for the many, many delightful hours I have spent poking around for useful snippets for the *Penrose & Pyke* books.

One never knows what one will come across, such as the gem about the first person to be prosecuted in New Zealand for taking lewd photographs, which I saw in the wonderful Port Chalmers museum. It was thanks to a fascinating talk on the history of the First Church that I learned about the repairs needed so soon after the church was built. As fate would have it, my hotel room looked out over the old Hallenstein Brothers clothing factory and the long roofs of the adjacent buildings that stretch between two steep streets, sparking the idea of the dressmaking salon and rooftop escape.

The blackmail plot is entirely fictional, as are all the characters depicted in the story. The places mentioned are also fictional, aside from the First Church and Southern Cemetery, which I have co-opted for my own purposes in the story. Māori prisoners from the Taranaki wars are buried in the Southern Cemetery, as noted in the story, and misdeeds and ghostly sightings were reported in historical records.

Acknowledgements

A huge thank you to my fabulous beta readers: Mary, Jenny, Kathy and Ross. Their dedication and enthusiasm are very much appreciated. Two writing friends have joined the beta reading group: Bronnie Thomas and Tracy Chollet. Check out their books at: www.tracychollet.com and www.bronniethomas.com.